Finding Each Other

Copyright © 2018 by Richard Alan and Village Drummer Fiction

This book is a work of fiction. Any names, places, characters, or incidents are products of the author's imagination or are used fictitiously. Any resemblance to actual events, locales, or people is entirely coincidental.

Cover design by AuthorPackages
www.authorpackages.com

www.villagedrummerfiction.com/

ISBN: 978-1-970070-04-0
This book is available at most online retailers.

Chapter One ~ *It's a Doozy*

DR. MORRIS KAPLAN, A world-famous geneticist, was attempting to give a lecture to a group of scientists and students at a university in Oregon. Just after he had begun describing current research topics, a number of loud and angry protesters started waving signs, yelling, and shouting obscenities.

They accused him of many things, saying he had a God complex and was trying to destroy the natural world by creating Frankenstein's monster. The protesters screamed that they wanted Morris's gene project terminated.

Morris was most disturbed when he saw signs comparing him to Josef Mengele, the sadistic German National Socialist doctor who cruelly experimented on Nazi concentration-camp internees.

He tried to explain how his genetic research might open the door to develop cures for many treatment-resistant diseases, but Morris was simply shouted down.

By the time police arrived, at least two of the protestors had tried to get to the podium to physically attack him, and many other protesters had handcuffed themselves to the permanent seating in the auditorium.

Morris finally gave up trying to speak and drove back to his home in Seattle. He believed in the promise of his research and was profoundly saddened by his reception. His wife, Michelle, was concerned about the protestors. Morris tried to calm her. "It's not that big a deal," he said. "They simply don't understand what I'm doing. Besides, most of the people arrested weren't even students."

The university in Seattle where he occasionally taught also offered to provide Morris with extra security, but he turned them down. Morris felt that if he did a better job of explaining what he was trying to do with the science of genetics that it wouldn't be a problem.

"Morris, please be careful," his wife pleaded. "These people threatened physical violence."

Again, he reassured her. "Michelle, I've been told I'll have security anytime I speak, so please don't worry."

Just then, Morris' twelve-year-old son entered the room. "Why do you need security, Dad?"

"It's nothing you need to worry about, Jonah. There were just some protestors at my speaking engagement. I'm sure this will all blow over once people understand the work I am trying to do. Now, what can we do for you?"

"Well, I was racking my brain trying to come up with an appropriate Christmas gift for Holly."

Morris raised his hands in surrender. "That's your department, Michelle."

She smiled and gestured for Jonah to sit beside her. "Tell me more."

"Mom, Holly is the first girl my own age I can really talk to. I know we're just kids, but we have fun when we talk and when we get together." He got comfortable on the sofa. "I'm not like the other guys at school. The girls think I'm nothing but a geek. Holly gets me. She and her family are coming up to Seattle the last two-weeks of December to visit her grandparents and celebrate Christmas with them. We hope to find some time to get together."

Morris smiled at his son's dilemma, grateful for the distraction from his own.

Michelle put her arm around Jonah's shoulders. "If Holly *gets* you then you need to get her a present you know she will enjoy — something that says you get her like she gets you."

***

Five-hundred-miles away in Meridian, Idaho, a similarly perplexed twelve-year-old Holly was striving to come up with an appropriate gift for the boy who had come into her life the previous summer. She had felt an immediate connection to him that didn't diminish with the five-hundred-mile distance separating their homes.

"I've been thinking about this, Mom," she said. "I like talking to Jonah, but how's the weather only gets us so far. We need to have more to talk about, and I really want to get him a great Hanukah present."

"Well, Holly, let's review what you enjoy doing."

"I love learning new languages—in fact I love learning almost anything. I also love romance novels where the hero saves the damsel in distress. I doubt if Jonah would have any interest in those kinds of stories."

"Then maybe there's something you two could learn together." "I'll ask Jonah. There has to be something we can do together even though we're so far apart."

"When children have their *Bar Mitzvahs* they usually do some kind of a charity project. Do you know what Jonah is doing for his *Bar Mitzvah* in May?"

"I'm not sure but he said something about it being a doozy— whatever that means." Holly rolled her eyes.

"That sounds like a clue." Her mother seemed to ponder that for a while. "The origin of the word doozy refers to an old car called a Duesenberg," she said. "But I don't see what that could have to do with it. Maybe you'll find out when we see him in a couple-of- weeks. By the way, Holly, I've heard you and Jonah greeting each other in a language I don't recognize. Are you speaking Hebrew?"

"No, Mom." Holly laughed. "The day of the car parade, back in September, we talked to a couple who were also riding in an antique Auburn car like Jonah and I. While we were

4

talking to them, the man turned to his wife and said something we didn't understand. When I asked him about it, he told me he was Navajo and was speaking Navajo."

"I've heard it's a difficult language."

"Maybe." Holly shrugged. "I was intrigued. I told him I loved learning languages and I spoke English, Spanish and was learning Italian. I asked if they would teach us how to greet someone in Navajo. They said they were happy to. I was kind of surprised at how excited Jonah was to learn something in Navajo as well. He said something about Navajo Code Talkers during the Second World War. The couple had huge smiles when they heard him mention the Code Talkers. Anyway, they taught us a greeting, so now when Jonah and I talk we always greet each other in Navajo. The sounds are neat. The woman said it was a tonal language. I want to learn to speak Navajo someday."

Her mother smiled. "My dearest Holly, if you continue down this track you will far surpass your mother in your language ability, and I love it!"

***

Holly and her family arrived in Seattle on December twenty-third. Since Jonah didn't celebrate Christmas and Holly didn't celebrate Hanukah, the pair decided to exchange presents the day before Christmas. They met at Jonah's house around ten o'clock in the morning and Jonah's mom, Michelle, described the house rules.

"Holly, I talked to your mom and she agrees with me on our house rules, so they will be the same in either of our homes. You may spend time in each other's bedrooms only if an adult is in the house, but the door will remain open. If you violate the rules you will be separated and not allowed to see each other. Jonah, is that clear?"

"Yes, Mom. That's clear."

"Holly?"

"It's clear to me, Mrs. Kaplan."

"Okay then, you two may go and exchange your gifts."

They went up to the second-floor media room. Jonah put a Brian Setzer CD on the audio system. Holly looked at the speakers and remarked that they looked like the same expensive speakers Michael Levin had at his home in Meridian, Idaho. "What did you call them again, Jonah?"

Jonah perked up. "They're called Maggies. That's the nickname for Magneplaner audiophile quality speakers — and yes, just like his, but much smaller. My brother, David and I received the audio equipment as Hanukah presents from Michael. It was to thank us for helping his wife, Anna, at the time of their son's delivery. He sent them along with the amp and preamp. We worked together to buy the CD player. I think he sent Linda's family a similar system for helping, as well."

"Jonah, they sound amazing," Holly exclaimed. "I can practically see the musicians in front of us."

"I agree. Sometimes I have to pinch myself just to remember I'm not dreaming."

They placed their gifts on a small table, off to the side of the room. Jonah's gift from Holly was wrapped in Hanukah paper and his gift to her was wrapped in Christmas paper.

"This is your house so you open your gift first," Holly said. Jonah shook his head. "I think ladies should go first." Holly was intent. "Please, Jonah. You open your gift first."

Jonah grinned and began to open his gift. Inside he found two books. The first was on the history of the Auburn automobile and the second about World War II aircraft engines.

"Holly, this is incredible," he shouted, eyes wide. "I can't wait to learn what's in these books. Thank you so much."

"You're welcome. I'm glad you like my gift."

Jonah stared at Holly. "These books are great," he said. "You really know me." Then he paged through his books for a few moments.

He looked back at Holly. "Okay, your turn to open your present."

Holly's present was shaped roughly like an eight-inch-cube. She was curious and excited to see what was inside. She tore the wrapping paper off. "Jonah! Outrageous! This is perfect."

Jonah was grinning as if he already knew how excited she would be when she saw his gift. "I thought you might like it."

Holly held it as if it were gold. Printed on the outside of the yellow box was *Rosetta Stone Navajo*. "I'm so pleased. Thank you, thank you." She placed her present on the table with care.

"A group called the Navajo Language Renaissance had it available on their website. Maybe we—"

Holly threw her arms around Jonah, cutting him off mid-speech.

"Boy, if this is what happens," he said as he returned her embrace, "I need to get you great gifts on a regular basis."

Holly let go. "This is one of the best gifts I have ever received.

Thank you so much."

"You're welcome. How did you decide what to get me?"

"I found the Auburn book online and the other book at the Outlet Mall in Boise. I thought you would appreciate them." Holly felt proud and happy that she had done such a good job choosing.

"I showed them to my dad, and he even bought his own copy of the aircraft engines book," she continued. "We were also at the mall to buy a blanket for my brother, Drew. I saw the beautiful Pendleton Code Talkers blanket, which has a few words in Navajo on it, but Drew wasn't interested. I guess I was staring at it, because my mom asked me if I liked it. She said she would buy it for me when I learned Navajo. Jonah, I'm proud to tell you I paid for the books myself. I've been getting paid five-dollars for each-hour I tutor language skills."

"That's great, Holly. My Uncle Meyer pays me twenty-dollars when I spend a day helping him work on one of his old cars. That's how I paid for the Rosetta Stone Language package. My mom paid for the tax and shipping. She thought it was a great gift idea for you."

"She was so right."

Jonah's mom walked into the media room then. "Well, let's see what you have." Smiling, she looked over the gifts. "Thoughtful gifts, I see."

"I can't wait to tell my mom," Holly said.

"She already knows," Jonah's mother said. "We talked about it a few-weeks-ago. I wanted to be sure that you would enjoy the gift, as it was a bit expensive. Your mom assured me you would, and of course, she was right. Seeing as Holly is still learning Italian, and Jonah has lots to study for his *Bar Mitzvah*, we propose the following for you two. As a gift for Jonah, we'll buy him the Rosetta Stone Navajo package at the time of his *Bar Mitzvah* next May. That way you can both start working on learning Navajo during the summer. Holly you are to concentrate on your school work and continue your Italian studies until the school year ends. When the two of you can demonstrate to Holly's mom that you have successfully completed the first level, I'll take you both to a two- week Navajo language immersion class in New Mexico at the end of the summer. Would you like to do that?"

"I would," Holly answered, trembling with excitement.

"Holly and I would have our own language," Jonah said. "Not exactly our own language, but it's going to be rare someone would understand us."

After another moment, his face lit up and his smile widened. "I would learn the language of the Code Talkers. I would *love* to do that."

"It will take lots of hard work. It is a difficult language to learn," Jonah's mom warned them as she left the room, "but I think you two have sufficient mental acuity to do this."

Jonah smiled at Holly. "If all it takes is hard work, we can definitely do it."

"I'll be looking forward to summer," Holly added.

Jonah and Holly talked for a while and then she asked about his charity project. "You said it was a doozy," she reminded him.

"It is," he replied with a smirk.

"A doozy refers to a car," Holly said, exasperated. "Not a charity."

"It's cool you knew that." Jonah grinned. "Uncle Meyer asked me to assist with the rebuilding of an old Duesenberg car. I'm doing as much of it as I can by myself, with his instruction. He's helping me get bids on the rest of the work. I should have it done by the time of my *Bar Mitzvah*. Uncle Meyer is going to have it sold at an auction, and I get the difference in price between what it cost to rebuild and the sale price at auction. I'm going to donate the money to the charity of my choice."

"What charity are you going to donate the money to?"

"I haven't decided. Everyone with a pet charity is pushing me. Maybe you can help me with that?"

Holly became excited. "That would be fun, and if you used some of my ideas it would be like we both were involved in your charity project."

"I already have two of the door panels off the car," Jonah said, enthusiastic. "I need to clean, sand, and prime the panels. If you help, then you're really part of it."

"That would be wonderful!"

So, the two friends dressed in suitable coats and gloves for the walk over to Meyer's garage.

Entering, Holly saw an older-looking car which had been mostly disassembled. The door panels that needed refinishing were sitting on two pairs of saw horses, and they sat in a bay isolated from the rest of the garage by large sheets of translucent plastic.

"That keeps the dirt and dust in here," Jonah pointed out. "This bay also has special air filtration."

The garage was heated so they removed their coats and since they were going to be sanding and painting, they each climbed into a Tyvek suit, put on goggles, dust respirators, hair covers, and booties.

Finally they started sanding off the old paint. It was a hard task and the main ingredient was a lot of elbow grease.

"I could have had a paint shop do this, but I save a fortune by doing it myself," Jonah said, then corrected himself. "Oops, I mean *we* save a fortune by doing it *our*selves."

"Thank you for the correction, sir." Holly grinned, as she turned over her sanding block to get some fresh sandpaper to work into the old paint. Jonah had explained how they needed to get down to bare metal, but not more.

"What about this ugly dent?" Holly asked.

"We get the paint off and Uncle Meyer will show us how to carefully pound it out."

Two-hours-later, Uncle Meyer came out to see why there were lights on in the garage. "Hey, you snow bunnies," he shouted. "How's it going?"

"It's going great," Jonah shouted back. "I have a co-worker today."

"Is Holly behind that mask?"

"Yes, Mr. Minkowski, it's me Holly," she yelled through her respirator.

"I'm glad to see you again, lady. I can't believe he convinced you to help with this messy part of his project."

"If we work on it together, it's kind of like the project belongs to both of us."

"That's true." Uncle Meyer ran his hand over the panels where the metal had been exposed. "Smooth as a baby's bottom. Good work kids—have you had lunch yet?"

Jonah said they hadn't.

Uncle Meyer turned to leave. "Report to the house in thirty

minutes and lunch will be ready for you."

After another twenty-minutes of sanding and priming, they removed their bunny suits and headed inside.

Joan Minkowski greeted and hugged each of them as they entered the kitchen.

"Typical holiday weekend," she said smiling. "I'm serving another lunch for more relatives. This is the best." She set a couple of plates for them. "Just leftovers, I'm afraid."

They were served her famous chili, and because Aunt Joan knew that Holly liked to cook she took time explaining all the ingredients she used. "I made it with of a mixture of half ground beef, half ground Italian sausage, onion, garlic, *Pasilla*, red and green peppers, fine-ground dried *poblano* peppers, *adobo* spice, plus the incredibly aromatic and flavorful New Mexico chili powder blend from the World Spice shop near Pike's Market in Seattle. A touch of Smoked Tabasco sauce was added at the end, to balance the flavors and enhance the smoky essence of the dried *poblano* peppers. I found I can use the Tabasco to replace most of the salt, and I love the smoky flavor it imparts."

She also served finely chopped raw onion and shredded cheddar cheese in case anyone wanted toppings on their chili. Next to each plate, she placed a piece of spicy cornbread which contained jalapeños and sundried tomatoes.

"What a great recipe," Holly commented. "Chili is perfect fora cool, damp day like this."

Jonah's aunt and uncle sat with them while they ate and remarked to each other they were delighted to find Holly was the same warm, charming, and happy girl they had gotten to know the previous fall. They also pointed out how Holly and Jonah laughed, worked as a team, and talked to each other, each listening carefully to what the other said.

As if to emphasize the point, when Holly finished her apple juice, Jonah jumped up and refilled her glass before anyone else could move.

***

Holly's twelve-year-old body began changing the following spring. It brought occasional pain and mood swings she didn't enjoy, but her mother explained it was part of developing a woman's body. By the time she and her family drove to Seattle to celebrate Jonah's *Bar Mitzvah* in late May, she was wearing her first bra and there was no mistaking her growing feminine form.

The week before they arrived, she was on the phone with Jonah. He'd teased her about her language ability and when Holly became quite angry, Jonah had sounded confused. He apologized and then made an excuse as if he was trying to get off the phone as quickly as possible.

Holly had hung up the phone, horrified she had gotten angry with him over such a silly remark. She had worried all week that he would still be upset with her when she arrived.

When Holly and her family arrived in Seattle, the usually self- assured Jonah seemed nervous. He took Holly to the media room at his house to show her the new Magnepan center channel speaker he had purchased for his family's audio system. He put on a CD and they sat quietly listening to it.

After the first song, Holly spoke. "I was worried you would still be upset with me, from our argument last week."

"I don't understand why you were angry with me. I've kidded you about your language ability many times."

"I'm not sure." Holly looked at the floor. "Your teasing rarely bothers me…but now, sometimes, the silliest things will suddenly upset me."

He shrugged. "Maybe you could warn me next time."

"I'll try."

"I feel bad if I hurt your feelings. I've been counting the days until you arrived so we could spend some time together."

"Thank you, Jonah." Holly said relieved. "I didn't know

what to expect."

"*Ya at eeh,* Holly," Jonah said in Navajo.

"Ya at eeh, Jonah."

Jonah put his arms around her and hugged her.

As she put her arms around his neck, Holly realized hugging Jonah made her body feel warm. She rather liked the sensation, she decided.

Chapter Two ~ *Trials and Tribulations*

AT THE END OF January, Chela and Warren became the proud parents of a baby girl, whom they named Carrie after Grandma Perla's mother of blessed memory. Grandma Perla was delighted. All the family came to their Seattle home to celebrate the birth.

Warren became a doting father to his new daughter and Chela continued her efficient running of their home.

Everything seemed good until mid-March, when Warren came home to find Chela sitting on the couch in their living room, staring off into space. He tried talking to her, but she didn't respond. He grasped her shoulders and shook her. He yelled at her as loudly as he could. There was no reaction. It was as if she didn't know he was in the room.

Carrie was screaming in the nursery. Warren ran to pick her up and dialed 911. Her diaper was soaked, and from the redness of her skin, had been for some time.

As he took care of his daughter, Warren's fear grew. He carried her to the living room and saw Chela still staring straight ahead. He heated a bottle of milk for Carrie who quieted down as soon as she started drinking.

The paramedics arrived and rushed Chela to the hospital. Warren arrived shortly afterwards and asked the doctor to check out Carrie as well—he didn't know how long she had been neglected.

After a few minutes, the doctor returned Carrie to Warren. "She's fine," he said. "We're waiting on some specialists to come down and check out your wife."

"How is she?"

"I don't have a good answer right now. We're going to have her examined by a neurologist and a psychiatrist."

"She was fine when I left for work this morning."

"I hate to speculate. Let's wait and see what the specialists say."

"We're going to begin running tests," the specialists said when they arrived. "As soon as we know something we'll let you know."

Trembling, Warren sat at Chela's bedside and cried. He couldn't imagine raising Carrie by himself. He tried to be positive, but everyone who examined Chela walked away, looking grim.

After three-days-of-tests, a doctor finally sat down and spoke to him.

"She's had a complete psychotic break. She has almost no awareness of anything or anyone around her. Sometimes people's brain chemistry changes without warning. We don't know why."

"Is there something you can give her?"

"Not really. She's going to need continuous care, perhaps for the rest of her life. I'm sorry, but there isn't much we can do for her. I know this is painful to hear, but she needs to be put in a long- term-care facility."

***

In Meridian, Idaho, at the home of Anna and Michael Levin, the phone rang. Michael looked at the call display. "It's Warren," he told Anna.

"Warren must have news about my sister," Anna said. "Pick up the extension, Michael. What if it's bad news?"

"Hello, Warren. Michael and I are both on the phone. Do you have news about Chela?"

"The doctors say that there isn't anything they can do," Warren blurted out.

Anna started shaking as tears formed in her eyes.

Michael had the cordless phone, so he walked closer to her, placing his hand at her back.

"Are you sure?" she asked, her voice trembling. "There's nothing they can do?"

"That's what they told me." Warren sounded as if he was holding back tears of his own. "They are going to be moving Chela to a long-term-care facility, Anna."

Anna's eyes glossed over and she shook her head slowly. "There isn't anything—I don't believe this is happening."

She turned and spoke to Michael. "My sister—it's like she died, but her body is still around—you talk to Warren." Anna dropped the phone and ran sobbing to her bedroom.

"Warren," Michael said, "would you like us to come up to Seattle…until you're settled?"

"Thank you, Michael, but you have Anna and your own newborn to deal with. No, I have to get settled taking care of Carrie myself, setup a routine, but I'm worried that it's going to be too much—never mind, I'll just have to find a way."

"If we can do anything for you, Warren, anything at all, please call."

"Actually, Michael, will you please call Chela's parents. I don't think I can handle telling them that their daughter is being institutionalized. Thank you." Warren hung up the phone.

On his way to the bedroom, Anna's Grandma Perla passed Michael in the hallway.

"I heard Anna crying, Michael."

He briefly told her about her other granddaughter, and she was visibly distressed by the news. When he said he would call Anna's parents after he went to check on her, Grandma Perla said she would do that.

Michael smiled and gave her an embrace, then went in to

comfort Anna. He sat next to her on their bed and she reached out to him immediately.

"Michael, I can't believe this is happening. Everyone liked Chela and I'm certain she would be a great mom for Carrie. Why would this happen to her? Why? I just don't understand."

"Warren wanted me to contact your folks and tell them what's going on. I ran into Grandma Perla outside her room and I had to tell her. She offered to call."

"Thank you, Michael." Anna began to sob harder. "I just realized, poor little Carrie is going to grow to adulthood without knowing who her mom is. She'll never go bird watching with her, or setup hummingbird feeders in their back yard, or hear her mother warn her about dating and boys. How can a little girl grow up with no mother?"

Michael held her tighter. "She has Warren, although…"

"Although what, Michael?"

"Well, he didn't finish his sentence, but it seems like Warren was thinking it may be too much for him to raise Carrie on his own."

"But, Michael, it has only been three-days."

Anna and Michael returned to their usual routine. That was the last they heard of Warren's distress. They assumed that Warren had worked everything out and had settled into being a single father to his beloved daughter. And so it went, until two-months had passed since Chela had been institutionalized.

Anna was hanging up the phone, just as Michael was coming home from work.

"Warren just called me," she said. "It was rather strange. He wanted to know what our work schedules were like. I told him I worked four-days-a-week from home and went in to the office all day Friday. I asked about Carrie, but he simply said good-bye and hung up."

***

The next Friday morning around eight-thirty, Warren arrived at Michael and Anna's door. A surprised Grandma Perla, alone at the time, greeted him, thinking he looked nervous and scared.

"I have a meeting in downtown Boise," he said. "Would you mind watching Carrie for me? I'll be back later today."

Although she had a bad feeling, Grandma Perla happily agreed and took the little girl in her arms. Warren gave her a hug, handed her a diaper bag, and left without saying good-bye.

She watched out the door as he climbed into a waiting cab, sure she saw him crying as the cab drove away.

As the day went on, she cared for the two infants, getting warier by-the-hour. By the time Anna and Michael arrived home from work around five o'clock, she felt quite certain that something bad had happened.

Anna and Michael were, of course, shocked to find an additional baby in their home. As it was dinnertime, they decided to sit down to eat, giving Warren a little more time and not wanting to call him if he was, indeed, in a meeting. But by seven o'clock, Anna said she was getting worried and tried to call Warren on his cell to see when he would be returning.

She hung up the phone without speaking or leaving a message. Both Michael and Grandma Perla watched her as she stood, shaking her head.

"What's going on?" Grandma Perla asked.

Anna's face reflected complete shock and disbelief. "The number has been disconnected."

Nervous, Anna called Warren's family. They were just as shocked, saying they had no idea what was going on with Warren. They too had thought he was coping with his new responsibilities.

***

The following morning, before they could report Warren as missing, a special-delivery-package arrived. It contained the titles to Warren's car and motorhome, along with a notarized letter stating everything in his home was now the property of Michael Levin. It further read Michael had power-of-attorney to sell his home and keep the proceeds for Carrie's education. There was the name of a lawyer in Seattle that Michael was to contact regarding Carrie, and a letter which Anna read aloud.

Anna and Michael, I tried, but I can't take care of Carrie. Raising her without Chela is proving to be impossible for me. She needs a home with two loving parents. I know you will provide that for her. When she's old enough, please tell her, her mother and father both love her. Please, don't hate me. I'm doing what I think is best for Carrie—I promised her a better life. Thank you, and love always, Warren.

"Why would he just leave his daughter?" Grandma Perla asked.

Michael shook his head. "In the note, it sounds as if he felt like he didn't have any other choice. I suspect he didn't want us to try to talk him out of leaving Carrie here, which is why he pretended to have a meeting."

"How can he give up his daughter?" Anna's eyes were wide in disbelief.

They all sat in shocked silence, until Michael spoke again. "If you have to quit work to take care of both little ones, Anna, it's okay with me," Michael said. "I certainly earn enough money to allow you to stay home with the kids."

"Let's just get through next week, and we'll see how it goes." She looked at her grandmother. "I think with Grandma here we can manage."

"I know we can," Grandma Perla assured them, as she rocked Carrie.

Around mid-afternoon on Saturday, Dell Beckham stopped

by the Levin home with their half of the brisket that she and Anna had purchased together and she had smoked for them.

Anna explained the new baby in the house. She told Dell how she had asked her brother, Steven, and his wife, Jackie to consider raising Carrie. Jackie and Steven had tried and tried, but couldn't seem to conceive. Their doctor had counseled patience, but Anna said Jackie would get depressed as each month's period arrived.

"They would be a perfect choice for Carrie," Dell said. "That's what I thought," Anna agreed. "But Jackie told me that if Warren returned and wanted the child back, she didn't think she could handle that. She said because I already have a child, it was different for me."

Dell placed a hand on Anna's shoulder.

"I just don't know," Anna said. "We're not prepared for this." "I have a crib and dresser," Dell said. "You can have them for Carrie. I'll ask Sherry Schulman and Ruth Holt. We'll see what they have. Let me call Wilson and have him bring the crib over right away."

Within-an-hour, there was a flurry of neighborly activity centered at the Levins' home. Tiny Carrie suddenly had her own crib, which was being assembled by Michael and Wilson. Pink blankets for the crib and a dresser also came over from the Beckhams. Baby girl clothing came from the Schulmans. From the Holts, Oliver and Drew brought over a rocking chair and a desk that would work as a change table.

There were endless offers of help from the neighbors, too. Everyone took a turn holding the baby girl and welcoming her to the neighborhood.

Just as things were calming down, Holly arrived. She asked if there was anything she could do to help Carrie. The usually self- assured Holly appeared quite nervous and concerned.

"Carrie is in her new crib," Anna said. "Why don't you hold her for a while?"

Michael looked more than a bit shocked. It was an absolute

rule of Anna's — sleeping babies were not to be disturbed. But Anna understood that on some level, Holly needed to hold Carrie, more than Carrie needed sleep.

***

"Hi, Carrie, I'm Holly." She picked up sleeping Carrie and carefully cradled her. "We're going to be friends."

Holly looked around the room. She saw the two rocking chairs, sat in one of them, and began to rock while she continued talking to Carrie.

"You're safe now. You're with a good family and they're going to take care of you and protect you. You don't have to worry about being abandoned — like some other kids. Anna and Michael will take care of you just like they take care of David Linn."

She pointed to the other crib. "See? You have a big brother to take care of you as well, and I just live a few blocks from here so you and I will be great friends. I'm going to teach you Spanish."

She leaned in to whisper in Carrie's little ears. "Keep this a secret, but I can teach you to speak Navajo, too. We'll have a great time speaking Navajo. And don't you worry — everyone will listen to you and respect what you have to say. Even when you're real little, they're going to listen to you."

When the baby started fussing, Holly began singing, "Sunshine, Lollipops and Rainbows." The warm bundle in her arms settled down, opened her bright blue eyes, and smiled. But after a couple-of-minutes, Holly stopped singing and began to cry.

"Holly, are you okay?" Anna called from down the hall.

"I'm fine. I'm happy, really. It's a long story, but I had some bad experiences when I was little so I just had to let Carrie know she would be okay and we would all be there for her, anytime she needed us."

Holly rocked Carrie quietly. "Mrs. Levin, would you mind asking Mr. Levin to play IZ's song 'Over the Rainbow' for me? I can't seem to remember the words, but I think Carrie will feel better if she hears it."

***

On Thursday night, the week of Jonah's May *Bar Mitzvah*, he and Holly were alone at his parents' home near Seattle, watching a sci-fi movie. His parents and older twin brothers were out with the rest of the family to see a late movie at the theatre.

The power in the house went out just after midnight, but Jonah noticed the house behind them still had power. He looked out the side windows and saw the houses on either side also had power.

When he heard noises coming from the first floor, Jonah remembered the protestors at his father's speaking engagement and immediately grabbed Holly's hand. They ran to the master bedroom and into his father's closet where Jonah quickly punched in the ten- digit-code that opened the gun safe.

He pulled out an AR-type-rifle and put a loaded magazine in it. After chambering a round he checked to make sure the safety selector was on safe, and then showed Holly how to hold it and aim it in the dark by finger pointing. The AR had little kick he reasoned, so it would be perfect for Holly to defend herself.

Jonah pulled out his favorite rifle, a Dash 91-main-battle-rifle. He knew the 91 kicked like a mule but he had heard his Uncle Meyer tell his dad that if someone wanted to have an argument with guns, a main battle rifle could be used to settle the argument. Besides, Jonah's dad had taught him how to properly hold the rifle, so he wasn't worried about the nasty kick.

He chambered a round in the 91 and stuffed an extra magazine for it in his belt, then set the selector on Holly's AR to fire and told her the next time she pulled the trigger a bullet would come out.

She whispered to him in the dark, "I'm scared, Jonah. Maybe we should call the police?"

"There's no time, Holly."

"Are you sure about this?"

"You can do this, Holly. I know you can."

They moved to the middle of the darkened bedroom where they could look down the thirty-foot hallway without being seen. The last fifteen-feet of the hallway lead to the master bedroom and was open on either side to the floor below.

Jonah stood sideways, parallel to the hallway. He brought the 91 up to his shoulder. Looking through the rifle's red dot sight, he strained to see in the darkened house. Holly looked at him and assumed a similar stance with the AR.

There was just enough light coming in the house from the streetlamps so they could watch as two shadowy forms moved up the open stairway to the second floor. The dark figures wore ski masks and carried weapons. At the top of the stairs they proceeded down the hall into Jonah's bedroom. Multiple barks came from what Jonah now recognized as silenced pistols.

"If they come toward us, one behind the other, we'll both shoot the lead person first," Jonah whispered. "But if they come down the hall separately, you take the one on the right and I'll take the one on the left. Don't start shooting until I do, or they do."

Holly didn't reply, but just nodded. "I have to concentrate on the job at hand, no matter how frightened I am, just like Dad told me," she whispered.

Jonah was scared too, but he'd been shooting enough times with his father, brothers, uncle, and cousins to know that he could hit what he aimed at. He watched as the two figures moved to each of his brother's rooms. He again heard the clicking sound of silenced rounds.

The figures quietly turned and started up the hallway to the master bedroom, separating to either side, then advancing slowly and quietly toward Jonah and Holly.

They had taken about four steps when Jonah decided they were close enough. He fired two rounds into the person on the left who immediately fell backwards.

Holly started pulling the trigger at the person on the right. Her target managed to fire a round at them, but luckily missed.

Just as Jonah had mentally rehearsed and practiced at the range hundreds of times, in a fraction-of-a-second, he had trained the red- dot sight of the main battle rifle at the second figure and fired twice, sending that invader flying backwards to the floor. Neither figure moved.

Jonah put his hand on Holly's shoulder. He could feel her trembling as she stopped firing. Then they walked out into the hallway and heard the back door of the house opening.

Jonah looked out a tall first-floor window in time so see someone running out of their back yard.

Just then, they heard a key going into the lock at the front door of the house.

***

Jonah's parents and brothers had pulled into the driveway of their home just in time to see flashes of light and hear a roar of gunfire. Morris jumped out of the car as Michelle dialed 911. Morris told the others to stay where they were and he raced toward the house while taking out his concealed carry pistol.

"Be careful," Michelle yelled at him as he dashed to the door.

Morris opened the front door a fraction and peered inside. His heart was racing at the thought that his son and Holly were inside. "Jonah?"

"We're okay, Dad, but there are a couple-of-creeps on the floor up here who aren't so great," Jonah called. "Also we saw a third person running out of the yard."

Relieved, Morris turned back to his wife. "Michelle, they're both okay." By the light of the streetlamp, he saw his wife's face relax at the news.

He went into the house, and using the flashlight on his pistol, he inspected the first floor. He stopped at the open back door and muttered. "The gunfire probably scared the hell out of him and he left in a hurry."

Morris called to Jonah again, telling him the first floor was clear, then he climbed the stairs to the second floor. His flashlight revealed two people in dark clothing and ski masks lying on the floor. Neither one had a pulse.

Jonah told him what had taken place.

"Thank God, you learned how to shoot and could defend yourself. These people had every intention of killing everyone in the house."

"Holly helped as well, Dad."

Morris smiled at Holly. "Good job, Holly," he told her. "Use my cell and call your mother. I don't want her to hear about this from someone else. Jonah, grab some flashlights."

***

Holly called and told her mom what had happened. "I kept thinking of the things Dad told us about being in combat," she said. "You know, how he said it's okay to be scared, but you have to concentrate so you can do the right thing. I was scared beyond belief, but I just kept repeating what Jonah told me to do, so when it was time to fire I just did it — and it worked. My ears are still ringing and I'm still scared as hell, but at least we stopped those fucking assholes."

Holly felt a pang of guilt when she realized what words she had just used.

25

"Holly," her mother began, "I'm quite glad you two stopped those fucking assholes."

Holly laughed. She had *never* heard her mother use profanity. "Thanks, Mom. I'm sorry I used swear words. Mr. Kaplan said he's going to have his wife drive me over to our hotel."

Just then, they heard sirens approaching the house. Holly told her mother the police were coming and she had to go.

"Jonah, clear the rifles and put them back in the safe," Morris said.

He studied Jonah with a puzzled expression for a moment.

"Wait a minute. How did you get into the safe? It has a ten-digit...never mind...I don't want to know. The police are arriving so I'm going outside to meet them—on second thought, maybe you should just lock the guns in another room. The police will want to see them."

Jonah nodded his head and stored the rifles in his parents' bathroom. Then he and Holly quietly followed his dad downstairs. Holly stopped midway down the stairs and broke the silence.

"I'm starting to shake." She looked down at her trembling hands. "I know what you mean," Jonah agreed. "I suddenly feel more scared now, than before."

"You saved me." She threw herself at Jonah and wrapped her arms around him.

"You helped," he said and pulled her closer.

"Ten-minutes-ago, I didn't know how to fire a rifle, Jonah. I couldn't have done that without you."

"Hey, partner, we did it. All the times I mentally rehearsed using the main battle rifle, I never imagined you would be depending on me to get it right. But just like I had rehearsed in my mind so many times, my plan worked."

Jonah raised his eyes as he prayed out loud. "Thank you, Lord, for making sure I had the skills necessary to protect Holly and myself in a time of great danger."

Holly squeezed his hand and smiled, raising her own eyes, too. "And I thank you, Lord, for putting Jonah at my side to protect me."

They embraced again, and Jonah put his lips on Holly's. It was a first kiss for each of them.

"That sure felt better than when I kiss my relatives," Jonah whispered.

"Thank you." She kissed his cheek. "I think I feel better now." "All the times I went to the range, I never thought…I mean, I pretended in my head sometimes. I guess I mentally rehearsed what I would do if someone invaded the house, I didn't have to think about it."

Jonah turned to lead the way to the front door, but Holly grabbed his arm and stopped him. When he turned back, she put her arms around his neck, her head on his shoulder, and softly started crying.

Holly was holding him so tight she thought she must be squeezing the air out of him, but he didn't complain; instead he just wrapped his own arms tighter around her.

"I was so scared," she told him. "I think I'm still scared. It is suddenly starting to seem so real. What if —"

"We stopped them." Jonah loosened his grip on her.

"Don't let go!"

He clutched her tightly again. "Hey, it's going to be okay."

After a few moments, Holly slowly let go. "Thank you. You saved me."

"We saved each other."

She put her hands on either side of his face. "Jonah Kaplan, listen to me," Holly said with utmost determination. "You saved my life. No matter what you say to other people, I know in my heart…you did that for me."

She leaned forward and kissed him.

They walked the rest of the way down the stairs and as they were rounding the corner, the police were heading up. Jonah and Holly followed them along with Jonah's father.

Jonah and Holly sat at the end of the hall and told one of the officers what had happened. Then, as the other officer removed the ski masks from the two bodies, they heard Jonah's dad say that he recognized them as protesters who had been removed from his lecture in Oregon. He told the officer all about it.

"I didn't realize how angry they were." Jonah's dad's voice was shaking. "They tried to kill my entire family."

At that, the officer said he was done talking to Jonah and Holly for now, and they walked out of the house. Michelle grabbed them both and embraced them tightly.

"Thank God you're all right. I was so frightened when I heard the gunfire. Holly, I'm going to drive you back to your hotel. We will all be staying at Jonah's Uncle Meyer's home tonight."

When Holly arrived at their hotel she sat with her mother. "No matter what anyone says, Mom, I want you to know Jonah saved me. He's the one who realized it wasn't a neighborhood power outage and that something was wrong. He's the one who got the rifles from the safe and showed me how to use one of them. Jonah even told me what to do depending on how they came up the hallway. He did all of that, Mom."

Holly cried quietly, wiping her tears away with her sleeve. "I have to thank Dad for being willing to tell us what it was like to be in combat, too. I think those conversations really helped me so I could do what needed to be done. I am so lucky to have you guys around me."

***

On Friday morning the families gathered for brunch at Meyer and Joan's home on Lake Washington. As soon as Ruth Holt saw Jonah, she walked over and embraced him.

"Holly told me what you did last night." She had tears in

her eyes. "God bless you for saving my daughter's life."

Much of the conversation remained centered on the shooting and there were lots of questions and compliments for Jonah and Holly. Jonah continued to insist that he and Holly had saved each other. Holly just smiled each time he said that.

Meyer saw how close they stayed to each other. He thought about how what they had been through had the potential to cement their relationship—not that they needed it. It was impossible to miss the glow on Holly's face whenever she looked at Jonah.

Ethan and David, Jonah's older twin brothers, looked like they were walking a foot off the ground with pride in their brother's actions.

"From the first time he went to the shooting range with Uncle Meyer's friend Gene, we were told Jonah was a great shot," Ethan's girlfriend, Sheryl, commented.

"And since he was little, he's always been calm in an emergency," David reminded them.

"The intruders were wearing body armor," Morris told the assembled relatives. "If Jonah hadn't picked up the main-battle-rifle, they might not have been able to stop them. From what I saw, Jonah managed to get two shots into each of them roughly center of mass. I'm sure that's what did it. The kids also must have surprised the hell out of them with all the sudden gunfire. From what the police told me, the intruders only managed to fire off one-round in their direction and it went into the ceiling."

Then Meyer and Joan took Jonah for a walk out to their antique car garage. They explained to him that the Duesenberg he had helped restore, had brought in a lot of money at auction which Jonah could give to the charity of his choice in honor of his *Bar Mitzvah*.

"You saved two lives last night, Jonah," Meyer said. "I can't begin to tell you how proud I am of what you accomplished. There are probably fewer than a half dozen boys your age in the entire state who could pick up a main-battle-rifle and put it to efficient use like you did."

"Thank you, Uncle Meyer. At first I was thinking I wanted to hide, but then immediately realized the best way to protect Holly was to be prepared to shoot them, instead of letting them try to find and shoot us."

"It's your *Bar Mitzvah* tomorrow," Joan said excitedly. "We had picked out a present for you, but after what you did last night, we think something special is in order." She reached into her pocket and took out a set of car keys. She handed them to Jonah.

He gasped as his eyes went wide. "The keys to the Auburn roadster?"

"You've earned it, Jonah," Meyer said.

"Wow. I don't know what to say except thank you so much." He hugged his aunt and uncle.

"Thank you, Jonah, for protecting yourself and precious Holly," Joan said. "Not to mention telling your brother how to get out of a snow bank in an emergency, and helping your uncle with a medical emergency when you were just little. This car is nothing compared to what you've accomplished in your young life. It's an honor to have you as part of our family."

"I was wondering about something, Jonah," Meyer said. "How did you get into the gun safe?"

"My father has a methodical mind. He thinks in patterns. Whenever he walked up to the gun safe, I watched his arm movement. I certainly couldn't see the numbers, but he moved his arm diagonal, reverse diagonal, horizontal, and middle top." Jonah shrugged as if it was the easiest thing in the world. "It wasn't hard to determine that the pattern was one, five, nine, three, five, seven, four, five, six, two."

Meyer and Joan both laughed.

***

Just as they started back to the house, Holly's dad, Oliver, came up the driveway. He parked and got out, heading straight to Jonah. "Holly told me what happened." He patted Jonah on the back and his voice was filled with relief and pride. "Your quick thinking and aggressive action saved my daughter's life. If I'm ever — God forbid — in combat again, I'd want Jonah Kaplan right next to me."

"Wow. Thank you, Mr. Holt."

Hearing an actual combat veteran saying those words was probably the greatest compliment Jonah had ever received in his young life. He immediately told Holly what her father had said.

"He has told me many times that when the you-know-what hits the fan, you want the most dependable people around you," Holly said proudly. "I have firsthand knowledge he's right about you. When the poop hit the fan last night, I was safe, because you were next to me."

"You helped," Jonah reminded her, accepting a warm hug.

A short while later, Holly and Jonah were introduced to Uncle Meyer's cousin, Isaac Rabinowitz. He had a PhD in psychology and specialized in family and grief counseling. Uncle Meyer had asked him to spend some time talking to them about what happened.

He had brought along his yellow Labrador, Jake. He said the dog helped him break the ice with younger patients.

Together, they all went into Uncle Meyer's office. Dr. Rabinowitz sat at the desk while Jonah and Holly each sat on one of the wide, leather chairs facing the desk. Jonah thought Holly seemed nervous.

Dr. Rabinowitz asked her if she would mind if Jonah sat with her in the same chair. He said it was so he wouldn't have to keep looking back and forth when he was talking to them, but Jonah thought it was to put Holly at ease. Since Holly seemed more relaxed after Jonah moved, he supposed he was right.

Dr. Rabinowitz leaned back in Uncle Meyer's desk chair and opened a leather clipboard. "So how about telling me what you were feeling last night."

They were quiet for a moment. They exchanged a glance, and then Holly spoke. "Something strange happened," she said. "Until it was over, I think I felt more angry than scared."

"Why do you think you felt that way?"

She became quiet again for a bit and then said, "Well, I was angry that these people, who didn't even know us, were trying to try to hurt me and Jonah — his whole family really."

"That's funny," Jonah said. "I remember being angry they were trying to hurt us, too."

"Is it bad we were angry?" Holly asked.

Dr. Rabinowitz looked pensive. "Let's think about this situation. You felt your lives were being threatened. The two total strangers in front of you were putting you in mortal danger...I think I'd have been angry as hell."

"But we killed two people." Holly said.

"Yeah. I feel bad they died," Jonah said. "But not that bad, because they were trying to kill us. They probably thought they had already killed me and my brothers when they came to my parents' room."

Holly seemed to carefully consider Jonah's words as she petted Jake, who had put his head across her knee. "Yes, Jonah's right," she said finally. "They shot into David's, Ethan's, and Jonah's beds so we knew what they would do to us. We didn't have a choice. We didn't go looking to kill them. They came looking to kill us. The only choice we had was to shoot them first."

"The *Talmud* says when someone is coming to kill you, go quickly and kill him first," Dr. Rabinowitz counseled.

"That's exactly what we did," Jonah said.

They talked awhile longer and then Dr. Rabinowitz nodded his head, shut his clipboard, and clicked his pen closed. "I think that's enough for now. Do you agree, Jake?"

Hearing that, Jake bounded over. Dr. Rabinowitz took out a tennis ball and Jake took the ball in his mouth, returning to Holly and Jonah. He then flipped his head to the side, neatly depositing the ball onto Holly's lap.

"Good boy, Jake."

Holly smiled then looked up at Dr. Rabinowitz. "He wants me to play with him."

"Why don't you take him down to the lake? He'd love to retrieve the ball for you."

"Did you train him to do that?" Jonah asked as they stood to leave.

"It was easy to teach him. He loves to play and he's absolutely wired to retrieve," Dr. Rabinowitz said with a smile.

"One more thing," he said. "I'd like permission to talk to your parents concerning our conversation today. I just want to reassure them that you two are dealing with this in a healthy way so far. I'd also like to talk to them about seeing you again in a month, just to be sure."

"That's okay with me," Holly said.

"No problem," Jonah agreed.

"If either of you need to talk, or become anxious before then, please call me."

They both nodded and then ran outside with Jake on their heels.

***

Jonah's *Bar Mitzvah* was a wonderful celebration. He chanted all the blessings and prayers in a strong and melodic fashion. Considering how the week could have been, everyone was relieved he could still perform so well.

Before he began his *Bar Mitzvah* speech, the Rabbi spoke to the congregation. "As I worked with Jonah to help prepare him for this special day, I learned quite a bit about him. He has a strong dedication to Judaism. With all he learned during this time, he evidenced a strong work ethic. I've also learned, just today in fact, Jonah is quite a straight shooter."

Most in the congregation groaned at the Rabbi's terrible pun. The Rabbi then proceeded to discuss the Jewish view of the importance of defending one's self. Then, Jonah's *Bar Mitzvah* speech described the week's *Parsha* and its significance. After he finished the last sentence, Jonah looked directly at Holly and said in Navajo, "I wish to thank the Great Spirit who brought Holly's sunshine into my life to lift my heart and protect me."

Upon hearing those words, Holly knew her heart had just been lifted. She replied in Navajo, "Thank you, Jonah."

Ruth leaned over and whispered to her daughter. "That didn't sound like Hebrew and from the confused look on the Rabbi's face, I'd say it wasn't."

"It wasn't, Mom. Jonah just said some lovely things to me in Navajo."

"You mean you two have been secretly learning Navajo this spring?"

"I hope you're not upset with us. I know you wanted me to wait, but Jonah bought the program in January and we've been working together for thirty minutes almost every night. I'm learning faster than he is, but if you knew what he just said to me you would know he's doing great."

Ruth shook her head in disbelief. She turned to Anna Levin. "I've been teaching advanced Italian to Holly the entire spring. She was also working hard enough to get great grades in school and all that time she was teaching herself Navajo."

"Holly," Anna said. "You are one hard worker."

Ruth smiled at her daughter. "I think your father is right about you. You *do* have a word magnet in your head."

"Did I just hear Klingon?" the Rabbi asked Jonah.

"No, Rabbi," Jonah smiled and replied. "That was Navajo." The Rabbi started to laugh, but then realized Jonah was serious.

"I guess I shouldn't be surprised that erudite Jonah would be speaking Navajo."

Chapter Three ~ *The Motorhome*

MICHAEL LEVIN, ALONG WITH Oliver and Drew Holt, flew up to Seattle on a Friday morning to bring Warren's motorhome and Jeep back to Meridian.

Michael planned to sell them and put the money in Carrie's education fund.

When they arrived, they checked out the motorhome and found it to be in excellent condition, so they drove the unit over to a trailer rental location and picked up a car carrying trailer to transport Warren's Jeep back to Idaho.

Later, they drove over to Oliver's parents' home for dinner. His wife's parents were there as well.

"Michael, what will you do with the motorhome?" Oliver's dad asked during dinner.

"I'm going to sell it and invest the money for Carrie's education. I'll be doing the same thing with the money we get for the Jeep and the house."

"What do you think the motorhome and Jeep are worth?" Ruth's father asked.

"The motorhome is worth one-hundred-and-a-half. The Jeep is old so it's only worth about ten-grand."

The two grandfathers smiled and nodded to each other.

"Will you take one-hundred-and-a-half for both?" Oliver's dad asked.

"Dad, what are you talking about?" Oliver asked, looking shocked.

"The parents-in-law have gotten together and we'd like to buy the motorhome and Jeep for Oliver and Ruth. We've done our research and we know Michael is asking a fair price—especially if he throws in the Jeep."

"Michael, what do you say?" Ruth's dad asked.

Michael considered their offer. "I need to get something for the Jeep to be fair to Warren and Chela," he said. "What would you say to one-hundred-and-fifty-five-thousand-dollars for both vehicles?"

The fathers-in-law looked at each other and then put out their hands to shake his.

"Wow, our own motorhome!" Drew yelled, unable to contain his excitement. "Thanks, you guys. And I'm going to learn to drive in a Jeep."

Oliver looked at the parents. "Thank you so much," he said, still appearing astounded. He stood up and gave each of them a hug. Drew did the same.

After some banking and signing of titles the next day, the threesome began the nine-hour drive back to Meridian.

Oliver said he was in heaven thinking of all the trips he was going to take his family on. "We'll definitely be on the neighborhood trip to Yellowstone this summer," he told Michael.

"This coach is identical to mine," Michael said. "So we can work together to maintain them if you'd like."

"Michael, I'll certainly be looking forward to that."

They stopped for a fast-food lunch, planning to eat in the restaurant, but Drew begged them to eat in the motorhome.

"It will be our first meal in there. I'll do the cleanup and throw out the garbage like I do at home."

They laughed at his request, but agreed, and an elated Drew ate his first meal in *their* motorhome.

***

The following day saw two motorhomes parked on the apron to the Holts' garage. Oliver had made up checklists and started a maintenance log book for each coach, and he and Michael started by checking on the driveline components. Afterwards, they checked out the electrical, water, and heating/cooling systems. Every time they found a defect they noted it in the coach's log and scheduled a time to repair the problem. Drew followed them everywhere they went including in, under, and on top of the coaches.

Ruth and Holly went out to the motorhome, and Ruth was sporting a big smile.

Holly looked at Ruth staring at the motorhome and she asked why her mom was smiling so much.

"Your grandparents spent an amazing amount of money for the motorhome and Jeep. They could have just as easily saved it for their own needs. As you go through life, people will tell you about many important things. Take it from your mom, the single most important thing is family."

Then Ruth turned to Michael. "And great neighbors don't hurt either."

"I'm happy to be able to see you guys enjoy this," Michael said. "Plus it will be great having you along on the trip to Yellowstone."

Just then, Anna called Michael over from their front door. He excused himself and went up to her. She asked him how everything was going.

"I'm going to have much more confidence in our coach now," Michael told her. "Oliver is methodical to a fault. He discovered a misaligned pulley which was causing excessive wear on a V belt. I wouldn't have discovered anything wrong until it broke. I'll pick up a new belt this week and we'll be installing it next Saturday. We made up a soap solution to check for leaks in the propane lines. The two of us are getting to be good friends. I'm sure glad we're neighbors."

Chapter Four ~ *Caravan to Yellowstone*

IN LATE JUNE, A caravan of motorhomes and travel trailers left Meridian, Idaho destined for Yellowstone National Park. The Schulmans had purchased a used fifth-wheel trailer and were busy learning its systems and how to drive the unit, and the Beckham family led the caravan as they had been to Yellowstone numerous times before. While they all had cell phones, they had also installed CB radios to talk to each other.

The Wagoner family, their friends from Nampa, Idaho also traveled with them and brought four horses for trail riding.

Sean and Trisha McCarthy traveled in their new, and quite large, fifth-wheel-coach. With three children to travel with, they needed all the space they could afford.

A few-days-earlier, Steve and Jackie Cardozo left southern New Mexico towing their camper with Steve's pickup truck. They planned on traveling about six- or seven-hours-each-day to arrive at the campground north of Jackson, Wyoming at the same time as those traveling from Meridian.

Jonah and David Kaplan, much to Holly's and Linda's delight, were invited to accompany the families. Ethan was busy with Sheryl and he wasn't too sad to see his brothers go without him. David and Linda were looking forward to starting college that fall in Seattle. Jonah and Holly would be starting high school.

In the back seat of the Schulmans' four-door pickup, David, Andy, and Linda kept each other entertained with word games and puzzles. In the Holts' motorhome, Jonah had six-or-seven-million- questions for Oliver about how the motorhome had different running gear requirements than a car. He was amazed the motorhome's diesel engine could develop so much power at such low RPM. Holly played some games with Drew and her mom for a while. Then Drew decided to do some drawings, at which point Holly and Ruth promptly fell asleep.

Half way through the drive they all stopped in the parking lot of a large mall to break for lunch and do some shopping.

Alex Schulman was nervous about towing their fifth-wheel- trailer. He was particularly worried about the next part of the trip where they would be traveling through mountains. "I haven't driven through anything but relatively flat terrain so far."

David volunteered to do some of the driving for him.

Wilson Beckham gave David a quick lesson on towing a fifth- wheel-camper. "You're going to follow me when we leave. If you can read the brand name on my camper, you're following too close. These rigs are heavy so we brake early and slow down gently. Going down big grades, I may radio instructions to you, to slow down and use a lower gear. If something goes wrong you gently, and I mean *gently*, slow down the rig, and after you've slowed to walking speed, get to the side of the road. You'll be driving a powerful diesel pickup. Even so, there's no reason to try to accelerate quickly. Keep an eye on the oil pressure, engine temperature, and the transmission temperature. Let me know immediately if any readings are out of the green. Lastly, watch your mirrors, watch your mirrors, and watch your mirrors. When you're making a turn, keep your eye on the wheels of the trailer to make sure you aren't cutting the corner too tight. We're all on CB channel fourteen, so monitor that channel and let us know if something doesn't look or sound right." Suddenly the gravity of what David had volunteered to do hit him.

"Mr. Schulman, would you mind if Jonah rode with us?" he asked. "He could help keep an eye on things for me."

"That would be fine, David, I'm sure Andy would like to spend time with Drew in the Holts' coach."

Jonah happily agreed to be the co-driver for his big brother. The other drivers were entertained by Jonah's regular CB radio reports to Mr. Beckham on the temperatures and pressures in the pickup his big brother was driving.

Just as they were entering the mountains and David was getting comfortable behind the wheel, towing a fifth-wheel-trailer, it started to rain.

Wilson Beckham announced they should put more distance between the units.

Everything was going well until they hit a long wet downhill section of road. David was about to shift to a lower gear to help keep his speed down but tried his brakes first. The pickup lurched and the trailer's back end was swinging out to the left.

Jonah coached David to get off the brake and open the throttle slightly. David did as his brother instructed him and the trailer swung back to the right and then centered itself behind the pickup.

Jonah continued to advise David, and he gradually slowed the unit down until they were at walking speed. He guided the pickup and trailer to the side of the road, and then applied the service brakes.

They all gathered at the side of the road. Oliver and Wilson ran up to David to find out what happened.

"Great driving, Tex," Oliver said to David after hearing an explanation. He looked at Jonah then patted him on the back. "Fast thinking and good instructions, professor."

Jonah grinned proudly.

After a brief discussion on what had taken place, it was decided to drive slowly to the next exit and attempt to diagnose and repair the problem on the wide exit ramp. David stood, looking frightened, next to Linda, while Jonah appeared as calm as can be. Holly was standing behind him with a huge smile, clearly proud of what he had done to help.

Oliver made a suggestion. "I think David needs a little time to calm down. Alex, would you mind if Jonah drives your rig the few miles to the exit ramp. Don't worry. Jonah's Uncle Meyer gave him some driving lessons in his old Mack semi and a flatbed. I'll bet that's why he knew what to do. Seeing as he can drive that old Mack with a trailer, I'm certain that he knows how to handle the fifth- wheel."

"In that case, I wouldn't mind at all."

Oliver turned to Jonah. "Okay, professor, you keep your speed down and no more than ten-miles-an-hour," he said in a stern voice. "The truck has a powerful diesel engine, so you shouldn't need more than a thousand-revs. Put your flashers on. I'll stay behind you with my flashers on as well."

Holly was imploring her dad with her eyes.

"Go ahead Holly, you can ride with him. You stay on the radio and let me know how things are going."

"Yes, Dad," Holly said excitedly.

Continuing in a serious voice, Oliver told Jonah, "You don't start moving until I tell you to. We'll let everyone else drive ahead and wait for us at the exit ramp. Is that clear?"

"Yes, sir, Mr. Holt."

As they walked back to their motorhome, Ruth expressed concern Jonah was so young to be driving a pickup and towing a trailer.

"He saved them, Ruth. He knew what to do and David didn't. Jonah received great grades in school this year so his Uncle Meyer rewarded him by teaching him to drive that Mack. He deserves a chance to be the driver of that big rig. We'll be driving slowly anyway. That kid must have been born with ice water in his veins. When there's an emergency, he manages to stay as calm as can be and do what needs to be done. As if that wasn't enough, Holly's riding with him.

There's no way he would let anything bad happen to her."

After the other units drove ahead of them, Oliver called over the radio to Holly to tell Jonah to put the pickup in gear in preparation for getting back on the interstate. Oliver waited until he couldn't see any cars coming up the highway behind them. Over the radio, he signaled to Jonah to pull out.

"Does everything look okay?" Holly asked.

Looks good," Jonah said after glancing at the gauges.

"Everything looks good Dad," Holly broadcast on the radio.

"This is me, Holly by the way."

She kept up regular reports during the fifteen-minutes it took to leave the interstate.

When they came to a halt on the long exit ramp, Oliver took out a coil of wire and a continuity meter. He and Michael started tracing the trailer's brake system. Jonah and Drew attached themselves to Oliver like a starfish trying to open a clam so they could watch and learn what he was doing. They eventually discovered a broken wire leading to one side of the trailer's brakes.

"Uneven braking," Drew said. "That's why it swung out."

Oliver smiled at his son. "That's absolutely right. It looks like we may have another automotive professor here."

Jonah looked at a grinning Drew and they high-fived. "Great call, Drew," he told him.

Michael and Oliver quickly spliced in a new section of wire. They each watched one side of the repaired trailer while Wilson drove the trailer forward at low speed and slammed on the trailer brakes. Both sides of the trailer's brakes locked up as they should.

Mr. Schulman kept patting David and Jonah on the shoulder, telling them they did great.

Wilson asked David if he was calm enough to continue driving. David confirmed he was, but asked if Jonah could ride with him again.

The weather cleared and stayed that way for the rest of the drive. The magnificent Grand Tetons came into view. Many "*oohs*" and "*ahs*" could be heard in each of the vehicles. As they pulled into the campground, they saw Steve and Jackie had arrived from New Mexico and were in the campground office registering. After signing in, the convoy drove to pull-through parking where they lined up adjacent to each other.

Chapter Five ~ *Ya at eeh*

THROUGHOUT THE WEEK, ANNA was delighted by the enjoyment her two little-ones brought to the group.

Everyone wanted a turn holding them. Holly certainly loved to be around them. She would immediately volunteer to help with anything concerning their needs and talked to them constantly. From feeding and changing diapers to bathing and dressing them, Holly, Linda, and Jackie gave Anna a tremendous amount of time to relax and enjoy Yellowstone.

With Grandma Perla visiting Anna's parents in New Mexico during the two-week trip, she was glad for the help. She was also looking forward to seeing her parents soon, too, as they would return to Boise with Grandma Perla to visit.

During a hike to the hot springs, Jonah had Carrie sitting in a baby support backpack while Holly walked next to him. Jonah and Holly spoke to each other in Navajo as much as possible, and Anna enjoyed watching and listening to them. Though, when Holly spoke to Carrie it was in Italian. Before the trip she had asked Anna if it would be all right if she talked to the little ones in Italian and Anna loved the idea.

Ruth had also given Anna and Michael some language learning tips to help them rapidly learn Hebrew to speak to them in that language, too. So when Michael saw the way Carrie seemed to listen intently to Jonah and Holly speaking in multiple languages, he had to make a joke.

"Great," he said. "As a teenager she'll be able to talk back to us in multiple languages."

Anna smiled, playfully defending her daughter. "She's

going to be a perfect little lady so that will never happen, Michael Levin!"

David Kaplan carried David Linn. He and Linda had demonstrated immense patience in dealing with the tiny ones, too. Linda had brought a list of developmental milestones she used to demonstrate what the eighteen-month-old babies were capable of. David Linn was at the age where he was making lots of little sounds and loved when someone repeated the sounds back to him.

"Carrie isn't making many sounds yet," Holly mentioned to Jonah.

"Carrie?" he asked. "How do you solve a differential equation?"

She was quiet for a moment and then started make a cute series of bubbly little sounds.

Holly laughed.

"See that?" Jonah said. "Carrie can talk. You just have to ask the right question."

Holly smiled and agreed. "Maybe she'll be a multi-lingual math geek when she grows up!"

Then, as if to emphasize the point, the two of them resumed speaking in Navajo again.

They had all stopped to admire a magnificent, rather large, blue pool with shades of copper along its edges, when a young couple walked up to Jonah and Holly.

"You speak Navajo very well," they said. "Where did you learn to speak the language?"

"We learned from the Rosetta Stone package we purchased," Holly replied. "We're just beginners. Please correct us if we say something incorrectly."

Scott and Katie Rollins introduced themselves and continued walking with them while speaking in Navajo.

Little Carrie, Anna observed, seemed to become more active and verbal while the four of them spoke in Navajo. "Maybe she wants to learn Navajo instead of Italian?" Anna said to Michael.

"With Ruth and Holly in the neighborhood," he replied, "there's no telling what she'll be able to speak."

As they walked, Katie taught Holly some simple Navajo songs to sing to Carrie and David Linn.

Jonah commented that he was fascinated by how quickly Holly learned new words and how fast she improved her grammar and pronunciation when Scott or Katie corrected her.

They all went to Yellowstone Lodge for lunch. Anna took little Carrie out of the backpack to feed her, but as she walked to their table Carrie started to cry, reaching back toward Holly.

"Holly, I think Carrie wants you to feed her," Anna said. "Would you mind?"

"I'd love to, Mrs. Levin," Holly replied, her voice full of enthusiasm.

After handing Carrie to Holly, Anna grabbed some of Carrie's pureed food and a bottle for her and placed them on the table in front of Holly. Carrie was still fussing when Holly held her, and much to their amazement, she was now reaching toward Jonah.

Jonah took her and placed her in his left arm and she immediately calmed down. "Carrie wants to be with the math people and hear us speak in equations," Jonah said as he began feeding her.

"It's the strangest thing," Anna said. "If David Linn is upset, he feels better when either Michael or I or Grandma hold him, but when Carrie is uncomfortable only Jonah holding her will do."

"We guys know how to take care of our women," Jonah said in a deep voice.

Yes you do!" Anna and Holly said simultaneously. They looked at each other and started laughing.

Holly placed a bib around Carrie and looked to be in heaven watching Jonah feed her.

After lunch, Scott and Katie, who were meeting friends on the other side of the park, said good-bye to Holly and Jonah.

"If you're ever in Sedona, Arizona, please stop by," Katie said. "We'd love to have another opportunity to speak Navajo. Scott's grandparents live nearby. They're native speakers so you can work on your language skills with them. Also his grandfather knows tons of old stories of Navajo life."

"He was one of the Code Talkers as well," Scott mentioned.

"It would be a great honor to meet him," Jonah answered.

Scott smiled. "He would be honored, as are we, because you've taken the time to learn our language."

"We have your email address so we will surely stay in touch," Holly said.

Chapter Six ~ *The Dinosaur Museum*

SOME DAYS THE FAMILIES traveled around the area together and some days they traveled separately. Jonah convinced a group to head over to Thermopolis, Wyoming, to see the magnificent archaeological digs and Wyoming Dinosaur Museum located there.

Holly enjoyed the museum as well, but enjoyed Jonah's excitement and enthusiasm even more. It was during the trip to the museum they started holding hands. Jonah saw an Archaeopteryx and wanted Holly to walk with him to see it.

She was standing and looking at an Allosaurus when Jonah slipped his hand into hers and guided her over to the Archaeopteryx display. Holly liked the display but was most excited he was holding her hand. *Such a simple thing and I'm enjoying it so much*, she thought.

A different day, Tina and Trace went trail riding and taught horse-riding skills to Jonah, Holly, David, Linda, Drew, and Andy.

David and Jonah, the big city kids of the group, weren't too sure if they wanted to spend a day on horseback, but since Holly and Linda were going, they tagged along. Holly thought it was rather funny that Jonah and David could safely tow a fifteen-thousand-pound RV with a pickup drum truck but they were nervous about riding a horse.

Jonah quickly discovered that traveling on a horse was a great platform for taking pictures with the camera his cousin, Leah, had given him to use during the trip. He was under orders from her to send back lots of pictures—which he dutifully did each night with a laptop connected to the internet.

The following week was filled with more exploration of the magical sights of Yellowstone, trips to Jackson, float trips on the Snake River, ATV rides, and more trail riding on horseback. Holly was pleased to have spent many hours with Jonah during the two- week vacation.

"Our relationship is growing," she reported to her mom. "It didn't matter what we were doing. We were happy just being together. I think that's great."

"I think that's great as well," her mother told her.

"Sometimes his excitement is contagious, like when we were at the dinosaur museum. His delight at what we saw kind of rubbed off on me. Is that weird?"

"That's a sign of a caring relationship."

"We have a caring relationship," Holly said slowly and quietly. She thought for a while, then added, "When we're together, it's almost like we're taking care of each other. Even when we had little Carrie with us, we both took care of her as well as watching out for each other. I wonder if it was easy to take care of Carrie because we have spent so much time taking care of one another."

"From what I've observed," her mother told her, "Jonah is spending nearly as much time taking care of Carrie as you are. That's quite mature of the two of you and speaks volumes about your relationship. You talk about how Jonah *gets* you. Well, he *gets* little Carrie as well, which is astounding for someone his age."

On Wednesday, everyone said good-bye to Jackie and Steven as they began their drive back to New Mexico, while Friday morning saw the Meridian caravan form up and begin the one-day drive home.

Then on Saturday morning, Linda drove David, Jonah, and Holly over to the airport for the Kaplan brother's flight home to Seattle. After long hugs and kisses good-bye, the girls watched as the brothers cleared security. They waved to the boys one last time and quietly drove home.

When they got home, Holly confided in her mom. "It hurt to say good-bye to him this time, Mom," she said.

"I know, honey. If the two of you are meant to be together then you'll have more opportunities to see each other."

"At least Linda will be in university with David this fall."

"That will be wonderful for them—I have a picture I've been meaning to show you. Remember the day we went on the long hike and ended up at Old Faithful?"

"Yes, I do. Jonah had Carrie in the backpack the entire day. She was so excited to see the eruption and watch the buffalo that trotted across in front of us. When we arrived back at our motorhome we were completely exhausted. Jonah and I curled up on the couch around Carrie and the three us fell asleep."

Ruth showed Holly a picture of the three of them fast asleep under her Code Talkers blanket. "Do you think we should frame this?" Ruth asked.

"I'd love this in a frame, Mom," Holly replied.

***

Three months after returning to Idaho, Anna received a good news phone call from Jackie.

"Holding the babies up in Yellowstone must have been good for me. Anna, I'm two-months-pregnant."

Anna screamed, "Yes," so loudly, the sound most likely registered on the Richter scale.

Much to Anna's amusement, Jackie suggested she should check with the Holts as Holly had spent nearly as much time holding the babies as Jackie had.

Chapter Seven ~ *Boyfriends Visit*

THE FOLLOWING YEAR IN early June, sixteen-year-old Holly and twenty-year-old Linda drove out to the Boise airport on a pretty Friday morning to meet Jonah and David. They were coming to town to travel with the Meridian families on their camping trip to southern Utah.

As they watched the people coming out of the security area, Holly couldn't stop smiling. All week long she had been planning what she would say to Jonah. When she finally saw them walking up the corridor, her heart started racing. Holly was so excited to see Jonah she ran up and threw her arms around him. As he held her, the practiced words disappeared from Holly's mind and all she kept saying was, "Hold me, hold me."

David picked up Linda and spun her around while they kissed. "I know it's only been two-weeks we've been apart but I missed you so much," Linda told him.

When Linda dropped Holly and Jonah off at the Holts' home, Drew came out to welcome Jonah.

"How's the Auburn running?" he asked as he picked up one of Jonah's bags.

"It's been running kind of rough. After the camping trip, I'm going to have to perform an ignition tune up on the old girl."

"Wow, I sure wish I could be there to help you."

They walked up to the house and Holly's mom opened the door for them. She had a huge smile as she welcomed the teenager who made her daughter so happy. "Welcome to our home, Jonah. I'm so glad to see you."

After some brief conversation, Jonah, Drew, and Holly took his things up to the study which also served as the guest bedroom.

"Don't unpack too much," Holly's mother called to Jonah. "We're only going to be here one night. Oliver will be bringing the motorhome back to the house shortly and we'll start loading everything for tomorrow's trip."

Multiple laundry baskets filled with various supplies had been lined up in the living room. As soon as they heard the rumble of the motorhome pulling into the driveway, Ruth called to them.

"Each of you, please carry a laundry basket out to the motorhome. White baskets get stored in the outside bays and yellow baskets go inside."

"Hey professor, how's life in the big city?" Oliver called to Jonah when he saw him. "How's your family?"

"Everyone's great," Jonah replied shaking Oliver's hand.

Ruth entered the motorhome and started directing where she wanted things stored. As more laundry baskets filled with goods were brought in and the contents stored, she joked, "My helpers look like ants bringing items into the ant hill."

As Holly helped Jonah bring his things out to the motorhome she saw something like a long mailing tube and asked him about it.

"I'll show you after we finish storing things in the motorhome," he answered with a big smile and a twinkle in his eye.

They finished loading up the motorhome, but then dinner also got in the way, so it wasn't until after dinner that Jonah brought the object down to the living room where everyone had gathered.

Seated together on a love seat, Jonah turned to Holly. "Holly, an older woman in our neighborhood died recently.

She left instructions to sell her collection of Native American art and give the proceeds to charity. I saw this and thought you would treasure it, as she did."

Then, Jonah un-wrapped the tube and removed a thirty-inch- by-fifty-inch Navajo woven rug with a black and gray border. The central area had dark rust, black, and different shades of gray in a white background.

"Oh my word," Holly said. "It's beautiful."

"It's called a storm pattern," a smiling Jonah said. "You can tell because of the central block with four arms extending to the areas near the corners which represent the four sacred mountains of the Navajo Reservation. This one includes lightening and representations of water bugs."

"I'm amazed the weaver managed such an intricate pattern in a hand-woven item," Holly's dad said.

"That's too pretty to put on the floor," her mother added.

"I'll make some brackets to hang it on the wall," Drew offered.

"Thank you. It would look lovely on the wall."

Holly smiled at Jonah, leaned toward him, and kissed his cheek. "Thank you, Jonah. This is such a thoughtful gift."

He could only mumble a brief thank you while he looked at the floor. He was blushing. Holly's parents exchanged a brief glance and smiled at Jonah's obvious discomfort.

Chapter Eight ~ *The Bryce Canyon Trip*

AS IN THE PREVIOUS year's trip to Yellowstone, Steven and Jackie would be meeting the Meridian families at their destination. Only this year, the trip was to the Bryce Canyon National Park area and they would be bringing their two-month-old son, Samuel.

They named him Samuel after his great-great-grandfather, of blessed memory. He was remembered as a kind man who was small in stature but big of heart.

As an added bonus, also joining them this year were Steven and Anna's parents, Arturo and Carmen Cardozo. Steven was quite concerned about all the extra weight they were carrying in their camper, so he had purchased a new tow vehicle. The truck had four- wheel drive, huge wheels and tires, a monster CAT diesel engine, and looked like a four-door pickup on steroids.

Jackie said she was certain Steven had purchased the truck because he liked driving the rig so much. He would look for any excuse to spend time behind its controls. He even had a huge winch installed in the front bumper, "Just in case we need it," he'd said. When they set out on their twelve-hour-drive to Utah, Steven and his father were in the front seats and Jackie, Carmen, and little Sam were in back. They, and the families from Meridian, decided to make the drive in two-days. The weather was beautiful for driving, and the scenery was magnificent.

Little Samuel wasn't too happy to be strapped into his car

seat, but the constant low-pitched rumble of the truck's big diesel engine quickly put him to sleep. The trip was easier for Steven this year as he and his father shared the driving duties.

***

The Meridian caravan headed out at ten o'clock on a bright, sunny, and warm day. Most of the group was wearing shorts and light shirts. They drove for two-hours and stopped for lunch at a big truck stop. While they were waiting outside for their name to be called, Holly held thirty-month-old Carrie, while Jonah stood next her.

"I don't think she remembers me," Jonah said.

"Carrie, do you remember Jonah?" Holly asked.

At first, Carrie looked at Jonah with no sign of recognition, but then she held out her arms toward him.

"Oh, so you do remember me," Jonah said, putting her in his left arm.

"Jonah," Carrie said, then rested her head on his shoulder.

He was pleased she remembered him and had pronounced his name. Jonah felt little arms and hands on his right leg. He looked down to see thirty-one month-old David Linn holding on to him.

"Hey, little buddy, so you remember me as well," Jonah said. Holly picked him up and put him in Jonah's right arm.

Little Carrie looked at her brother and said, "Jonah." "Jonah, Jonah." David Linn replied in a happy voice.

"You both know my name now. I appreciate that."

Anna and Michael enjoyed watching their little ones hanging onto Jonah.

Just then a huge California condor came into view circling above them. Carrie pointed to it. "David, *uccello*! Jonah, *uccello*!" shesaid in an excited voice.

David Linn also pointed. "*Sie uccello.*"

"*Ché uccello grazioso.*" Jonah immediately told them.

Holly smiled at Jonah and explained to Michael that *Uccello* meant bird in Italian. "Jonah just told the kids it's a pretty bird."

"Jonah, have you learned Italian?" Michael asked.

"Just a little. At least enough to say something is pretty. I wouldn't have known what *uccello* meant but Carrie was pointing to the bird. I mean, really, I hang with Holly so some of her language skill had to become part of me." He turned and smiled at Holly.

Then Anna mentioned that Carrie notices birds the way she remembered Chela doing. She put the tiny ones in highchairs, and Anna took out some small food containers, placing them on the trays in front of the children.

David Linn ate for a while and then scooped up some mashed peas in his hand and offered them to Holly. She let him put the peas in her mouth and did her best to smile at him while everyone else laughed.

When Carrie finished her food, she struggled to get out of her highchair. Her face was getting red from anger and frustration as she strained against the straps which held her. She started making loud noises while Anna and Michael warned her to sit still and be quiet while everyone else finished eating. Carrie wasn't listening.

"Carrie, that's enough," Jonah said in a firm voice from across the table.

Carrie looked at Jonah, her eyes went wide, her little lip quivered, and she started crying.

"All right, Carrie." Anna sighed and took her out of the highchair.

Jonah felt guilty he had made Carrie cry. "I'll hold her so you can eat," he told Anna.

She smiled and handed Carrie across the table to him. "Thank you, Jonah."

He held her in his left arm and continued eating with his right, telling her that her behavior was unacceptable and she needed to wait sometimes.

Carrie cried harder for a few moments and then began to calm down. She put her tear-streaked face on Jonah's shoulder with her forehead against the side of his neck and within a couple-of-minutes was fast asleep.

Jonah managed, with occasional assistance from Holly, to finish his meal using only his right hand.

"You better be as good with babies as your brother," Linda said to David.

"Don't worry." David laughed and grinned. "I'm taking notes over here."

He took a photo with his cell phone of Jonah holding a soundly sleeping Carrie. "I'm going to send this to his Mom and Ethan," he said.

His phone chimed when they texted him back. David laughed and then told Jonah what they said. "Ethan showed the picture to Sheryl and she said, 'So Jonah has a new love in his life. Does Holly know about this?' And then Mom replied, 'Jonah?' You're not going to live this down, Jonah," David teased.

Jonah just grinned and rolled his eyes.

After lunch they drove for a few hours until they were just south of Ogden, Utah. They stopped for their group dinner at a lovely campground with a magnificent view of the surrounding mountains.

Mr. and Mrs. Holt prepared a Heavenly Hash salad of pineapple, pears, coconut, sour cream, and miniature marshmallows. Dell Beckham served pulled pork in barbeque sauce. Anna brought out corn on the cob, while Linda Schulman brought baked beans which had been slowly simmered for seven-hours and Jackie served sweet potato fries. Trisha finished off the meal by serving pecan pies.

"If anyone goes hungry on this trip, it's their own fault," Jonah whispered to David.

Seven-year-old Cathy McCarthy whispered something to

her mother who nodded.

"Go ahead and tell them, Cathy."

"When we get to the campground tomorrow night, we're going to be eating an Irish dinner," she said in an excited and proud voice. "My mom, Mrs. Levin and Linda are going to make colcannon for everyone. Mrs. Beckham and Mrs. Cardozo, who is coming all the way from New Mexico, are going to make barley pudding for desert."

"Colcannon is my favorite," the McCarthy's six-year-old son yelled.

David looked at Jonah. "Like you said…"

After dinner, Jonah and Holly, along with David and Linda, went for a walk around the campground.

"Holly, do you mind my spending so much time holding Carrie and David Linn?" Jonah asked.

"Jonah, you have no idea how happy it makes me. Those little babies don't know how lucky they are. They have so many people around to love them and make them feel secure."

Jonah looked at Holly, and although she was smiling, she looked like she was ready to cry.

"Are you okay?" Jonah asked.

With tears in her eyes, Holly nodded. "When I was a little girl, I had an awful time," she told him. "I would have given anything to have had so many loving people around me. Jonah Kaplan, you have no idea how happy I was when I saw little Carrie calm down and fall asleep on your shoulder."

"You had a difficult childhood? You never mentioned that before."

Holly nodded. "I know. I'll tell you about it sometime, but not today."

She stopped walking, wrapped her arms around him, and kissed his lips. "Thank you, Jonah Kaplan, for being the person you are—and for making me so happy."

Jonah couldn't imagine more loving parents than Oliver and Ruth. He was quite confused, but realized Holly would tell him about her childhood when she was ready.

"Do you ever think about those two people we shot?" Jonah asked her as they continued walking.

"Every now and then. Sometimes at night when I'm in bed I think of what happened, and I start to get scared. I called Dr. Rabinowitz a few times and he talked to me for a while. He said it's a normal reaction to be afraid and think about it sometimes. And, well, I did find a way to get over being scared and get back to sleep."

"How do you do that?" Jonah asked.

"I'll tell you, but you have to promise not to laugh." "I promise."

"I wrap myself around one of my blankets and pretend I'm holding you. Everything's fine after that."

Jonah stopped walking this time and opened his arms toward Holly. "Here I am. You don't have to pretend."

She wrapped her arms around him. "This is much better than my blanket."

Jonah put his lips on Holly's and kissed her for a long time. "Hey you guys!" Linda teased them. "This is a walk—not a stand-in-one-place-and-kiss."

Jonah and Holly looked at each other and laughed, then started walking again.

***

Holly walked with Linda for a while and the guys walked ahead of them.

"I've seen you guys are touching each other a lot more this year," Holly said, a little unsure of asking such a personal question, but too curious not to. "Has something changed in your relationship?"

Linda smiled and looked out at the shallow river running next to the trail as a fish jumped out of the water. "David and I each had our own rooms at the dorm last year, but toward the end of the year we rented an apartment for next year. We lived there the last month of school." She giggled. "Honestly, Holly, we started doing it the day we moved our stuff in. Our parents probably know we're living together, but they pretend as if we're not. Ever since we did it, we can't seem to keep our hands off each other."

"How did you decide it was the right time?"

"Well, we've been together for a number of years, and every day we're together, David does things to remind me why I love him so much. I started on the pill in January, but we didn't do it until we moved in together. Plus, our relationship reached a stage where we stopped talking about individual goals and started weighing our decisions based on our lives as a couple. I knew we'd be staying together, so I was willing to move to the next stage with David."

"Was it scary?"

"Like everything else in our life as a couple, it was more beautiful to do it with him than I can tell you. When David and I first met, I wouldn't let anyone put their arms around me because I had been sexually assaulted when I was fourteen."

"Oh, Linda. That is horrible."

"Don't feel sorry for me, Holly. I'm okay now. I mean, it was awful and hard to get through, but in the few days after David and I first met, he did such kind things for me—he made me feel so appreciated, I had to hold him. That was the day when the last pain from the assault disappeared. It was replaced by David's love. The relationship we put together repaired my soul. When I watch you and Jonah, I think you have the same future as David and me."

"Thanks for saying that, but we have a long way to go."
"How do you feel when he holds you?"

Holly thought for a moment and then smiled. "Remember when those two people were going to kill everyone in Jonah's house? After we stored the guns, I was standing next to him and my whole body started to shake. I put my arms around him and he held me. It doesn't make logical sense but his holding me made me feel better. It was as if he was taking the bad feeling right out of my body. In fact, anytime he holds me, I feel a sense of peace come over me."

"Work things out, Holly. It will be worth it, believe me. The two of you fit together like you were designed for each other."

"Thanks for talking to me about this stuff, Linda."

"Hey, we might both be married to Kaplan boys." Linda smiled. "We better be able to talk."

Chapter Nine ~ *The Plane Crash*

AFTER A FEW HOURS of driving, the Meridian neighbors arrived at a campground near Cannonville, Utah. An-hour-later, the New Mexico contingent arrived.

All the guys wanted to know the details of Steven's new hauler. He let each of them drive it around the campground. Alex Schulman thought it was too big, but said he loved the view from the elevated cab. From the over the road horn to the deep throated CAT diesel, Drew and Jonah loved *everything* about it.

In fact, the first time Jonah saw the truck, he rushed up to Steven and proclaimed, "I didn't know it was possible to fall in love with a truck, but I think I just did."

After dinner they met with the guide who would be taking them to a remote campsite, southeast of their current location.

"We won't be driving for very long before we'll be heading onto a narrow dirt road," he told them. "We'll drive this road at low speed as the surface can be bumpy. I've gotten fifth-wheel-trailers, travel-trailers, and diesel-pusher-motorhomes up there, so I know we'll all get there safely if we take our time. Once we're there, you'll see one of the greatest and most scenic views in the state. I'll lead the way and will have a trailer with six-side-by-side All-Terrain-Vehicles. The trails and areas we'll be exploring are magnificent. Remember, we'll be dry camping so make sure you have enough water and fuel for four-days. I'll be returning here at nine o'clock tomorrow morning and we'll head out."

Everyone thanked the guide and then spent some time

catching up with each other before turning in for the night.

They woke up ready to get going and it was indeed a long four- hour-drive at low speed to the campsite. It was located in a combination of state and national park areas, and when they arrived at a large flat area they arranged the campers in a circle, like the spokes of a wheel with the front of the units at the hub.

They put up portable picnic tables and started serving lunch. Tina's parents and grandparents helped them setup a portable coral for their Percherons and two other horses.

Their tour leader, Sam Martin, was a trained botanist who grew up in southern Utah and he loved sharing the beauty of this area of the state with new friends from around the country. He was constantly in communication with the park's rangers who advised him of everything from closed trails to migrating birds.

The tours began as soon as lunch ended. The ATV trail rides took them up narrow trails to magnificent vistas along the surrounding mountains and down into deep canyons. The stark landscape was a far cry from the lush growth of Yellowstone, but it had a unique beauty in the jagged shape and hues of pink, red and tan, in the many geological features they observed.

Jonah and Holly, plus David and Linda, were each given their own side-by-side ATVs to share. Drew and Andy shared a side-by- side as well.

"There'll be no showing off," Oliver reminded each of them. Ruth told Oliver she was concerned Jonah would be driving Holly around.

"Don't worry, Ruth. Jonah would put his life on the line to take good care of Holly — in fact, he already has."

"Oliver," she joked, "I have to worry. It's in my motherly DNA."

He laughed. "I love how those two treat each other, and I'm amazed how well they take care of the Levins' children.

They're going to be amazing parents one day."

Ruth leaned over and kissed his cheek. "Holly had, and has, a great example of how a couple should treat each other," she said. "Plus a marvelous example of what kind of man she should choose to be a father for her children."

"Thank you for thinking that, lady," he replied as he leaned over and kissed her lips.

It was a clear day and the sun shone down on them, making the day rather warm. During one break in the driving, Ruth was putting sunscreen on Oliver when she saw Holly doing the same for Jonah.

"She takes great care of him," Oliver noted. "They take good care of each other. I sure hope they can keep their relationship growing."

"Holly's telling Jonah about her childhood today and how she and Drew came to live with us," Ruth said.

"I think her telling him is another sign of how close they are. She doesn't tell many people about the time before she became a part of our family."

After dinner, everyone gathered around a small campfire, under a clear and cloudless sky. Michael had setup a couple of his telescopes and passed around his pair of binoculars, which were optimized for nighttime sky viewing.

Around eleven-thirty, a number of the campers saw the red and green lights of an aircraft come out of the sky to the south. It seemed to fly lower and lower.

"That plane is way too low," Mr. Martin said. "I don't hear any engine sound," Jonah added. "Neither do I," Oliver confirmed.

The plane seemed to disappear behind a mountain to their west. Everyone watched to see if it came out from behind the mountain. Instead, they saw nothing and heard only silence.

A park ranger who had been backpacking while doing an animal study, called for help over his radio, announcing a plane had crashed. The transmission was heard by the Mr.

Martin. He called the ranger who told him the location of the crash and said he could see there were survivors.

"It's about seven-miles up one of the trails we were on today. The plane went down in a narrow ravine," the tour leader announced. "It will take at least a few hours to get professionals up here from town to start rescue efforts. There is a tiny rocky footpath off the main trail, barely wide enough for a man to walk down. I'm heading up there to see what I can do."

"Let's gather up first-aid kits, flashlights, water, and blankets," Michael said. "We can put them in the two ATV trailers and haul them up there. Anyone who knows first aid or doesn't mind helping treat bloody injuries should come along. Although, it might be good to have at least one medically trained person stay here in case some of the injured need additional help once we get them back."

"Sir," Trace asked Mr. Martin. "Do you think a horse could get down the footpath?"

"A horse just might make it," he told Trace.

Tina and Trace raced off to saddle the Percherons. They took ropes along with them just in case they were needed.

The tour leader gave Anna an extra radio so he could relay information back to her. Jonah looked at Holly. "I'm going to help at the accident scene," he said. "It may be gory, but I could use a partner up there."

"I'm going with you." She grabbed a couple-of-hydration packs and energy bars.

They climbed into the side-by-side they had used during the day. David and Linda, plus Michael and Oliver, each took one of the side-by-side ATVs, too. Andy and Drew climbed on Oliver's ATV. Steve and Tina's mom, who had been a nurse, took another. With a sound reminiscent of loud angry bees, the ATV caravan motored off and up the trail toward the crash site.

Chapter Ten ~ *First Responders*

THEN THEY ARRIVED NEAR the narrow entrance to the ravine, all the ATVs parked at the side of the trail. They walked down the narrow footpath to a ghastly scene.

The air smelled of jet fuel and people could be heard moaning and crying. The airplane's silvery fuselage had been ripped open like a sardine can. One of the wings had separated from the plane and slid up and over the forward part of the fuselage.

Jonah and Holly walked over to the first injury they saw. It was a man with a broken leg. One of his shin bones was sticking through his skin. Oliver described how he wanted them to splint and bandage the terrible wound. Holly started to help but the bloody sight caused her to become sick to her stomach. She quickly moved away and began vomiting.

"When you're finished puking, I need more help over here," Jonah called after her.

Oliver walked over to his daughter and put his hand on her shoulder. He considered reminding Jonah not everyone can look at bloody injuries.

Holly took some water and rinsed her mouth. "I'm okay, Dad." She took a deep breath and headed back to help.

Tina's father and grandfather, along with Trace and Tina, began constructing litters for the Percherons to get people back to the campsite. Tina's grandfather had the foresight to bring along two hand-axes and a roll of duct tape.

For the next-thirty-minutes, the woods echoed with the sounds of small trees being cut down and trimmed, accompanied by the sound of duct tape being stripped off its roll.

Andy and Drew looked at the horrific scene. "This is bad," Andy said.

Drew observed the litters being made for the Percherons. "Come on, Andy," Drew said in an excited voice. "We can make litters like we did in Boy Scouts and attach them to the ATV trailers."

"What can we use to secure them?"

Drew reached into his father's tool box and pulled out a roll of duct tape and a small axe.

"Yes!" Andy yelled.

They ran to the two little trailers. Using duct tape and small saplings, they started building a litter for each one. Towing straps were put in place to help keep an injured person steady and secure during transport.

As the first two injured came up the steep narrow trail on the Percherons' litters, Oliver was shocked to see what the boys had created. He checked to see if the litters were sturdy enough and if they were attached to the trailers with sufficient strength.

He smiled at the boys. "Good job, Boy Scouts."

Trace and Oliver moved the two injured onto the ATV trailers and secured them with the straps.

Oliver looked serious. "Do you think you two are mature enough to carefully drive these people back to the campsite so the rest of us can continue to help the injured?" he asked.

"Yes, Dad," Drew told him.

"We can definitely do that, Mr. Holt," Andy added.

`Drew and Andy started their slow and careful seven-mile drive down the mountain. They kept their human cargo under a watchful gaze by regularly looking in their rearview mirrors.

Oliver watched them until they were out of sight. "Not bad for a couple-of-oversized twelve-year-olds," he said to himself with a smile as he headed down the path back to the accident scene.

***

The people at the campsite had been advised two casualties were being brought down by horseback. Sherry Schulman and Dell Beckham decided to use the bunks in the back of their toy-hauler fifth-wheel-trailers for the first injured to arrive.

As they awaited the arrival of the horses, they heard ATVs rumbling down the trail at a slow speed. When they came into view they were surprised to see Andy and Drew carefully driving the side- by-sides with litters on the trailers behind them.

Ruth immediately motioned them over to the back of Dell's trailer. The boys, Ruth, Jackie, and Anna moved the injured to the bunks and covered them with blankets. Dell Beckham, who had some first-aid training, checked their bandages and looked for other injuries.

"Are there more injured people coming down?" she asked the boys.

"Yes, I think there will be a lot more," Andy told her.

"You guys get going back up the trail. Drive carefully," Sherry Schulman reminded them.

Dell turned to her neighbors. "Andy said they need more bandages. We need to cut some clean sheets into strips."

"I can do that," Anna's grandmother called out. "Our little ones are asleep, so I have time now."

Jackie smiled at her grandmother-in-law. "I'll help you, Grandmother."

"From what the ranger told me, they may be up there most of the night," Anna said. "They may be getting hungry. We need to think about getting some additional water and food up there, plus jackets and sweaters."

She turned to Dell. "I have a ton of tortillas I was going to use for a couple of group meals. I can make a meat, garlic, cumin, eggs, potatoes, and onion filling, wrap it in the tortillas and send them up the mountain in coolers. We can have Andy and Drew transport them on one of their trips back up there."

"We can help," Tina's grandmother said. "Anna, please give me half the tortillas and I'll get busy cooking as well."

"I'll help you, Mrs. Wagoner," Ruth volunteered. "I'll help Anna," Mrs. Shulman said.

***

At the accident site, surprise registered on many faces when they saw the Percherons coming back so rapidly. Word quickly spread. Andy and Drew had made transports out of the ATV trailers.

Mr. Wagoner was working with his dad. A number of injured were trapped below fuselage parts and twisted seats. They cutdown small trees to use as levers to open the twisted wreckage.

"We need to get ropes on some of these parts and use the Percherons to move some of this heavy debris off these people," Mr. Wagoner said.

They took ropes from the Percherons and instructed Trace and Tina to take the litters off the horses next time down the trail and use them to help get people dislodged from the rubble.

Tina said she was nervous about using the young Percherons — the horses still had many months of training in front of them to be considered fully trained.

When she and Trace had removed the litters from the Percherons, they moved them into position so they could pull on the ropes which were being attached to various parts of the airplane's broken structure. The Percherons lived for pulling and being gentle giants, they followed every instruction Trace or Tina gave them.

"It's almost like they knew they were doing an important

job," Trace said.

After numerous people had been freed, the Percherons went back to litter duty.

The ranger and Michael looked at the wreckage and found a number of people were trapped under the broken wing which covered the forward part of the fuselage. Michael called Oliver over and they could see the only way to get those people out was to lift the heavy wing.

"I don't think the Percherons are capable of lifting such a heavy load."

"Steve has a winch on the front of his big truck," Michael pointed out, "but how could we get it down here?"

"There used to be mining in this ravine years-ago," the ranger said. "There was a road from further up the mountain which came down here. We felled a huge tree at the entrance to the road to keep vehicle traffic out. We'd have to get the tree moved. That was twenty-years-ago so we'd also have to clear a path to get a vehicle all the way down here."

He pulled out a map. Steve was called over and the ranger indicated to Steve the route he should take from the campsite to get to the head of the old road.

"The paint on your truck will get scratched to beat hell if you bring it down here."

"That's not a consideration," Steve told them. "My truck is designed for rugged use. I can always repaint it."

Steve excitedly drove an ATV back to the campsite and grabbed Jackie to help navigate.

Forty-five-minutes-later he was in front of the big log which blocked the trail's entrance. Steve ran the cable from his winch around one end of the log and hooked the cable back onto itself, and put the truck in four-wheel-drive.

With Jackie observing, Steve shifted into reverse and slowly took up the slack in the cable. As soon as it was taut he added throttle to the engine. The truck and its big CAT engine were more than up to the task as he pulled the log aside.

Some of the others had arrived and began clearing the small trees which blocked the truck's path to the aircraft.

Finally, with the truck near the airplane, they ran the cable from the winch over a sturdy tree and easily lifted the wing off the trapped passengers. Injured were loaded into the truck's box and the more mobile survivors climbed into the cab of the truck. Jackie rode in the pickup's box to keep an eye on the more severely injured, while Steve carefully drove them down to the campsite.

Andy and Drew occasionally brought buckets of water up the trail for the Percherons.

Jonah came across a woman who was breathing hard and whose skin tone was blue. She looked weak and tired.

"I've heard this song before," he said. "Holly, please get me a roll of gauze."

He kneeled next to the woman and gently lifted her left arm. Moving her shirt out of the way he found a hole in her side which was foaming. He put his latex-gloved hand over the hole.

Holly returned and Jonah explained what a sucking chest wound was. The woman started getting her color back.

"Is that better?" he asked.

"Much better," the woman replied. "Thank you so much, young man."

"Uncle Meyer showed me how to treat this type of wound when I was little," he told Holly.

Jonah replaced the latex glove with the appropriate type of bandage and held it in place while Holly wrapped gauze around the woman's body to secure the bandage. With Oliver and Michael's assistance, they carried her over to Steve's pickup.

"When she's down the hill, tell Mrs. Beckham she has a sucking chest wound." Jonah told Jackie. As they moved to look at another injured person they saw the ranger was watching them.

"Great job, kids," he told them.

They thanked him, smiled briefly at each other, and started helping another injured person.

As Holly worked with Jonah to bandage a particularly bloody leg injury, there was a child's voice in the distance yelling. "Mommy! Mommy!"

"Can you finish this?" she asked Jonah. "I'm going to look for that little voice."

Holly walked some distance off to the side of the wreckage and found a girl, who looked to be around seven, crying quietly, her little body shivering from the cold.

"Jonah," Holly yelled. "I need you over here—like yesterday!"

"My arm and leg hurt a lot," the little girl told Holly through her tears.

"We're going to take good care of you."

"My mommy is supposed to meet me at the airport."

"We're going to fix you up so you can see your mommy in a little while. Is that okay?"

The little girl nodded. "That's okay," she said in a weak voice.

"What's your name?"

"Shelly."

Jonah came running over to Holly.

"My name is Holly and my friend here is Jonah. He's going to put some bandages on you."

"Will it hurt?"

"It may hurt, but I'll hold your hand while he puts on the bandages." Holly took Shelly's little hand in her hers.

"Her left arm and left leg need a lot of help." Jonah spoke in Navajo so the little girl wouldn't be afraid.

Holly nodded and Jonah straightened out her left leg.

Little Shelly screamed and started crying as Jonah worked on her. After a few minutes bandaging to control bleeding and splinting her leg, Jonah gently put a splint on her left forearm and made a sling to hold it across her body. Holly pinned the sling to the girl's clothing to keep her arm still.

Oliver walked over. "What have you got?"

"I think both the left arm and leg are broken," Jonah informed him. "I splinted both of them and Holly pinned her sling to her shirt so she can't move the arm."

"See if her tummy is sensitive to pressure, and if not, let her have a little water. Great job troops," Oliver said smiling.

"Let's get her out of here," he added. "The horses are coming back and the ranger said she should be taken out next."

"Shelly, this man is my dad. He's going to carry you over to some people who will get you out of here and down to a warm place, okay?"

"Holly, will you still hold my hand?"

"Of course, I will."

"Ow," Shelly cried as Oliver gently lifted her. "That hurts so much."

When she was placed on one of the Percheron's litters, she asked Holly, "Will you come with me?"

"I'm right here, Shelly. I'm going to walk right next to you and hold your hand."

When they arrived at the ATVs, they moved Shelly onto the trailer behind the ATV that Andy was driving. He covered her with a blanket.

"Shelly, this is my brother's best friend, Andy. He's going to drive you down to where some other people will take care of you."

"Are you coming with me?"

"I have to help some more people up here, but when Andy gets you down the mountain, I want you to do something for me. I want you to ask for Ruth. She's my mom. You tell her Holly said she should hold your hand. Can you remember to say that?"

Shelley nodded. "Ask for Ruth and tell her Holly said she

should hold my hand."

"Perfect. If you forget, Andy is going to help remember for you."

Holly leaned over and kissed her little patient on the forehead. "I'll see you later, Shelly."

Then Holly looked at Andy. "No problem," he told her. "I'll take good care of her."

***

All during the ride down the mountain, Andy talked to Shelly and tried to say silly things to make her laugh. When they arrived at the campsite, Andy drove over to where the Holts' motorhome was parked.

"Mrs. Holt, someone needs you," Andy called out.

Ruth hurried over as Andy began undoing the straps which held Shelly during the ride. "Are you Ruth?" Shelly asked.

She looked down at Shelly. "Yes, I am."

"Holly said to tell you, you should hold my hand."

Ruth was visibly affected when she heard Shelly's words. "Well, of course, I'll hold your hand. While I do that, Andy is going to move you into my motorhome where it's warm and we have a place for you to lie down."

Andy gently lifted Shelly and carried her into the Holts' motorhome. He placed her on the pull out couch in the living room. Ruth gently put a colorful wool blanket over her.

"Thank you for driving me down here, Andy," Shelly called to him. "And as soon as I can, I'll count my toes again."

Ruth looked at Andy who had a huge smile.

"We talked about toes on the way down here," he told her.

Dell stopped by and checked Shelly over. "Someone's doing an excellent job up there," she told Ruth.

"Did Holly put bandages on you?" Ruth asked Shelly.

"No, she was holding my hand while this man did that stuff. I think his name is Mona."

"Do you mean Jonah?"

"Yes, that's it. He said some funny words to Holly and she held my hand real tight while he put that stuff on me. It really hurt. Holly put this on and pinned it to my shirt. I forgot what it's called."

"It's called a sling, dear."

"Why don't you stay with her?" Dell said. "If you need something just yell."

Ruth asked Shelly about the ride down to the campsite.

She started giggling. "The guy who brought me down here kept making me laugh," she said through her giggles. "His name is Andy and he kept telling me funny things about my toes and stuff. He's very funny. I like him."

***

After a few hours, paramedics began arriving. By then it was quite cold, and sweaters and jackets had been sent up to the first aiders. Steve and Jackie indicated to them how to get to the old mining road, which had been reopened. Much to Steve's delight, he continued to use the truck to bring paramedics up to the wreck and take injured back.

Holly and Jonah arrived back at the campsite just as the sun was beginning to rise.

"A-2-2—we are the Tigers!" Jonah proclaimed. Holly looked at him bewildered.

"Holly, I'm too tired to tell you about A-2-2, but believe me, it's a cool thing."

They went to see Shelly, but just after they started talking to her, paramedics arrived with her mom. They loaded her into an ambulance and drove to an area where a medevac helicopter was waiting.

"You guys take what you want to eat," Ruth said as she left the motorhome to see what else she could do to help.

Holly looked at Jonah. "I'm not hungry," she said. "I need

to get some sleep."

"I'm so sleepy," he told her, "I'm sure I could sleep standing up."

Holly turned and started walking to the rear bedroom of her parents' motorhome.

Jonah followed, but stopped at the entry to the bedroom. "Maybe I should sleep in Michael's unit like I did last night."

Holly walked back and grabbed the front of his shirt. "If we can spend the entire night together helping the injured," she told him, as she pulled him into the bedroom, "we can spend part of the day sleeping in the same bed."

She opened a closet and pulled out her Code Talkers blanket.

Jonah took his shoes, jacket, and sweater off. He sat on the bed and helped Holly pull the big blanket over them. Then he lay on his back while she curled up against him, and they both fell fast asleep.

***

Thirty-minutes-later Oliver and Drew arrived back at the motorhome. Drew took one look at the pulled out couch and immediately went to sleep on it.

"I'm gonna shower and go to sleep," Oliver told Ruth.

"You can shower, but you need to sleep out here. Holly and Jonah are asleep in our bed."

"What?"

"Believe me, Oliver, as tired as they are, they're just sleeping. Please do quietly look in on them, though. Holly took out her Code Talkers blanket to cover them. They look so cute—I took a picture of them after they were asleep."

Oliver opened the door to the bedroom and quietly looked in on them. He smiled. "What a great couple."

He showered and dressed in clean clothes. "My Lord, Ruth," he told his wife. "You should have seen Holly and

Jonah. From one bloody mess to another, they smiled and stayed positive as if it was nothing. And some of those injuries were as horrible as any war wounds I've seen. If it bothered those two, they didn't let anyone see it. Holly was sick at first, but just rinsed her mouth and went back to helping Jonah. Michael, the ranger, and I kept checking on what they were doing, giving them pointers to treat different wounds. David and Linda, being future med students, did great as well. Quite a few people owe their lives to those kids."

"I suspect some of them owe a debt to the rest of you as well," Ruth said.

"Did you see the litters on the ATV trailers? Andy and Drew built them. Those two boys kept driving the entire night. I don't know how they stayed awake, although at one point early this morning, I saw them doing jumping jacks and pushups. What a great family we have! Not to mention amazing neighbors. It was so easy to work as a team because we know each other so well. Steve didn't know anything about first aid, but assisted Michael and did exactly as he was told. Steve's dad stayed with the ranger and assisted him. Now, Ruth my love, I'm so tired I'm just going to lie down next to Drew."

"Heroes." Ruth smiled at her exhausted family. "Heroes, everyone." She settled into a reclining chair and promptly fell asleep.

***

When Michael arrived at his motorhome, Carrie and David Linn were both awake and chattering away. He was so tired he ignored them and fell fast asleep in the bedroom.

Anna looked in on him, and with tears in her eyes, she walked over and kissed her sleeping husband. When she returned, she told her grandmother, "My firmware-guru husband transformed himself into a mountaineering-paramedic again tonight. I'm sure he took care of those people just like he took care of me when I was severely injured. I'm so proud of him and so glad he's my partner."

***

Back at their coach, Jackie told Steven, "I've never done so much for so many strangers in my life. I can't believe how busy we were and how proud I am of what we accomplished. You know, sometimes we dream about being the rescuers at an accident scene. Tonight we did it. I'm so excited I may not be able to sleep for a week."

"Many of those people would have bled out by the time paramedics managed to get up there," Steve agreed. "I think we saved quite a few lives last night."

"I have to admit," Jackie told Steve as she tightly embraced him, "last night, the monster truck you bought justified all the money you paid for it."

***

Although the rest of the camping trip was scenic and full of lovely memories, nothing would compare to the seven-hours where neighbors, husbands and wives, and boys and girls all worked together at maximum capacity to rescue an airplane full of strangers. Once rested, most reveled in the joy of their life-saving accomplishment and knew they had bonded with their fellow rescuers in a manner which would make them lifelong friends.

Chapter Eleven ~ *Wheelbarrows and Mathematics*

BACK AT HOME IN Seattle, the Kaplan family finished dinner and was still sitting around the dining room table chatting.

Jonah spoke up. "I don't think genetics will advance until it's based in mathematics."

His brother Ethan immediately jumped on him. "You're not even in college yet," he said. "You don't know what you're talking about."

"What do you mean, Jonah?" Morris asked him.

"What if you wanted to design a wheelbarrow to carry concrete blocks? First you would have to calculate the weight of the blocks which could fit in the wheelbarrow. The weight would be represented by a number. The concrete blocks don't know what they weigh, but we give them a numerical representation which represents their weight."

"Wheelbarrow?" Ethan said. "You're going to compare wheelbarrows to genetics? You must be nuts."

Morris looked at Ethan. "Ethan," he said, "there is an old saying—it is better to keep one's mouth shut and be judged a possible fool than to open one's mouth and remove all doubt. I strongly suggest you shut your mouth and listen."

Jonah continued. "How do we know what the bucket of the wheelbarrow should be made of and how thick it should be to carry the weight? We find a materials book and look up the strength of the material we're going to use to carry the load. It is the same thing with the handles and the frame and the fasteners. We mathematically calculate the forces which will be applied to the fasteners and choose the correct fastener based on our calculation. The forces aren't visible and the fasteners don't have a clue how strong they are, but the engineer does see all these things. All these things are invisible just looking at a wheelbarrow but mathematics makes them visible to the engineer so he can design a proper wheelbarrow."

Ethan's face was turning red by now. "I still don't think there's a comparison."

"That's because Jonah has a gift which you and your brother don't have," Morris told Ethan in a stern voice. "Jonah can understand concepts in an abstract manner, in a way I suspect you and your twin brother will never be able to grasp."

"Dad, I could design a wheelbarrow!" Ethan protested trying to salvage his pride.

"Yes, I believe you could, but could you design one if you'd never seen one before? I think not. But Jonah could and that's the difference between you and your younger brother."

A frustrated looking Morris pushed away from the table and announced he was going to his lab to do some work.

Around nine-thirty, the phone rang. David answered and called to his mom, "Mom, it's Dad's work. They need to talk to you."

She took the phone. "This is Mrs. Kaplan. Yes. What? Oh, my God. Yes. Thank you for calling."

She called to her sons. "Boys, that was the security company at your father's lab. They just rushed him to the hospital. Let's hurry.

We need to get to the ER. David, call your Uncle Meyer on your cell and tell him to meet us there."

She shook her head as she grabbed her coat and purse. "He's been complaining of back pains," she mumbled in a quivering voice. "I've been telling him to see our doctor, but your father is so stubborn when it comes to interrupting his work."

***

When they arrived at the hospital, Meyer and Joan were just rushing in the doors, too. They went straight to the triage desk and Michelle gave the nurse her name. They were all immediately taken to a small room and a grim-faced doctor came in to talk to them.

"I'm sorry to inform you—Mr. Kaplan had a massive coronary infarction. He died at-least-an-hour before he was discovered. There really was nothing we could do."

The doctor lowered his eyes and stepped back as Michelle dissolved into massive sobs. Meyer and Joan grabbed her as she collapsed, and then Meyer moved her to a couch but continued to support her.

Ethan and David were beside themselves with grief while Jonah stood off to the side. His eyes were filled with tears, but he didn't cry.

A sobbing Joan walked over and put her arms around Jonah.

He held her as she cried.

"He was a good dad," he told her. "We all loved him a lot." Meyer was horrified to observe Jonah was comforting Joan—not the other way around.

At the funeral it was the same. David, Ethan, and Michelle were visibly devastated, but Jonah showed little emotion. His brothers seemed sure this was a sign of disrespect toward their father. Dr. Isaac Rabinowitz, the family friend who specialized in family dynamics and grief counseling, volunteered to talk to the family a few days after the funeral.

"Michelle gave me permission to discuss this with you, Meyer. She hoped you might have some thoughts on Jonah. She and the twins are dealing with their sudden loss in a healthy manner, but I'm worried about Jonah. He won't discuss how he feels. No matter what I ask, he just replies that he's fine. When I asked about his friend Holly, he told me they won't end up together because she's not Jewish."

"He never mentioned that to me," Meyer said.

"I know he's close to you. You might want to go out of your way to spend time with him and see if he'll talk about his dad. Don't push it. Just give him the opportunity to talk."

Meyer agreed that it was important and he said he would be there for Jonah.

Chapter Twelve ~ *Bellissima*

OLIVER AND RUTH FINALLY took their family on their previously-promised honeymoon. Because of Oliver's job change, and the move to Meridian, it did not occur until four-years-after they were married. But now, they were flying to Italy, with a stop in New York.

Ruth and Oliver had kept sixteen-year-old Holly and thirteen- year-old Drew in suspense about their intended destination until they were in New York. All they told them was they would be going to see a car factory. Holly and Drew made themselves crazy trying to guess the destination.

When they arrived in New York, Ruth gave them their tickets for the next leg of their trip.

Holly's face lit up like fireworks. "Italy! I can't believe we're going to Italy!"

Drew was puzzled for a moment and then his eyes slowly widened. "Maranello? Are we going to Maranello to see the Ferrari factory?"

"You got it!" Oliver happily told him.

During the flight, they reviewed travel brochures and the itinerary Ruth had prepared for their trip.

They spent two-glorious-weeks touring the sights of Italy. During five-days of their trip, Ruth's former student, Francesca, came from Florence to visit them in Rome. She took them on a tour of the Vatican and then played tour guide, escorting them to many other locations to see numerous Italian art treasures and historic sights.

The trip to the Ferrari factory was everything Drew had

imagined it would be. They went over to the Fiorano test track and were lucky enough to see and hear the banshee wail of a Ferrari F1 as it hugged the track, keeping a steady pace at well over a hundred miles an hour.

Then, on their last night in Italy, Holly received a call on her cell phone. "Jonah, it's so kind of you to call. We've been having an incredible time here. I've been speaking in Italian all week long and just loving it. You have to see this beautiful country sometime."

She spoke excitedly for a few more minutes and then the pitch in her voice dropped. "What? Oh, Jonah, I'm so sorry. I know you and your father were close."

She said good-bye to him and closed her cell phone. She turned to look at her parents. "Mr. Kaplan had a heart attack three-days- ago. He died. His funeral was yesterday."

"Oh my," Ruth said.

"He wasn't much older than we are," Oliver added.

Holly shook her head. "I'm a bit perplexed. Jonah talked like nothing had happened until the end of the conversation. Then, in a matter of fact voice, he mentioned his father had died. He didn't seem upset or anything."

"I'll call Michelle when we get home," Ruth said.

Chapter Thirteen ~ *The Notebook*

JONAH AND HOLLY HAD fallen into a routine where he called her every Sunday at seven o'clock, Boise time. They would each review what had happened during the previous week.

His Uncle Meyer managed to find projects where he needed Jonah's help around the antique car garage and Jonah would talk to his uncle about many things, but never talked about his father. Uncle Meyer would often come in and find him cleaning and waxing his Auburn—even when it didn't need cleaning or waxing. When his father's office was cleaned out, all of his papers were moved to the house. Jonah had spent time alone, going through his father's laboratory notebooks. He'd read the last dated notebook, written before his father died. It had an indication that there was a following notebook. His father had been scrupulous in dating and tracking his notes and Jonah thought it was odd the last notebook was missing.

One Sunday morning, he decided to clean one of his father's rifles. He went to the safe, entered the pin, removed the main battle rifle and carried it over to his father's workbench where he cleared it and started disassembling it. Jonah then spent an hour lovingly cleaning and lubricating the rifle that had served him and Holly so well.

As he was placing it back in the safe, he noticed the edge of a lab notebook sticking out from a pile of papers in the safe. Jonah removed it. From its date, he knew it was written the day his father died. He started looking through the notes and studied a section that had symbols he didn't recognize. After two-and-a-half-pages of the strange symbols, his father had written two-horizontal-lines following the last entry and scrawled across the bottom-half-of-the- page "Jonah is right!"

He closed the safe, but took the notebook to his room where he carefully hid it. He wondered if someone might have hidden the notebook from him because of what his father had written in it.

Two-weeks-later, Jonah was looking around his Uncle Meyer's extensive math library. He took a piece of paper out of his pocket. He had transcribed some of the strange notation from his father's notebook. "Do you recognize these symbols?" he asked his uncle.

"That's p-adic numerical notation."

His uncle pulled a book from his library entitled *p-adic Analysis* and handed it to Jonah. When Jonah opened the book, he saw many of the same symbols his father had used in the last entries in his notebook. Jonah asked if he could borrow it.

"You can certainly borrow the book, but it's way over your head. That's master's level stuff."

Jonah took the book home and then opened his father's lab notebook. The symbols were clearly the same, but the concepts were indeed over his head.

The following Sunday Holly and he had their usual what-happened-that-week phone conversation. Almost as an afterthought, he mentioned he had found his father's notebook and it had p-adic numbers in it. She said she had never heard of p-adic numbers.

"Neither have I, but I'm trying to figure them out so I can understand what he was trying to express."

"Jonah, I'd like you to do me a favor, please," she asked him. "I've started running every morning with Drew. Would you start running every day so we can run together the next time we meet?"

"Sure, I'll do that."

When Holly and her family came to Seattle to visit her grandparents she and Jonah were together for brief visits but they never talked about anything more than what was happening at school. They did occasionally run together during the visit, which they both seemed to enjoy.

Chapter Fourteen ~ *Mourning*

ON A VISIT TO Seattle in late fall, Holly borrowed her parents' car and drove over to Jonah's home shortly after lunch; she found him standing outside waiting for her.

Her heart began beating faster as soon as she saw him.

It was a cloudy and cool day with a light mist in the air. Jonah suggested they go for a walk around his neighborhood. "We need to talk about some stuff."

"I'd love to," Holly told him. She grabbed his hand as they started walking.

After few steps he pulled his hand away. "We need to talk about something," he said. "I don't have feelings like I had before my Dad died. I don't get excited and I don't get sad like I used to. That includes us."

"I see."

"I'm sorry, Holly. You seem to have hitched your wagon to an unfeeling zombie. I think you deserve better than that."

"Do you think we should stop seeing each other?"

"I don't know what to think, other than you shouldn't be spending time with someone who is an emotional train wreck."

"Shouldn't that be my decision?"

Jonah didn't answer, but stared blankly ahead as they continued walking.

Holly used both hands to pull up her collar as the wind increased and the mist began changing into rain which pelted their faces.

"I hardly have a thought that doesn't include you, Jonah.

When I bought this jacket last week, my first thought was whether you would like it. Whenever I think about my future, it always includes thoughts of you."

"I'm not the same person, Holly. I don't enjoy talking to anyone other than you and Uncle Meyer. When Dad was alive he understood me. He would talk to me about my future, give me advice on my values, and occasionally mentioned things that he wanted me to research for our business when I finished school. He always referred to it as our business when he talked to me, and never mentioned my brother's names when he talked about research. It was going to be us. Our research, for our company, he always said."

"Doesn't it make you happy he thought of you as his future partner?"

"It did at the time, but not now. If I think about it now I start feeling sad, and I don't want to feel like that so I think about something else. As unfeeling as I've become, even things that should make me happy don't."

"Do I make you happy?"

"I don't know anymore."

"Jonah, I do need you. More than you can imagine. When someone doesn't understand me, I remember that Jonah understands me and cares about me. Those simple thoughts make me feel like everything's all right in my world. I know you've suffered a terrible loss, but somehow you have to figure out how to get over it so we can have a life together."

"How can you need someone who can't feel anything?"
"Because you're the one who makes me happier than anyone else does. Because thoughts of you bring joy to my heart. Only you do that for me."

"How can I do that for you when I can't even do that for myself?"

"I don't know how and I don't care. I'm just happy that you do."

"Holly, you deserve someone else—someone who can

feel."

Holly threw her arms around him and held him as tight as she could as the rain turned into a downpour. Wet, cold drops coursed down her face and inside her collar onto her neck, making her shiver.

"Like the song says," she told him, "I love you—always—forever."

Jonah put his arms around Holly in a gentle manner.

"Maybe you should talk to Dr. Rabinowitz," Holly suggested.

They returned to his home. Jonah's mother met them at the door. "You two must be soaked, staying out in the rain like that."

"We're okay, Mrs. Kaplan. We had some things to talk about."

"Take some towels from the linen closet upstairs and dry yourselves off."

As Holly dried her hair, she studied Jonah. "You look exhausted, Jonah."

"I haven't been sleeping well."

"Come on." She led him into his room. "We'll lie down for a while."

They left the door open as first Jonah and then Holly lay down. She had to guide his arm around her as she wrapped herself around him. For the first time since she had met Jonah, Holly began to worry that he would try to end their relationship.

***

Twenty-minutes-later, Michelle was on her way to her bedroom to put some laundry away. As she walked past the door she looked in on them and found them fast asleep. She covered them with her Pendleton Father's Eyes blanket which was created as a tribute to the fathers who watch over and guide us as we grow.

"Watch over them, Morris," Michelle whispered to her departed husband. "They need you to guide them."

A tear slipped down her cheek and she went and sat on the side of her bed. "Oh, Morris, I miss you so much. Why did you have to leave us? You have three growing sons that still need their father— Jonah more than any of them. I am so worried about him, Morris. He's still hurting so bad because you're not here. He's polite to the rest of us, but he only has conversations with Meyer and Holly. And Holly, well, I don't know what they had to talk about that was important enough to stay out in the rain, but—" Michelle began to sob. "The worst part is, Morris, he never talks about you."

She leaned her head into her hands and released the flow of grief that she had been keeping inside, away from her children as much as she could. Just then a breeze blew in the room and the wedding photo on her bedside table toppled over. Michelle stood up and went to check the window, but it was closed.

As she set the photo back up, she smiled through her sadness. "You are watching over us, aren't you, Morris."

***

Jonah had taken the college entrance exam and earned excellent scores. Michelle started talking to him about choosing a college and thinking about a major.

"I just want to go to the university here in Seattle. I'm going to major in mathematics."

"I know you don't like to talk about your father, Jonah, but I have to tell you something. You know we both love all three of you boys, but your father never for a moment kidded himself about one thing. You, Jonah, are the only one with the intellectual capacity to do work at your father's level. David and Ethan will do fine at whatever they decide to do, but you have the ability to become the best of the best at whatever area you decide to tackle. Your father would have given anything to see you go into genetics. If we could have kept his company afloat after he died, you would be the one who he expected to run it. You don't have to believe me, ask your Uncle Meyer."

"Thanks for telling me, Mom, but I only have an interest in mathematics." Jonah walked out of the room.

Michelle began quietly crying and pleaded with her absent husband. "Morris, please help me. He could do so much, but you're not here to give him direction. I don't know how to get through to him. You and Jonah spoke the same language. Please find a way to guide our son, please, Morris."

***

As he had planned, Jonah was accepted at the university in Seattle. Holly was happy for him. Things had changed between them somewhat, although, they remained friends and the phone calls continued.

She went out with a few boys during high school, but she knew Jonah's social life remained a complete zero. Dating was fun for her, but Holly primarily looked forward to the Sunday night calls from Jonah and opportunities to get together with him when she and her family visited Seattle.

Her parents said they were concerned Jonah might never get over the loss of his father and they had hinted that she might want to reconsider her relationship with him.

Holly was adamant. "He's still hurting and he still needs me," she would say. "As long as he keeps calling me, I'm not changing anything."

Chapter Fifteen ~ *A Soldier's Thoughts on Death*

IN LATE OCTOBER THE Holt family was visiting Ruth's and Oliver's parents in Seattle. Jonah drove over one morning to go for a run with Holly, Drew and Holly's dad. Holly said she had twisted her knee during the week so Jonah ran with Oliver and Drew. For the first mile, Jonah didn't say anything.

After a long uphill run, he asked Oliver, "Would you mind if I asked about something that happened when you were in combat?"

"Ask away."

"When one of your friends died in a battle, how did you get over that?"

"First, I did my best to end the fire fight we were in. Later I would cry and feel like part of my soul was missing."

"How did you replace the missing part of your soul?"

"I never did. The damage will be with me until I die. I just learned to deal with it. Do you know what survivor's guilt is, Jonah?"

"I think so. It occurs when someone is one of a few survivors and feel guilty they didn't die like everyone else."

"You got it. I had a problem with that. I went out with a twelve-man squad and only two of us survived. After the army, I started getting headaches so bad they nearly incapacitated me. I was dating Ruth then and she encouraged me to continue getting help. Also her unconditional love and support enabled me to confront my feelings. I don't get the headaches any more, but the pain of the loss is still there."

"Do you think about the men who died?"

"I think of them every day of my life. When I get up in the morning I say a prayer asking the Lord to remember them and take good care of them. Then I ask Him to help me live that day in a way my lost buddies would be proud of."

They had stopped running and were walking to cool down. Oliver had tears in his eyes. "They were such great men, Jonah. One of them could play violin in a way which could make you laugh, cry, or dance. Another one was absolutely brilliant in science and he was going to go to med school. I couldn't understand why I survived and they didn't. My God, I miss them."

"Do you understand now?"

"No, and I probably never will. I've just learned to live with the pain."

"What happened to the other guy who survived?"

"He couldn't deal with his feelings. He ended up in a VA hospital in San Diego and will most likely remain there the rest of his life. I still visit him at least once a year."

He put his arm around Jonah when he saw the tears running down his face.

"Losing someone we love is the worst shit we can face in our lives," Oliver told him. "The pain of losing your dad isn't going to go away. You're nearly a grown man now, and you need to figure out how to get on with your life—be someone your dad would be proud of. If it means getting professional help, then you need to do that."

Drew put his hand on Jonah's shoulder, as he too felt sorry for his pain. "I don't know what I'd do if I lost my dad," he said.

"No one knows until it happens, Drew," Oliver told him.

Jonah thanked Oliver for talking to him about his combat experience.

After the run with Drew and Oliver, Jonah talked to Holly.

She again suggested that he should talk to Dr. Rabinowitz.

Chapter Sixteen ~ *Seeking Help*

JONAH FINALLY FOLLOWED HOLLY'S advice and called Dr. Rabinowitz. Jonah's session with him allowed him to realize that he was extremely angry with his father. He loved his dad, but was angry with him for no longer being a part of his life.

"Dr. Rabinowitz, people tell me I'm pretty smart, but why couldn't I see for myself what was happening?"

"Sometimes extreme emotions can blind us, Jonah. From what we've talked about, it's obvious your father was a huge part of your world. When he left, no one could take his place."

Dr. Rabinowitz paused, looking contemplative. "I think in some respects your father looked up to you."

"What? What do you mean?"

"After the shooting, he told me he never could have done what you did when he was your age. When he found out what you and Holly had done at the accident scene in Utah, he was so proud of you he was walking on air for weeks. Again, he told me he couldn't have done that when he was sixteen. I can't begin to tell you how excited he was when he found out you had learned to speak Navajo while you were studying for your *Bar Mitzvah*. Possibly the one thing that gave him the most joy was your relationship with Holly."

"I had no idea he felt that way."

"Well, Jonah, some men have a tough time telling their sons how they feel about them."

"He always taught me and my brothers that we had a responsibility to use the gifts God gave us."

Dr. Rabinowitz stared at Jonah for a few moments. "And that's going to be one of the next big challenges in your life."

"What do you mean?"

"You mentioned you are going to major in mathematics."
"Yes. Math is the only subject I enjoy."

"What will you do with that knowledge when you graduate?"

Jonah went completely blank. "I'm—I—I absolutely have no clue." He sat in stunned silence for a while. Then a smile started spreading across his face. "I'll talk to Holly and Uncle Meyer. They'll help me."

As he shook hands with Dr. Rabinowitz, Jonah thanked him. "I'm not going to suddenly stop being angry at my dad overnight, am I?"

"You suffered a huge wound, Jonah. It requires time to learn to deal with the pain. By acknowledging your anger you have a good place to start healing. Anytime you want to talk, just call me."

"Thanks, Dr. Rabinowitz. Talking to you has been a huge help."

Chapter Seventeen ~ *Holly to the Rescue*

HOLLY APPLIED TO, AND was accepted at, the same university as Jonah. She'd decided to take a class which started in June but had difficulty finding housing over the summer. She had mentioned her housing problem to Jonah and the next day his Aunt Joan called and excitedly told Holly she could stay in their in-law apartment.

"It has its own entrance so you can come and go as you please," she'd told Holly.

Both sets of Holly's grandparents also offered to let her stay with them, but they lived much further from the university. She also liked the idea of having a place with its own entrance which meant more privacy.

On Sunday morning, Holly filled the little minivan her parents had given her as a graduation present, said good-bye to them, and started the nine-hour-drive to Seattle. As she drove through the scenic Blue Mountains of Oregon and the desolate desert areas east of Yakima, Washington, she wished Jonah could have been with her to share in their beauty.

She arrived to see Meyer and Joan looking ecstatic to have her in their home. They helped her unpack her things and fill closets and dressers. Then they asked Holly to join them for dinner. Joan was positively glowing as she talked excitedly to Holly about all the things they could do together around Seattle.

When Jonah's name came up, Holly mentioned she thought he still wasn't dealing with his father's death.

"None of us have been able to get through to him," Meyer said. "He's not the same person. He's not happy and he's not sad. It's as if he's just going through the motions of life with no feeling. A few- weeks-ago he asked me what it was like when one of my fellow soldiers died in combat. I told him how awful it was, but we still had to continue doing our job. I also explained how the pain of the loss never goes away, but we do our best to learn to live with it. I think your father had a similar talk with him the last time you were out here."

Holly listened and was glad to be around people that cared as much about Jonah as she did. After dinner at six o'clock, she returned to her apartment to wait for Jonah's weekly call.

***

At six-fifteen, Holly's apartment doorbell rang. As she hadn't been expecting anyone, and she'd been so focused on Jonah's call, she picked up her cell phone. Then she gave her head a shake, realizing it was her doorbell.

She opened the door to see Jonah standing there. He was at least a head taller than she was. Her heart jumped in her chest as soon as she saw him.

She invited him in and he started telling her about the new CD transport he had added to his audio system. She didn't understand most of the discussion, but loved having all of his attention and simply hearing his voice.

As she listened, she thought Jonah didn't look like a boy any longer. His body had become muscular and firm. After she talked about her upcoming class, they agreed they would get together again next Sunday evening.

The couch they were sitting on looked out onto the lake through an open screened-in sliding glass door. The sun was low in the sky over the lake and many boats were cruising by, probably heading home. The beautiful scent of the lake air filled the little apartment.

Holly had been sitting next to Jonah, but then she kneeled on either side of his legs, sitting on his lap facing him.

"You're still in pain about your father, aren't you?" she said.

He looked at her as his eyes filled with tears. It was as if a veritable tsunami of sadness overwhelmed him as he began to cry. "I miss my dad, Holly—and Lord knows I've missed you."

She pulled his head to her chest and held him there with both arms. He wrapped his arms around her and sobbed. A little at first, but then a torrent of pent up pain and sorrow came pouring out.

Holly held Jonah as tight against her as she could. She cried with him, knowing how much pain he had suppressed since his father died. He had his arms around her as if he were clinging to a life preserver. She felt his hot tears running down her chest and it was a long time before he completely stopped crying.

Jonah finally began to talk. "The day Dad died, we had a talk at dinnertime. I told him some stuff about how his research should change. Then, he went to his lab and I never saw him again. Sometime-later I went through his lab notebooks. I thought the last one was missing, and I discovered it in my dad's gun safe. The last entry in the lab notebook was on the day he died, Holly. He wrote, 'Jonah was right, in big letters.'"

Jonah took a big breath. "After all his years in research, I'm afraid my seventeen-year-old-mind showed him how all the work he had been doing was wrong. That could have been the stress which caused his heart attack. I feel so sad about doing that to him."

"Jonah, you don't know if that caused his heart attack. Ethan told me he was overweight and never exercised. At the funeral, I overheard your mother telling people he had been having severe back pains for weeks, but wouldn't go to the doctor. From what I've read, those pains could have been small heart attacks. All of those things occurred before you talked to him. He also felt a tremendous amount of stress after those people tried to kill us. He believed it was his fault we had been put in so much danger."

Jonah stared at her for quite a while. "Is that why you asked me to start running? You wanted me to run to help get rid of my stress?"

Holly nodded. "I was hoping it would help."

He put his head back on her chest and quietly cried while continuing to hold her tightly. "You are so good to me," he told her.

Holly ran her fingers through his hair and massaged the back of his neck as she continued to hold his head against her. She wished she could take his pain away.

After he once again stopped crying, Jonah looked at Holly. "I guess I knew those things about my dad, but I was so angry, I ignored them. Only my dad, Uncle Meyer, you—and come to think of it, your dad—understand me. I can barely talk to the kids my own age. I love my mom, and she's the perfect mom for Ethan and David. I know she loves me, but she doesn't *understand* me. If it wasn't for you and Uncle Meyer, I don't think I could have managed the time since Dad died."

"It's going to be better in university. You might find people as geeky as you are," Holly teased. "Besides, I'll be there with you."

Jonah smiled up at her. "So, this is what being loved by a partner feels like," he said. "I'm amazed how your embrace is making me…well, finally start to feel some sense of peace."

He briefly kissed her lips. "I love you, Holly. I don't know what I would have done all this time without your phone calls to look forward to. I feel bad though, because we never talked about anything serious."

"I know you love me, Jonah. That's why I didn't care we couldn't talk about serious things. I was just glad you called."

"But I'm sorry I couldn't tell you how I felt. You deserve better than that."

"You don't have to be sorry for the way the conversations went. I know you loved your dad and I know how much he meant to you. Losing a parent is not an easy thing to deal with. Believe me I know. There is nothing to be sorry about."

She leaned forward and put her lips gently on his. They enjoyed a long kiss.

"I tried to tell you what I was feeling so many times," he told her, "but it just wouldn't come out. I'll never understand why."

"You just weren't ready. It doesn't matter, as long as we can talk about things now."

Holly leaned forward and they kissed again. "*Ya at eeh*, Holly."

Holly saw his smile was returning. "*Ya at eeh*, Jonah."

In perfect Navajo Jonah said, "Holly's love for me surrounds and comforts me like the warm desert wind. That warmth has sustained me through this troubled time."

"Jonah, that's beautiful." Holly put her hands on either side of his face and put little kisses all over it. "You continued practicing Navajo," she exclaimed, delighted as they continued their conversation speaking Navajo.

"Yes, I worked and studied the language of the *Dine*, so there would be a time when I could express the great love in my heart for you."

"You are so special," she told him. "Thank you for continuing to study, and for saying something so beautiful to me."

"We have a lot to work out if we're going to stay together."

"No one knows what the future holds," she said. "My wise father once told me we need to live our lives like things will work out."

"Your father is, indeed, a wise man."

"Hey, let's walk down to the lake," Holly said reverting to

English. "I've never lived in a house on a lake before." She started to get up but Jonah held her on his lap.

"Thank you, Holly. You are so good to me. I'm so happy you're going to be living near me. I love you more than I can tell you."

"I know. I've felt your love for me since we first met. Our time together has brought me more happiness than any one person deserves."

They kissed again then walked down to the lake hand in hand. They stood at the lake's edge for a while when Jonah suddenly reached down and picked Holly up, acting as if he was going to throw her in the water.

She screamed and yelled at him to put her down—most of which was unintelligible because she was laughing so hard. When he put her down, she put her arms around his neck, and they kissed again.

Holding hands once more, they walked out to the end of the pier and began to converse in Navajo again.

"Okay, Mister Jonah. It's time to dump all of your bad thoughts into the lake."

"I might fill it up," he warned her.

"Not anymore," she told him with a laugh. "The partners are together again. When one of us sees the other having a cloudy day, it will be our duty to fill our partner's spirit with sunshine."

Jonah stared at Holly with a huge smile, then he wrapped his arms around her. "Yes, the partners are together again and that makes all the difference."

***

Meyer and Joan watched them from their perch on the balcony. "He was laughing about something," Joan said to Meyer. "You're right," Meyer agreed. "I haven't seen him laughing since Morris died."

Joan opened her cell and called Michelle. "You won't believe what's going on over here. Holly arrived today, and she and Jonah are out on the dock laughing and joking. I can't understand what they're saying. I think they must be speaking Navajo. Yes, I'm serious. They're out there laughing and joking. Michelle, quit crying. This is a good thing — Meyer, talk to your little sister. All she wants to do is cry."

Meyer chuckled and then took the phone. "Michelle? We're not kidding. He came over around six. They talked for a while and we heard him crying. He must have cried for quite some time, but I'm telling you — oh my Lord, you won't believe this, but Jonah just started walking up the pier toward the house. Holly hung back for a second then she ran and jumped on his back. He's laughing so hard he can hardly carry her. They're coming up to the house. We're going to invite them for coffee and desert on the patio. Why don't you come over? See you in ten-minutes."

When Michelle arrived, they all gathered on the patio overlooking the lake to enjoy apple pie and coffee. Michelle was beside herself listening to Jonah and Holly joke and laugh.

"A neighbor of ours taught me to bake apple pie with a tiny amount of fresh ginger," Holly told them. "My mom says you add just a whisper. You can barely tell it's there, but the ginger adds substantially to the flavor."

Joan looked at Holly, a smile spreading across her face. "Kiddo, you and I are going to be great friends. I have recipes for using nectarines and rainier cherries in northwest-style cooking which are to die for."

"I've never made anything with nectarines," Holly excitedly told her.

"How about getting the family together next Saturday night, Holly?" Joan suggested. "I think you should invite your grandparents as well."

"Only if Jonah and I get to do the cooking," Holly insisted.

"Okay with me, but only if I pay for the groceries," Joan said.

"Great!" Holly told them. "We can get up early next Saturday if you like. We'll start by shopping at the farmers' market in Issaquah."

Holly turned to Joan and asked, "Do you keep kosher?"

"No, but some of our relatives do."

"No problem, I can make everything dairy."

"I thought you weren't Jewish," Meyer said. "How do you know about kosher cooking?"

"I have this amazing neighbor in Meridian, who I think you met, named Anna Levin. She decided to keep kosher at her home. She's been teaching me kosher-style cooking."

"Is she the one who taught Linda to make those incredible rainier cherry blintzes she serves with homemade yogurt?"

"Yes, that's Mrs. Levin. Mrs. Minkowski, do you have a pasta machine?"

"Yes, but it's one of the old hand crank types."

"That's great. I think the hand types are the best for homemade pasta."

Meyer's eyes widened and he looked at Joan — she knew exactly what he was thinking — homemade pasta!

***

Holly turned towards Jonah. "You had better be doing pushups on your fingertips all this week to get your wrists in shape to turn the pasta machine crank, Jonah."

"Oh, that's just great," Jonah complained in a sarcastic voice, "I have something to look forward to. My first full Saturday with Holly and I'll never get closer to her than the end of a pasta machine crank."

Everyone laughed at their jovial banter, but Jonah's mom excused herself and walked down to the water's edge. Holly quickly stood and walked down the lovely flagstone path to talk to her. She found Mrs. Kaplan had tears rolling down her cheeks. "Are you okay?" Holly asked.

"Precious Holly, I am happier than you can imagine. Jonah hasn't made jokes like that since his father died."

"I guess he wasn't ready until today."

"Thank you, Holly. I'm so appreciative of what you've done for him."

"It's not a big deal. Sometimes we girls have to rescue our guys."

"Believe me, it's a huge deal." Jonah's mom embraced her. "God bless you, Holly."

They walked back to the patio. "When we first saw you and Jonah together we all thought it was cute," she continued. "Except for Morris who told me you were perfect for each other and you would end up together. I remember laughing at the time, but he was right."

"We still have some things to work out," Holly said. "Judaism is important to Jonah. I don't know how we'll work that out."

"Morris was much more religious than I was. I think my becoming more religious brought us closer together. I don't know what will work for you two, but I hope you'll work out your differences. Believe me, it will be worth it."

***

Holly and Jonah returned to her apartment. They started making plans to get together during the week when she wasn't in class, then they held each other in a tight embrace.

"Thank you, Holly, for being you." "I love you, Jonah."

"And I love you so much."

They kissed one last time and Jonah headed home.

As Holly went to sleep that night, her thoughts turned to an angry and scared young girl who had felt every adult in her life had abandoned her—and to the man whose love made her feel so protected that she wasn't scared of relationships any longer. Her anger was completely defeated by the man's unconditional love for her. Holly realized that her unconditional love for Jonah had done the same for him.

"Thank you, Dad," she whispered to her pillow. "If you hadn't done that for me, I wouldn't have been able to do the same for my beloved Jonah."

Chapter Eighteen ~ Seeing Double is the Bee's Knees

ON THE FOLLOWING SATURDAY morning Meyer and Joan took Jonah and Holly on a trip to the farmers' market in Issaquah.

"Let's hit the flower vendors last," Holly suggested.

They went to the stall of a local baker. Holly and Joan selected a few savory rounds and some sesame baguettes. A local dairy farmer had fresh ricotta cheese, rich cream, and just-churned butter.

Holly and Joan chattered like sisters as they examined the fresh vegetables and fruit. Based on what was available, they were putting together a menu which had Jonah's and Meyer's mouths watering. Into bags went zucchini, onions, shallots, turnips, crimini and shitake mushrooms, Japanese eggplant, spinach leaves, Bibb lettuce, red and green bell peppers, *Pasilla* peppers, celery, Roma tomatoes, and pickled *gardiniera* for the *antipasto*.

They also bought a couple of infused olive oils plus a bottle of eighteen-year-old balsamic vinegar. At the fresh-herb stand they bought garlic, rosemary, basil, thyme, bay leaves, and dried oregano. "I like to use dried oregano. I think the flavor is intensified when it's dry," Holly told Joan.

Meyer and Jonah were carrying so many bags they asked the girls to take a break to let them put their purchases in the car. By the time they returned, the girls had picked out seven huge bouquets-of-flowers.

After the farmers' market, it was off to the Italian deli for more *antipasto* ingredients like pickled eggplant, peppers in olive oil, mozzarella, provolone, *Provola affumicata*, marinated artichoke hearts, and pickled herring.

Joan found sharp, flavorful *Pecorino-Romano* and full bodied

Parmigiano-Reggiano cheeses, both for grating.

Holly put dried porcini mushrooms-in-a-bag. She'd been smiling all day as if she was in heaven. She once again thanked Joan for treating her like family.

As they walked back to their car, Jonah and Holly started laughing about something and Meyer turned to Joan. "Do you see it?" he whispered.

"Of course I do," Joan agreed. "They have magic between them like Ari and Leah. They act and sound the same as when Ari and Leah were their age. I'm so happy for them."

***

When they arrived back at the Minkowskis' home, they found Ari and Leah had arrived with their five-year-old identical twins, Marsha and Esther.

"Hi, Uncle Jonah," they screamed and ran over to him.

"Oh no! It's the twins I can't tell apart," Jonah yelled as he gave them each a hug. Then he stepped back and gestured to Holly. "Ladies, this is my good friend, Holly."

She greeted them and Esther informed her, "It's easy to tell us apart, because I'm Esther and she's Marsha. I don't think it's difficult."

"I'm sure that won't be a problem," Holly said, smiling widely at the girls.

"Hi, Aunt Holly," Marsha said.

"Marsha, she's not your aunt," Jonah corrected her. "Are you guys together?" Esther asked Holly.

"Yes, we're good friends, like boyfriend and girlfriend." Marsha looked at Esther. "We're going to help her cook and

116

Mom said she's really nice, so I think we should call her Aunt Holly."

Esther stood with feet spread, folded her left arm over her head, pointing to Holly, and extended her right arm pointing in the same direction. "That's settled then," she said. "Aunt Holly, how can we help?"

Everyone was smiling and laughing at the twin's antics just as David and Linda arrived to a noisy greeting by the twins.

"Aunt Linda, come over here," Marsha yelled in an excited voice. "I want you to meet my Uncle Jonah's Aunt Holly."

"Hey, Uncle Jonah's Aunt Holly," Linda shouted with laughter as they walked into the kitchen.

"Hey, Aunt Linda." Holly giggled in return.

"I see you've realized the twins make up their own rules as they go," David said.

"They couldn't be more precious," Holly told him, clearly already in love with the twins.

"Look out now," David declared as he looked around the kitchen. "Linda and Holly have the kitchen."

"And I'm stuck over here on this pasta machine," Jonah complained.

"Be quiet and crank!" Holly ordered.

As everyone laughed, Linda asked, "Where can I start?"

"How about making two fillings for the ravioli? It's going to be a dairy meal, so I was thinking ricotta with butternut squash and ricotta with porcini mushroom. After that, I'll need a filling for the *gnocchi* and later a dessert filling for cannoli."

"I'll start on those right now," Linda said in a happy voice.

"How about cream, vanilla, lime juice, sugar, cinnamon, and nutmeg for the dessert filling?"

"Aunt Linda, that sounds perfect," Holly replied.

Leah had her twins put on tiny, light green aprons, each with their name embroidered on it, then Holly, Jonah, and the twins, who were standing on step stools, started making the pasta.

Linda instructed David on what ingredients to start prepping for the marinara sauce and the *pasta e fagioli.*

Ari looked ecstatic watching his daughters learn to make pasta with Jonah and Holly.

"Look how the twins follow exactly what they are told to do," he quietly said to Joan. "They are absolutely in heaven cooking with them. Holly is so special and so perfect for Jonah. They really know how to make the twins feel special."

"Leave it to Jonah to find a partner who is a brilliant cook and great with children," Leah added.

"Mom," Esther called to Leah. "When am I going to be an aunt?"

"You'll be an aunt when your sister has children."

"Sorry, Sister, you can forget that," Marsha told Esther. "Children are home-wreckers. I could never put up with them."

"Sister, I know what you mean," Esther said. "You guys are children," Jonah informed them.

"Do you believe your Uncle Jonah said that?" Esther inquired of Marsha.

"Maybe you should tell him," Marsha suggested. "I don't think he's listening to me."

"Uncle Jonah, we are not children. We are *sisters.*"

Amid the laughter, Joan was thinking there couldn't possibly be any more fun activity going on in her kitchen. That is precisely when her pregnant daughter, Samantha, arrived with her seven- year-old son, Sam.

"Aunt Samantha," Esther yelled. "Come over and meet my Aunt Holly and my Aunt Linda."

They greeted each other with hugs.

"Uncle Jonah, I want to help you," Sam said.

"Thank heavens you're here, Sam, I need help turning the crank on this pasta machine."

"Sorry I can't help cook today," Samantha said. "If this kid gets any bigger I'm going to need a wheelbarrow to carry my belly around." Samantha was eight-and-a-half-months pregnant with her second child.

"Well," Leah said, "seeing as nearly everyone is here, I have an announcement of my own — I'm two-months-pregnant!"

Everyone cheered and congratulated Leah and Ari.

"Mom," Esther asked, "are you going to have more twin sisters like me and Marsha?"

"I don't know yet," Leah replied.

"Maybe you're going to have twin brothers," Jonah suggested to her.

Marsha looked at her mother and put her little hands on her hips. "Mom, you wouldn't."

"Maybe I would. Maybe your father would like to have a boy at our house."

Esther rolled her eyes, and looked at her sister. "Marsha," she said, "you need to have a talk with your father to tell him he doesn't need a boy in our house."

Soon the kitchen was turning out ravioli, *gnocchi*, cannoli, and *pasta e fagioli*, while Linda and Holly's marinara sauce was filling the air with the rich fragrance of tomato, basil, garlic, and oregano.

Samantha's husband, Moshe, arrived. He and Ari started making up the *antipasto* trays. Linda prepared a nectarine-lime- mango sauce for the cannoli.

"Uncle Moshe, we made ravioli and gnocchi and cannoli for you," Esther yelled, her voice filled with pride.

"Thank you, guys. It sounds like I better be hungry."

Leah told her twins it was time for them to nap. They both groaned.

"Mom, can we sleep in the playroom?"

"You can, but you better sleep."

"I'm not tired." Esther pleaded.

"If you guys sleep now," Jonah told them, "then I'll take you to the store in my old Auburn car to buy spumoni ice cream."

"What did your uncle say?" Marsha asked her sister.

Ari interrupted them, speaking in a stern voice. "He said the two-of-you better be on your way to a nap immediately."

The girls quickly started walking to the playroom and Joan followed.

"Come on, girls. I'll tuck you in," she said.

"When Dad uses that tone of voice," Marsha said, "we need to start moving right away, because if we don't, we get in *big trouble*." Esther nodded in agreement.

As they entered the playroom, they decided they needed to wear a hat to get to sleep. Putting on old lace hats they each lay down and Joan pulled an Afghan over them. They were soon fast asleep.

***

Two-hours later Leah and Holly came into the playroom to wake them.

"Wake up, girls. Holly and Uncle Jonah want to take you to the store in Uncle Jonah's old-time car," Leah told them.

"Can we wear our hats?" Esther asked.

"Why don't you both put on your old-time outfits?"

"Aunt Holly, will you wait for us to put on our old-time outfits?"

She smiled. "I'll help you get dressed."

The girls dressed in white long-sleeve shirts, long paisley-patterned skirts, pink boas, and their wide-brimmed lace hats. They stood in front of a long mirror in the playroom admiring their outfits.

"You guys are the bee's knees," Holly proclaimed.

"Did you hear what your Aunt Holly said?" Marsha asked Esther.

"I think you need to talk to her. She's starting to sound like your Uncle Jonah."

"I think you guys are the cat's pajamas," Leah told them

with a grin.

Esther put her hands on her hips. "These are not pajamas, Mom."

The twins walked into the family room where everyone had gathered. They looked pleased to hear everyone praise their lovely outfits.

"Seeing you guys in period clothing gives me the heebie-jeebies." Holly giggled.

"Looks like you're ready to twenty-three-skidoo," Jonah added.

The twins stared at Jonah for a while and then Marsha looked at Holly. "Are you guys speaking that Navajo stuff?" she asked.

While everyone laughed, Leah explained to her girls about 1920's slang.

They went outside and Jonah helped the twins into the rumble seat of his car. Holly had them take their hats off during the ride to the store. Everyone who saw them couldn't help but smile.

Jonathan Rifkin and his wife Ileana arrived. He was a well-known author of children's books but had been restricted to a wheelchair since childhood due to a neuro-muscular disease. Their sons, Ryan, Benjamin, and Avram came with them.

"Ryan, over here," Jonah called.

Jonah and Holly greeted him. "I hear you're taking math classes at the university this year," Holly said.

"I'm lucky. I was born with a special gift for mathematics. I'll start full time at the university in another year. I hear both of you will be attending. It will be fun to see some family members over there."

"We're looking forward to it," Jonah said. "Us math guys have to stick together."

"That's for sure!" Ryan said.

*****

Meyer was in heaven watching Joan all evening. With their children and grandchildren, cousins, aunts and uncles, significant others and some of their other family members at her home, he thought she was positively glowing from happiness.

"The kids wouldn't let me do any of the cooking," she told Holly's grandparents as everyone began eating. "The twins and Sam helped as well."

"Holly's been great in the kitchen since she was twelve." Holly's grandmother proudly told Joan.

"Then David brings Linda into the family and it's one feast after another when she's around," Joan said. "And they're both learning to cook kosher meals from a wonderful neighbor of theirs, Anna Levin."

"We've had meals at Anna's home," Oliver's father said. "Just when you think there's nothing new to taste, she comes up with a twist on an old recipe."

"Linda cooked pumpkin soup last fall," Joan related. "It's made with chicken broth, pumpkin spice, and pureed pumpkin. It was Anna's recipe and everyone just loved it. She served it in a pumpkin shell."

After an amazing dinner everyone moved to the media room where a concert took place with Jonah and Meyer taking turns on the drum set—both with Sam's help. Linda played guitar and sang while David sang and played trumpet. Ethan also played trumpet as well as trombone while Sheryl played the keyboard.

They passed out song sheets for some audience participation and Leah setup a video camera to record the evening's performances for each family.

*****

At the end of a wonderful and fun-filled performance,

Holly approached Joan. "I want to ask you something," she said in a quiet voice.

"You're a grown woman, Holly. Of course he can stay with you."

"Thank you, Mrs. Minkowski." Holly gave her a hug.

"And thank you for putting on a gastronomic feast for everyone, but especially for all you do for Jonah."

The evening ended and Holly said goodnight to the two exhausted twins, and then Jonah walked her to the entrance to her apartment. She invited him in and the two-of-them sat in the living area on the big couch, Holly on Jonah's lap facing him.

"I asked Aunt Joan if it was okay that you spend the night here. She said yes."

He smiled and they kissed passionately. Holly took off her shirt and bra while Jonah pulled his polo shirt off.

Jonah put his hands on her breasts.

"Oh my lord, Jonah, your touch feels wonderful."

"I love touching you, and I can't believe how great it feels to have your hands on me."

Holly could barely breathe—Jonah's caresses made her feel so wonderful. She lifted Jonah's face to bring his lips up to hers and pressed herself against him.

In response Jonah moved his hands up and down her back, gently massaging her.

"I've waited so long for you to touch me like this," Holly said. "Remember when we first met at the Levins' home? As we sat together our shoulders were touching."

"I remember. I kept waiting for you to move away but you didn't."

"Something inside me wouldn't let me move away. I thought I should—it wasn't sexual or anything, but it just seemed to feel so right to be leaning against you. I felt like we had a connection between us. That feeling has continued to grow since then."

"Remember when we first kissed?"

"It was that crazy night when you saved me. I loved kissing you, but I was so scared, it was more important that you held me…and you did. That was the night when I began to realize I wanted to spend my life with you, Jonah. It wasn't a complete thought then, but whenever I considered what I wanted to do in the future, it always included you."

She gave him a kiss. "When we spent the night at the accident scene and slept together for the first time, I remember thinking we did a wonderful thing for all those people and my reward was getting to fall asleep while we held each other. I'll always remember that night, as one of the most beautiful moments of my life."

They started moving toward the bedroom, shedding clothing along the way. As each additional item of clothing dropped, they caressed the parts of each other's bodies that had been exposed. When they finally slipped nervously into bed, each one of them seemed concerned about the other.

When they were through, Holly had no regrets. Although it had been uncomfortable at first, she thought it was worth it. She lay close to Jonah and sighed. "That was one of the most blissful experiences of my life," she told him.

"I love you, Holly."

"And I love you, Jonah."

They lay still in each other's arms for a long time and drifted off to sleep.

At five-thirty the next morning, Jonah and Holly were awakened by Jonah's cell phone ringer. Jonah answered in a groggy voice.

"Sure, we can do that," he said. "Okay. We'll get ready right now."

"That was Ari," he told Holly. "He said Samantha went into labor last night and delivered her baby. Apparently she's in good health but the baby is having respiratory problems. Ari and Leah want to go over to the hospital to stay with his parents. They want us to watch the twins for them. They'll be here as soon as they get the girls dressed. Do you mind?"

Holly smiled. "I'm honored they would think of us."

A short time later Ari and Leah arrived. Each of them was carrying a still-sleeping twin and they passed them to Jonah and Holly.

Esther opened her eyes long enough to see who was holding her. "Hi, Aunt Holly. I'm still sleepy."

She wrapped her arms around Holly's neck and promptly fell back asleep. They put the twins to bed and covered them with Holly's Code Talker's blanket.

Leah hugged Holly and Jonah. "Thank you so much for doing this."

"It's an honor you would think of us," Holly repeated.

Ari laughed. "You're barely family yet and we're dumping our kids on you," he said. "Seriously, though, the twins adore you guys."

"Go! Take care of your family," Jonah told them.

When the twins awoke, they were overjoyed to find themselves with Jonah and Holly.

As they ate breakfast, they tried to decide what to do that day. "There is a *Concourse d'Elegance* this morning in Kirkland," Jonah suggested.

The twins looked at each other and Esther asked, "What's a — what did you call it?"

"It's a kind of car show. We could take the old Auburn over there for everyone to see. It takes place near the waterfront so there's quite a lot to do. We could have a picnic by the lake."

"Would it be the bee's pajamas to do that?" Marsha asked.

"You would have to dress in 1920's clothing again," Holly told them. "Jonah and I will also, so it will definitely be the bee's knees."

"Wow!" Esther declared.

"We would all look like the cat's pajamas."

Holly put on her period dress and then helped the twins

with their outfits and added a pair of white gloves for each of the girls.

As they were admiring themselves in the mirror of the playroom, Esther asked, "Can Marsha and I ride in the — what do you call that place where we sat yesterday?"

"The grumble seat," Marsha told her.

"Thank you, Sister." She turned back to Jonah. "Can we ride in the grumble seat again?"

Holly and Jonah smiled at them and Jonah said, "Certainly, you can ride in the rumble seat."

They drove over to Jonah's home so he could put on his 1920's clothing and his mother was in heaven talking with the twins.

"We're the bee's knees today, Aunt Michelle," Esther told her.

"You certainly are, young ladies," she agreed.

Holly asked if she had heard any more about Samantha's baby, but Jonah's mom said it was still touch and go.

Jonah came down, and then, on a beautiful day with warm sun and a nearly cloudless sky, Jonah slowly and proudly drove his Auburn to the car show. As he entered the grounds, he was directed to drive to a grassy area and park with cars from a similar era. He was driving at walking speed so Holly told the girls they should stand up, put their hats on, and wave politely to the onlookers.

The twins were pleased at people's reactions, which consisted of smiles and many returned waves.

Once the car had been parked behind a roped-off area, Holly explained to the girls they could tell people about the car. The crowds were gathering and many people started coming down the aisle where the Auburn stood, so the twins continually chatted with the onlookers about the Auburn.

When three judges stopped by, they asked Jonah if he wanted the Auburn judged. Jonah said no, as he hadn't prepared the car for showing.

"If you are the judges then you have to let us tell you about our Uncle Jonah's car," Marsha informed them.

"I think we have time to let you do that," one of the judges said.

"Well first," Marsha said, as she used a pointing and sweeping motion with her arms, "you have long swoopy fenders which start in front right over here and twenty-three-skidoo to the back of the car."

Esther ran over and stood on the running board. "This car has welcome doors," she said. She pulled the handle down on the rear hinged door and swung it open.

Marsha stepped on the running board, grabbed the steering wheel, and pulled herself into the car and onto the driver's seat. "Thank you for opening the welcome door for me, Sister. I feel quite welcome sitting here."

The judges were all smiles by now. "Can you tell me about the engine?" one of them asked.

Marsha stood up on the seat and pointed to the long hood. "Yes, it's a big engine, with an old-time sound, and it lives right under there."

"We have to show you the grumble seat," Esther exclaimed.

They ran to the back of the car and Jonah helped them into the rumble seat.

"A grumble seat is the bee's pajamas," Marsha informed the judges. "No wait, it's the bee's knees."

"Now," Esther told them, "you have to take off your hat if your Uncle Jonah is driving fast."

Marsha added, "But you can put your hat on and wave to people if your Uncle Jonah is driving slowly. You just do it like this."

The twins stood up in the seat and demonstrated waving to the crowd.

"Thank you, young ladies," the judge told them. "This has been a real education."

He quietly whispered something to Jonah. Jonah smiled

and whispered something to Holly who smiled as well.

"Hey, you guys, telling secrets is mean," Marsha complained.

"I'm sorry, ladies," Jonah said.

"It's lunchtime," Holly added.

They had a lovely picnic lunch at the water's edge. Holly was in heaven as the twins demonstrated how much they loved and respected Jonah. She thought she had been specially blessed by being the woman who would bring Jonah's children into the world.

Jonah and Holly just started to pack up the lunch things when an announcement was made that trophies would be awarded in a few minutes.

"Let's go see if you won an award," Holly told the twins.

A number of awards were handed out when one of the judges said, "The award for best car presenters goes to Esther and Marsha Minkowski."

The twins looked at each other in astonishment.

"Walk up there straight and tall," Holly quickly advised. "Shake the judge's hands when you thank them."

The twins made sure their hats were on straight and walked proudly up to the judges. They shook their hands and were given a lovely plaque with their names on it. They walked back to Holly and Jonah, with each of them holding up one side of their plaque. Jonah took a picture of them holding their plaque while standing in front of his Auburn.

To say the twins were proud of their achievement was an understatement. They were positively glowing, but as soon as the drive home started, the exhausted twins fell asleep.

They carried the sleepy twins up to Holly's apartment. "I can't wait for the day when we'll be carrying our own children," Holly said. "You will be such a wonderful father for them."

***

Jonah's phone rang. He answered and then told Holly, "It's still rough with the baby. Apparently they won't know until tomorrow. They want to know if we can watch the kids until later today."

"That's certainly not a problem," Holly said.

"That's what I told them."

When the twins woke up from their nap Holly explained why their parents were at the hospital.

"Why does the baby have breathing problems?" Esther asked.

"Sometimes babies are born with problems," Holly told her.

"Is he real sick?"

"Yes, he is."

"How will the doctors fix him?"

"It depends on what's wrong," Jonah told her. "The doctor might give him extra oxygen, or some type of medicine."

Esther's eye's started to fill with tears. "If I was his doctor, I'd know what to do and I'd fix him. He'd be happy by now if I was his doctor."

Marsha had little reaction to the news about Samantha's baby, but Esther not only became sad, but angry as well.

"When you become a baby doctor, Esther, I'm sure you'll know what to do," Holly told her.

"Yes I will!"

An hour later Ari called Jonah again.

"They know what's wrong and he's doing much better. You're going to love this. The obstetrics team leader here in Seattle is brilliant at diagnosing neo-natal problems, but today he was apparently assisted by this medical student who has developed an encyclopedic knowledge of neo-natal diseases. You might know him."

"Oh, my Lord...you're talking about David."

"Call your mom. She'll be happy as can be to know David

was involved."

Holly told the twins that Samantha's baby was on the road to recovery. Esther was most pleased.

"What did the doctors do for him?" she wanted to know.

"I don't know, but the next time you see your Uncle David, you can ask him."

"I will ask him for sure!" Esther exclaimed.

Chapter Nineteen ~ *New Friends*

SEVENTEEN-YEAR-OLD DREW and his best friend Andy went to the big mall in Boise. They were sitting in front of a coffee shop talking about the fun they had at the previous week's car show. Drew saw a lovely looking girl sitting near them. He recognized her as a model from one of the car show's truck displays. She was sitting alone, sipping a tall latte. Drew tried to think of something he could say to start a conversation with her.

A man sat down at her table and said something to her which Drew couldn't hear. The girl looked nervous as she glanced around at the people sitting at the other tables. After some heated conversation she started to look scared.

In a voice that tried to sound tough she told the man, "Look buddy, that big kid over there is my brother and if you don't leave, I'll have him bend you into a pretzel."

"Easy, baby, I just think you should get to know me. Come on, let's go for a little walk."

Drew and Andy weren't tall but had been working out with weights since childhood. They each weighed over two-hundred pounds and had builds that mostly resembled a fire plug.

Drew had heard the girl's last remark. When he saw the man grab the girl's wrist, he stood up and walked over to her table. Andy quickly followed.

"Is there a problem over here, Sis?" Drew asked. She looked at Drew and smiled at the man.

He scowled. "No. I was just leaving."

As the girl stood, she accidently dumped the rest of her latte on the man's crotch.

"You fucking cow!" he yelled as he jumped up.

With Drew and Andy standing at her side looking like a pair of Chicago Bears linemen, the jerk wasn't going to do anything with his anger other than curse. He turned and walked away yelling over his shoulder, "It's not over, you fat cow!"

"It better be or I will twist you into a pretzel," Drew's voice thundered after him.

"I'm Karen Wilson," the relieved-looking girl told them," and I'm glad to meet you."

They introduced themselves too, and then invited her to join them for an afternoon of Afro-Cuban music.

"It's a tradition at our high school. Every fall after school starts, the drumline and our friends from band head to a park to play. At first we just had percussion, but the last few years we've had horns and guitars as well."

"Thank you, but I don't think so," she told them.

Andy tried to persuade her. "Playing music is a lot more fun than sitting in front of a coffee shop getting hit on."

Karen laughed.

"It's a friendly crowd," Drew told her. "If you don't like the get-together, one of us will drive you home."

Karen looked at the two-of-them. She looked nervous about getting into a car with two guys she had just met.

"Hey, let's get going or we'll be late," a petite young lady called out as she and a female friend walked up to Drew and Andy.

"Kim and Beverly, this is our friend Karen."

"Are you coming with us?" Beverly asked. "It's a party to die for!"

Karen looked at them, seeming reassured she wouldn't be the only girl, and slowly nodded. "Sure. I could use a good time."

Drew picked up her shopping bags and Andy pushed in

her chair. She reached out as if she was about to take the packages from Drew, but realized he was going to carry them for her. Andy helped the other two girls with their packages.

As Drew drove them over to the park, Kim and Beverly told stories of how the tradition of music in the park started, saying it was after one of their friends had been sexually assaulted.

"Is she okay now?" Karen asked.

"Not only is she okay, but she's engaged to the love of her life." "That must be great for her," Karen said, then related the story of how Andy and Drew had interceded on her behalf.

"Oh yeah," Kim told her, "that would be Andy and Drew."

"If they're not around next time, you kick that bastard where you dumped coffee on him," Beverly angrily advised her. "You use enough force to make him choke! You can tell him you did it for Beverly."

The girls laughed, but Drew and Andy groaned knowing how painful a blow like that would be.

***

When they arrived at the park, Karen found a broad grassy area surrounded by tall trees waving in the cool fall air. A small bandstand was located off to the side of the park. Drew opened the trunk of his car and took out a number of Latin percussion instruments.

Everyone seemed to have something to do. Just as Karen was starting to feel out of place, Beverly called to her. "Hey Karen! Will you please help me cover the tables?"

Kim began directing some of the guys on where to place the tables while others were setting up the instruments in the small bandstand.

"I'm new in town," Karen told Beverly while she helped with the table coverings. "My family just moved to Boise a short-time- ago. I don't know what high school I'll be attending."

"I think this is a great area," Beverly told her. "There's always so much to do, especially if you like outdoor activities. Like, once the snow flies, you'll be able to meet this same great crowd on the ski slopes just north of here."

"I'll look forward to that," Karen replied. "Having spent most my life in southern Florida I can't imagine snowfall."

She busied herself helping Kim get tableware and food setup. She noticed Drew was keeping an eye on her. She wasn't sure if that was good or not. She asked Beverly about him.

"Drew is as sweet as he is strong—and believe me, he's strong as an ox. Everyone likes him and Andy. They're kind of the social spark plugs of the group."

"Is he dating anyone?"

"He dates a lot—I've never known him to be serious about anyone, but he's sure keeping an eye on you, girl."

During lunch Karen found herself sandwiched between Andy and Drew. Drew kept making sure she had a chance to taste everything on the table. When her drink emptied, he jumped up quickly to get her another one. Many of the other guys were doing the same for their girlfriends.

When the meal ended, Drew opened a big plastic trash bag and Karen helped him collect waste from the picnic lunch.

Drew asked her if she played an instrument or sang. "Negative on both of those, I'm afraid."

"That's okay. Just stay close and I'll help you."

Karen smiled. "Oh right! You're going to teach me to play an instrument in one day. This should be good."

Drew just smiled as he dumped the garbage and the two-of- them proceeded to collect recyclables.

The group organized themselves into a semi-circle and began to warm up. A number of neighbors had come into the park with lawn chairs in anticipation of the music to come.

Drew walked over to a large conga drum that was mounted on a stand. He waved Karen over. "This is an easy instrument. All you need are a pair of hands. Now count with me and hit the drum starting with your right hand. Copy me and count, one, two, three, four."

Karen felt silly but did as she was instructed. "We have another drummer!" Drew shouted.

Karen laughed. "Not yet you don't."

While the others continued warming up Drew showed her how to play three-beats and a double-beat with her left hand on the fourth-count. It took a few tries but she did it.

"Now play louder with your left hand than your right. Just lift it higher."

It took a bit longer but she did that too. The group's first song was "*El Manisero*."

As the music began, Karen felt awkward playing the big drum, but Drew kept encouraging her. Gradually, she started to feel how her little part added to the music. As she was playing she swayed in time to the music's strong percussive beat.

When the song ended Drew spoke. "Okay, now that everyone's warmed up let's do the same song with more feeling." He counted off the song and Karen started playing on the downbeat.

"Right on the down beat! Great drumming, conga lady," he shouted to her.

This time, Karen felt the music from the beginning of the song. She tried to keep a smile off her face, but just couldn't. This was too much fun. She grinned at Drew as he added various rhythmic patterns while she continued to keep time. Occasionally he would play the pattern she was playing for a few bars. Each time he did he would look right into her eyes. Playing together, she started to feel there might be a special place in her heart for him.

It was so much fun Karen could barely believe it was happening to her. When the song ended she heard applause from the gathering crowd.

"For the next song you have to make the sound of a

galloping horse," he said. Drew did it a few times and Karen managed to copy him.

Drew counted off and they started playing "*El Rancho Grande.*"

The music ended. "We don't have a part in the next song, so we'll have to dance," Drew told her.

"I don't know how to dance to this type of music."

"If you can walk, you can dance to this."

They moved out onto an open grass-covered area in front of the bandstand. Drew stood at Karen's side and put his arm around her waist.

"Starting with your right foot, we'll take three steps, pause on the fourth step, and do three steps again. Let's try."

They did, and a number of other couples were watching them and copying their movements.

"Now pause on the second count. When you count one, come up slightly using the foot which touches down on the first beat."

They tried the new step a few times and Drew suddenly spun and was in front of her. He put his right hand on her waist and held her other hand up with his left hand.

"You've got it!" he told her.

The band started playing "*La Paloma.*" It was perfect for the step Drew had taught her. As she moved with him, he turned and pushed her into simple spins, occasionally moving to her side.

The six couples, who were dancing the same step as Drew and Karen, moved in a large circle. She couldn't believe how fun this was and how easy it was to dance with Drew. As big and strong as he obviously was, she was surprised at how gracefully he moved and how gently he held her when they danced.

After they danced another moderately-paced tune, some of the band members starting looking at Drew and calling out, "*Suavecito.*"

"Hey! I'm dancing over here."

He looked at Karen. "I think they want me to sing '*Suavecito*' by the group Malo," he told her.

Karen smiled at him. "Go ahead."

"I can't do it alone, Karen."

"Oh no! I don't sing, and besides, I don't think I know the song."

"I don't need you to sing."

Drew smiled at her in such a warm manner she felt she had to accompany him to the microphone.

The song began with a simple percussion rhythm behind a solo trumpet and bass guitar.

Drew stood at the microphone with Karen next to him. After the instrumental intro, he took both her hands in his and started singing the beautiful love song, looking right into her eyes.

As the song continued, Karen could hardly believe Drew was singing such a beautiful song to her. If her smile grew any bigger she might break something.

She held tight to Drew's hands. It seemed like he was radiating pure exultation as he sang. When the song ended, she put her arms around Drew's neck and hugged him.

"Thank you. No one's ever sung a song to me. That was incredibly kind of you."

"My pleasure," Drew told her. "Come on, conga lady, we need to play percussion on the next song."

Karen drummed, danced, and laughed with her new friends until five o'clock.

"We have to break up the party now, because most of us have to be at the high school in an hour to play with the marching band during tonight's football game. Would you like to come with us?" Drew asked.

Again she was somewhat hesitant, but the day had been glorious so far and she didn't want it to end.

When they arrived at the school's band room, Karen found

a group of enthusiastic musicians getting ready for the evening's performance. She was shocked as they started undressing down to their underwear right in the band room. Her shock must have shown.

"Nearly all of us have been in band together since fifth grade," Kim told her. "It's like changing in front of your brothers and sisters."

Karen tried not to look directly at anyone, but in the reflection of the window to the music director's office she saw Andy and Drew peel off their t-shirts. They were muscled like statues of Greek gods. Karen felt herself blushing.

She looked at a smiling Beverly.

"I know what you're thinking," Beverly told her. "I'd love to have either one of those bodies at least once before I graduate high school."

Karen wasn't sure how to respond, but was sure Beverly understood what she was feeling.

The drumline formed up in a slight arc to begin warm up exercises. Drew was middle snare so he called the line to attention. Upon his command, a group of laughing, joking teenagers transformed into a deadpan-faced drumline which stood rigidly to attention.

Even their warm up exercises sounded great. Ten-minutes passed by while they played various exercises.

"Cadence," Drew said.

For the first time since they started drumming he glanced to the side as if checking to see if Karen was watching. After seeing she was, he had the tiniest bit of a smile. He then counted off to begin playing the high school's marching street cadence.

She saw some cheerleaders walking by and they began moving to the beat of the cadence. When the cadence ended, the band's director had all the musicians form up to march into the stadium.

A side gate opened at the end of the field. Karen watched

as they entered. She looked up at the already cheering crowd which was clearly looking forward to the evening's football game.

She was astounded at the enjoyment they were experiencing from a game which hadn't even started yet. This was the polar opposite of what she felt during her high school and junior high years.

She saw a man with a big video camera shooting tape of the crowd. The camera had a logo of the local television station on it.

"Great," she said under her breath. "All I need is to be on the news tonight. Sorry, Karen, but this magical day has come to an end."

***

The day with Drew and his friends had indeed made a huge impression on Karen. She felt bad ducking out on them.

As she took a bus back to her apartment, Karen was amazed at how much fun the band members created for each other. Even better, they'd made her feel like she was a part of their group from the first moment they arrived in the park.

"It's not fair," she said to no one in particular, as she considered the years of abuse she had endured growing up. Her former happiness changed to sadness and anger. She had tears running down her cheeks and the bus driver asked if she was okay.

"I'm good enough," she replied.

The evening was getting quite cool and the building she lived in wasn't particularly warm. At home, she wrapped herself in a blanket and tried to watch some television, but her mind kept reviewing the happy day at the park when she was surrounded by happy people who were kind enough to take a total stranger into their midst and ensure she had a good time.

She broke into tears again, wishing she'd had a normal

childhood and happy experiences instead of dreading her existence. Drew and Andy had treated her like a queen. She smiled, thinking back on how the two-of-them stood at her sides like big brothers defending a sister when the jerk became obnoxious with her.

"Oh well," she said quietly, "back to the real world tomorrow. Karen the waitress goes back to work."

Chapter Twenty ~ *True Confessions*

OVER THE NEXT FEW weeks the Idaho weather turned cold and snowy. Karen, who was accustomed to Miami's tropical temperatures, didn't have a clue how to dress in Boise's cold weather. She couldn't believe how downright painful the cold could feel. Blowing snow felt like tiny shards of glass crashing into her face. One of her fellow waitresses told her she needed to purchase some serious cold-weather clothing or she would freeze to death.

Karen took the bus to a used-clothing store and found long underwear, some sweaters, a huge parka, warm gloves, and a ski mask. She next traveled to an outdoor-sporting-goods store and bought a pair of cold-weather hiking boots. She put on a pair of knee length wool socks and tried out her new hiking boots.

"I don't think my feet have been this warm since I left Florida," she told the clerk.

She kept them on for the trip home. As she stood at the bus stop in front of the outdoor-sporting-goods store, her hands filled with shopping bags loaded with her new purchases, Karen felt a hand on her arm and heard an angry voice.

"I don't see your brother around this time, you little whore."

In one motion, Karen rotated toward her antagonist and speedily dispatched one of her brand-new, Russian leathered, over- the-ankle, insulated, hiking boots into his crotch with enoughforce to lift the jerk off the ground.

The guy tried to yell, but nothing came out but a small squeak as he grabbed his crotch and fell over backwards.

"That's from Beverly!" Karen raged at him.

"You tell him, honey," an older woman yelled. She was suddenly standing at Karen's side, aggressively brandishing her walking stick.

"You better get out of here, creep, or I'll be demonstrating some of my best Karate moves on your head," another woman told the would-be attacker.

The guy staggered up and left as quickly as he could, which wasn't all that quick as he looked to still be feeling the effects of Karen's boot.

***

Karen had been pleased with herself. She'd wished she could call Drew and his friends to tell them what had happened. She kept thinking about him—Drew dancing with her, Drew drumming with her and the elation of Drew singing to her.

She'd desperately wanted to see him again, and had wondered if the band members would be happy to see her again, too. She had disappeared so suddenly, without so much as a thank you, maybe they wouldn't.

Using a computer at the restaurant, Karen had found Drew's high school was having their last home football game of the season that Saturday evening. So, on a windy and cold Saturday in late October, Karen put on all her warmest clothing and took a bus ride out to the high school.

The ominous black clouds in the distant western sky were nothing but a chilly backdrop as she walked the two blocks through three-inches of hard-crusted snow to get to the school from the bus stop. As she trudged along, she felt the needle-like sensation of windblown snow on her face.

Karen took out her ski mask, pulled it over her head, and

closed the hood of her parka as tightly as she could.

People would have to be crazy to go out in this stuff to have fun.

There'll be no outdoor activities for me until spring.

When she arrived, the band was on the field doing their pregame show. She climbed the stands and found a seat next to the empty section which was reserved for the band. She saw Drew, Andy, and the other band members she had met at the park. Karen was nervous as the band came off the field and began filling their section of the stands.

What if Drew was angry with her because she had disappeared?

What if he had a girlfriend now?

As Drew came up the stands she smiled at him when he looked at her. She gave him her prettiest smile, but felt foolish as he just looked away. A saddened Karen looked down, which is when she felt her ski mask bunch up under her chin.

Of course, he didn't smile at me because he couldn't see me in this silly mask. Oh well, it's now or never.

Andy and Drew were sitting two rows below her. Andy sat on the end of the row next to the stairs with Drew to his left. The row was completely full.

Karen summoned all her courage and removed her ski mask.

She walked down to their row. "Is there room for one more?"

Drew looked up. "Yes!" His eye's widened and a broad grin immediately appeared, he rapidly slid to his left to make room. In the process he nearly crushed two freshman cymbal players. Drew stood up and reached out to take Karen's hand and guide her to the space between him and Andy.

"It sure is cold this evening," Karen said to Drew.

"These are aluminum stands. They suck the heat right out of you," he said. "Here, sit on this blanket with me." Drew opened the blanket he was sitting on so they could share it.

Karen was still shivering, so Drew unfolded the blanket and wrapped it around them as well, putting his arm around her too.

"Is that better?"

"It's great," she told him.

She saw that he was smiling at her, just like he did previously. She thought they were starting where they left off last time. She certainly hoped that was the case.

The icy wind kept blowing and a light snow started falling. At halftime the band headed back to the field for their halftime show. By the middle of their performance the snowfall had gotten serious. As the band moved back into the stands, it was hard to see the yard markers on the field.

As Drew walked back up the stands, Karen was bundled up in his now snow-covered blanket. Steam was rising from the blanket just below her chin. As he sat down next to her, she opened the blanket to make room for him, revealing that she was holding a hot chocolate.

"Thanks for the hot chocolate, Drew."

"You're welcome, Karen, but I didn't buy you anything."

"That man over there gave this to me when you were on the field and he said it was from you."

"The guy with the same patterned blanket as we have?"

"Yeah, that's him."

Drew smiled. "He's my dad."

"You have a cool dad."

"Karen, you have no idea how cool he is."

Karen related the story of the creep putting his hand on her at the bus stop. "I let him have it and told him it was from Beverly."

A mitten-covered hand shot out from under a blanket in the row in front of her. "High-five, girl," Beverly yelled. "Did you let him have it in a big way?"

"I'm sure he's still trying to get the shoe polish from my new boot off his crotch."

Everyone around them laughed and Karen heard a number of people shouting, "Way to go, Karen."

"I'm sorry I wasn't there for you," Drew whispered to her.

Karen looked at him and kissed his icy-red cheek. She wrapped both her arms around his arm, holding it tight against her. "You were there. You and all your friends were with me. Where do you think the courage came from to kick that creep?"

Drew looked a little confused, but smiled and leaned closer.

They watched the game as the home team was getting crushed by the best team in their division. Then, as yet another touchdown was scored against them, Andy turned to Karen. "At least we have the best band in the division."

All the band members nearby cheered.

In the waning minutes of the game, their team scored their only touchdown. The stands erupted as if they had just won the game. Karen jumped up and yelled with everyone else as if it was her team, too. Here she was, surrounded by these people she barely knew, and she had experienced so much fun and excitement with them. She felt close to them—almost like family.

"We have to go over to the band room to wipe off the drums and get out of these wet uniforms," Drew told her when the game ended. "Please, come with us."

As the band members started walking back, the drummers formed into their marching formation. They started playing their cadence as they marched.

Karen walked next to the row Drew was in. As she did, she joyfully marched in time to the cadence.

When they arrived at the band room, Drew's parents came over and introduced themselves to her.

"I'm sorry I tricked you into accepting the hot chocolate, but you looked so cold, I thought you might need that," Drew's dad told her.

"Thank you, Mr. Holt. That was kind of you. I'm from

Miami and I was freezing sitting up there. At least when the band members were sitting around me they helped to block the wind."

"How are you getting home?" Drew's mom asked while the musicians changed back into their street clothes. "I'll catch a bus. In fact, I have to leave pretty soon or I'll miss the last one."

"This is going to be a terrible storm," Drew's mother said. "Why don't you come home with us and Drew can drive you home in our old Jeep. It would be safer than taking the bus. Not to mention warmer."

"I'll be okay."

Drew's dad smiled at her. "Why take a chance? If you don't want Drew to drive you home, I'll be glad to."

Karen realized that even though the Holts didn't know her, they were trying to take care of her. "It is bad out, so I guess a warm Jeep ride would be a good idea," she told them.

They headed back to the Holts' home. The roads were getting slick and snow-covered. When they arrived, Drew and Karen climbed into the old Jeep. It had a small lift kit on it and large off- road tires. The body was in rough shape, but Drew said he and his dad had rebuilt all the running gear so it was reliable and warm, if not pretty to look at.

"There will be no showing off, Drew," his father said sternly.

"I won't, Dad."

"What was that all about?" Karen asked as they drove out of the neighborhood.

"Dad caught me doing donuts in this rig last winter. I caught hell. I'm pretty good at off-road driving technique, but he doesn't want me to demonstrate my ability in this awful weather."

"Just get me home safe and I'll be happy. I have to go to work tomorrow."

"Where do you work?"

"I have a job in a dress shop at the mall," Karen lied.

As Drew drove Karen to her apartment, the temperature was dropping, the streets were getting icy, and the traffic was getting snarled. The normal trip to Karen's apartment would have taken twenty-five-minutes. Instead it had been two-hours so far. The traffic seemed to be getting heavier as the time passed. Many people were abandoning their cars, which caused more congestion and slowed them down further.

The old Jeep was keeping them warm, but when they were a few blocks from Karen's apartment, they became completely stalled due to an accident in an intersection one block in front of them. Drew ran up to the accident site to see if everyone was okay.

"Only dented fenders and wounded pride up there," he told Karen, climbing back into the Jeep. "But we aren't going anywhere for a while. How far is it to your home?"

"We need to go one block to the right and then two blocks to the left."

"There's a big park on our right. The Jeep could make it, but I'd get in big trouble for driving through there."

Drew's cell phone rang. "Hi, Dad," he answered. "It's going okay, but we're stuck behind a few fender-benders."

Drew continued to tell his father about their situation as Karen looked ahead at the long line of frustrated drivers.

"Okay, Dad." Drew closed his cell phone. "What did he say?" Karen asked.

"He said to remember I'm in a Jeep." Drew grinned and put the Jeep into low gear. "Hold on. We're going through the park."

The little Jeep began clawing its way through the large snowdrifts like a wheeled polar bear. Drew carefully guided it over the large hill in the center of the park. He kept a constant speed, and quickly corrected any sideways motion of the rear end with smooth, controlled motions of the steering wheel.

Karen was holding onto the armrests of her seat with so much force, her knuckles were turning white. She had never experienced a vehicle trying to go in so many different directions at the same time. As they turned back onto the street, she finally relaxed her grip.

"You *do* know how to drive in this stuff," she said with relief. "You'll have to teach me someday."

Drew grinned. "I will, and we'll have a blast."

Karen had him park in the lot of the small three-floor apartment building. She stared at the floor of the Jeep for a while and finally spoke.

"Drew, the weather is bad and the streets are awful. It would be safer for you if you stayed with me tonight. I don't want you driving home through this mess."

"Will it be okay with your parents?"

"Please come upstairs with me. I have to show you something." They walked up two flights of stairs and entered Karen's tiny studio apartment.

"This is where I live. Please, sit down. I have some things to tell you."

They took off their jackets and boots and sat down on her couch, which was the only furniture in the little apartment.

Without looking directly at Drew, Karen clasped her hands in her lap and began talking. "I've been lying to you. It is hard for me to say this, because you've been nothing but kind, but as you can see, I live alone. My name isn't Karen Wilson. It's Karen Steele. I'm a runaway, Drew. I left my family in Florida two-months-ago when I managed to buy a fake ID. I'm not eighteen like my ID says. I'm seventeen, until next month. I've run away before but I didn't go far and they found me. This time I decided to go to a town as far from Florida as I could afford. Until I received my first pay check, I lived in a shelter for a couple-of-weeks. I don't work at the mall. I'm a waitress at a deli near here. I bought this couch and some kitchen stuff with the temporary modeling job I took at the auto show. I'm so sorry I lied to you."

Karen lifted her gaze to look directly at him. "When you

and Andy stood up for me the other day, it was probably the first time in my entire life someone was on my side. You have no idea how wonderful it was. I'm sure that's where I received the confidence to kick that jerk. I finally felt like I had someone in my corner, even if you guys weren't there next to me. I wasn't kidding when I said it was as if I felt you guys, Kim, and Beverly were there with me. I'm sorry I lied to you, and I swear, I'll never do it again. If you don't want to spend more time with me I'll understand, but with this awful weather you should stay here tonight."

Drew was quiet for a moment and then spoke in a serious tone. "Karen, I just have one question. When we get together next Saturday to go Lindy dancing, who will I be going out with—Karen Steele or Karen Wilson?"

"Drew, I have lots of problems. I'm going to need time to work them out. In fact, I'm not comfortable even thinking about sex."

Drew smiled. "Then we are certainly in luck. Lindy dancing doesn't involve sex."

"Drew, please be serious."

"Okay, I'm serious. You're a runaway—I don't care. You're seventeen, not eighteen—I don't care. You're a waitress—I don't care. You felt like you had to keep your identity a secret to protect yourself—I don't care. You have issues with sex—I don't care. You haven't answered my question about who I'm going dancing with next week. This I care about."

Karen stared at him and a smile started spreading across her face. "Who are you?" she asked.

"I'm just a drummer from Idaho who likes to drum with you, dance with you, sing to you, and sit in freezing cold weather watching a football game with you. Truthfully, I don't care what we do as long as Karen Steele or Karen Wilson is with me. Either one, or both, will do."

Karen pushed him onto his back and kissed him.

"I should call my folks and let them know I'll be staying

here." After he ended the call, Karen asked, "What did he say?"

"He said he expected us to treat each other with our utmost respect or we'd be in big trouble."

"Wow. Your dad is something special."

As Karen made tea for them, her cell phone rang. The owners of the deli told her not to come into work the following day, as they weren't going to open due to the storm.

After they finished their tea, they opened the sofa bed. "I can sleep on the floor," Drew told her.

Karen shook her head no. "Tonight is the first night since I can remember when I won't be dreading the thought of being alone. Drew Holt, you will spend this night in the same bed as me—or else."

He smiled at her. "Yes, ma'am."

"I'm sorry, Drew, but it gets cold in here at night."

Drew and Karen stripped down to their long underwear. He whistled at her.

She rolled her eyes.

"What? Even in waffle underwear, I can see what a shapely body you have." He shrugged and grinned.

Karen didn't think about Drew's body—she was more concerned if she really could deal with having someone in bed with her without flashing back to the painful recollections of the previous times she had company there. Karen pushed the awful thoughts from her mind, and they both lay down.

Drew pulled two thin blankets over them. "Should I stay on my side or would you like me to hold you?" he asked.

Karen was quiet for a moment and then whispered, "I'm nervous, Drew, but I'd like you to try holding me."

Drew asked her to lie on her left side and he did the same, putting his arm around her. "Is this okay?"

"This is wonderful."

"Goodnight, snow angel," he told her.

"Snow angel?"

He grinned at her. "Yeah. When I saw you freezing cold in the stands, wrapped in my blanket, I decided you looked like my snow angel."

She held his arm against her. "Goodnight Drew. Thank you for a super fun evening."

They were asleep for about four-hours when Karen started having a nightmare. Drew was awakened by the sound of her whimpering and making small jerky movements.

"Karen, it's okay," he said in a gentle voice. "It's me, Drew."

Karen awoke with a start. She grabbed Drew's arm and started to push it away. Then she woke enough to realize she was listening to Drew's voice, and it reassured her.

"It's Drew, it's Drew," she kept repeating.

Karen placed his arm back around her. "Thank you, Drew." She was soon fast asleep again.

***

Drew awoke before Karen. He picked up a pad of paper and opened it to a blank page. He looked at her bundled up in the blankets and pillows, and drew a portrait of her, as if she were wrapped in clouds, only her pretty face showing. He titled it, *The Snow Angel.*

Then he went into her bathroom and showered. When he returned to the living area, he found Karen staring at his drawing.

"Do you have any other talents I should be amazed about?"

"I've been drawing and painting since I was six. It's one of my favorite hobbies."

Karen walked over to Drew and embraced him.

"Thank you for holding me last night. When those nightmares occur, I can't get back to sleep, but with your arm around me, I quickly fell asleep again."

She started making coffee. "We need to talk about

something, Drew. I know sex is a normal part of a relationship when you have someone you care about."

"Karen, we don't have to do anything."

"I like you a lot, and from the way you take care of me, it's obvious how you feel about me — the thought of anyone doing anything to me, well, it makes me tremble just thinking about it."

"Karen, I repeat, we don't have to do anything."

She gave his hand a squeeze. "Thank you, Drew. I'm going to shower. I have orange juice and I can toast some bagels for us to eat if you like."

Drew folded their bed back into a couch. He looked around her kitchen and sure enough, the only thing to eat was coffee, orange juice, cream cheese, and bagels. When he heard the shower turn off, he put the bagels in the toaster and poured each of them an orange juice.

"I don't know what we can do in this tiny place," Karen stated while they ate.

"It's a beautiful sunny day. We need to get out there and go for a hike."

"You people up here are crazy. I don't think normal people should go out in freezing cold weather."

Drew laughed. "You'll be plenty warm once we start hiking through the snow."

"I'm willing to try, but I doubt I'll feel warm."

They started pulling on their cold-weather clothing. Drew kneeled in front of Karen and laced up her hiking boots.

She smiled. "Thank you. That's considerate of you to help me."

As they went outside, Karen agreed it was, indeed, a beautiful day. There was no wind and the temperature was still quite cold, but there wasn't a cloud in the azure-blue sky. The snow-covered scene in front of them had all the beauty of a Thomas Kincaid painting.

They proceeded to trudge through the knee-deep snow.

After one block, Karen pulled off her hood.

Drew smiled at her.

"Be quiet, Drew Holt!" she said. "Don't you dare say I told you so."

He laughed and partially opened his jacket, as he was getting warm as well. They found a neighborhood grocery store which was open. Drew bought bread, garlic, ground beef, onions, red potatoes, olive oil, broccoli, and a loaf of Italian bread.

As they were crossing the park, Karen told Drew her legs were exhausted, so Drew had her jump on his back.

"Mush, you husky, Mush!" she joyfully yelled. "On to the Yukon River, King old dog."

"My legs are getting tired and weak!" Drew exclaimed as they approached a rather large snowdrift.

"Oh no! Don't you dare drop me, Drew Holt!" Drew started wobbling from side to side.

"Drew, no!" she squealed through her laughter as they fell into the snowdrift.

"Bad dog! Drew Holt, you're a bad sled dog!"

They were both laughing hysterically. As Drew helped her up, she kissed his cheek.

Two preschoolers were watching. The little boy turned to the little girl. "I don't understand big people. First she thinks he's a dog and then she kisses him. Yuck!"

As they were brushing each other off, a couple came gliding past them wearing cross country skis.

"Drew, that looks like great fun. They seem to be floating on top of the snow instead of trudging through it like we are. Can you do that?"

"My whole family goes out to cross country ski every winter. If I know my dad, he's probably out in our garage waxing our skis right now."

"Someday I would love to have you teach me to ski like

that."

"I'd love to, but really, my dad is the one to teach you. He explains what you need to do in a way which makes it easy to learn."

Over the next two weeks Karen spent quite a bit of time at the Holts' home. She seemed to love being around Drew, but she also had many long talks with his mother. They discussed everything from cooking to relationships. Karen told Drew she admired the way his mom and dad related to each other.

"They have a special bond," she said. "Even when they tease each other it's always with the utmost respect. That's the kind of relationship I want."

Chapter Twenty-One ~ *November with the Holts*

TWO-WEEKS BEFORE THANKSGIVING, Karen, Drew, and his parents piled into the old Jeep and drove out to the Nordic ski center in the mountains north of Boise.

Drew's father rented skis, boots, and poles for Karen, and under his watchful eye, she began learning to use skinny skis. Excited and nervous at the same time, Drew's dad had her start out by simply walking around on the skis.

"I'm just shuffling across the snow. How do I make them glide?" Karen asked.

"You have to push off real hard on one ski and glide on the other."

After some practice she began feeling her skis begin to glide. They headed out on a green-level beginner trail, which was the easiest for learning. They hadn't gone far when Drew's mother asked to stop so she could take pictures.

Karen looked around and was astounded by the view. Up to now, she had been concentrating on her skis so much she hadn't noticed the beautiful terrain. She could see other mountain ranges and the city of Boise in the distance.

"No wonder people like to come out to play in the snow," she told the Holts. "What a magnificent view!"

She wasn't comfortable yet on the slight downhill runs of the beginner trails, but with Oliver's constant instruction she began to look forward to them. Of course she fell a lot, but Drew was always close by to hoist her back on her skis.

"I've never had to work so hard in my entire life to enjoy

something," she said at the end of the day. "I feel it was completely worth it. After all this exertion, even my teeth are tired, but I can't wait to do this again. Thank you so much for introducing me to this sport."

"It's our pleasure," Mrs. Holt told her. "Do you have time to go to dinner with us?"

Karen agreed and they drove to a small restaurant, south of downtown Boise. Near the end of a lovely meal, the waiter brought out a birthday cake, which he placed in front of a surprised Karen. The waiter lit the candles and they all sang *Happy Birthday*. She felt as if her face was glowing as brightly as the eighteen candles adorning her cake.

"Thank you guys so much," Karen told them sincerely. "You can't imagine how much this means to me."

Drew's mother handed her a small envelope.

She found a lovely birthday card inside, signed by Drew and both his parents. Below the signatures his mother had written, *Thank you for sharing your jubilant spirit with us.*

Mr. Holt put a big shopping bag on the table, right in front of Karen.

"Sharing my jubilant spirit…Drew, you didn't. You guys! You didn't."

She removed a large gift-wrapped box from the shopping bag. "We thought you might like this," Drew said with a proud grin.

Karen removed the wrapping paper from her gift and found a box inside labeled PENDLETON. She slowly opened the box and saw the "Shared Spirits" blanket. She had seen it in a store and told Drew that she liked it, because it had the most beautiful pattern and thoughtful message.

With tears in her eyes now, she stood up and walked around the table embracing each of them in turn.

"I'd like to tell you this is the best gift I have ever received, but the truth is, the best gift I have ever received is the time you guys are willing to spend with me."

"Let me tell you, young lady," Drew's father said in a sarcastic tone, "we certainly find it a strain to have to share your joyful spirit."

They all laughed at him.

***

The Friday before Thanksgiving, Drew told his mother Karen was feeling tired, had stayed in bed that day, and didn't have her normal energy level. His mother was immediately concerned.

"That worries me," she said. "Karen usually exhibits an energy level that could power a small city."

She quickly called her family doctor and with sufficient urgency in her voice managed an appointment for Karen that same day.

"I don't have insurance," Karen said when Ruth picked her up at her apartment.

"Let's get you to the doctor first and then we'll worry about medical bills later."

The doctor examined Karen. "I'm going to have some tests run, but I'd say this is a classic case of mononucleosis. You'll have to get plenty of rest the next-few-weeks and possibly for as long as two months."

"But I have to work. I have a waitressing job."

"Unless you can waitress from a sitting position, it's out of the question."

Karen looked frightened.

"Karen, look at me."

A teary-eyed Karen turned toward Ruth.

"First you have to get well. Then we can worry about other things."

"If I don't work, I won't have a place to live," Karen said in a thoroughly defeated tone.

"Karen Steele, you listen to me. You can have the guest

bedroom at our home. You can stay with us. Oliver and I have already been talking about offering you a place with us. We were going to wait to discuss it with you until after the Thanksgiving holiday, but we'll just have to push up the timetable. Oliver and Drew can pack and move all your things from your apartment, so you can move in tonight."

"Mrs. Holt—"

"Karen, there's nothing to say. You are sick and if you don't take time to heal, you'll just get worse. You have family here that cares about you. Whether you and Drew stay together or not is immaterial. You're one of us now. This is how we treat family and that's all there is to it."

Karen began to cry. "I can't believe you're willing to take me in."

When they arrived at the Holts' home, Ruth suggested that Karen go upstairs. "Why don't you head up to the guest room— your room—and rest for a while. I'm sure today has been exhausting. I'll call you when dinner is ready."

"Thank you so much," Karen said as she embraced Ruth. "I don't know how I can repay you."

Ruth smiled at her. "Get well, Karen. That will be payment enough."

Oliver and Drew cleaned out Karen's apartment. They moved her clothing into her bedroom and after wrapping her couch in plastic, stored it in the garage.

"This is a big commitment," Oliver said to Ruth later that night.

She smiled. "This wise man once said to me, sometimes there are situations where we shouldn't take counsel of our fears, but rather just get busy doing to help someone. I think Karen is a special young lady. Whether or not she and Drew continue as a couple, I think she deserves our help. I'm going to talk to her about finishing high school and considering college."

Oliver embraced his beloved wife and partner, saying in

Italian, "*Ti amo*, Ruth."

"*Ti amo*, Oliver," she replied.

***

Karen slept most of the next day, underneath her Shared Spirits blanket, of course. When she returned from a shower, she found pink soft-sculpture letters on her bedroom wall which spelled out, *Karen's Cabin*.

As she ran her fingers over the letters, she thought, I'm going to marry Drew just so I can keep these kind people close to me.

Ruth and Oliver established house rules for Karen and Drew. They explained these were the same rules they had for Holly and Jonah. They were simple rules, and Karen knew she and Drew weren't going to disappoint his parents by breaking them. Obviously, she and Drew had to keep apart to some degree, so she didn't pass the disease on to him, but they still managed to do household chores together as often as her strength allowed.

Karen loved how Drew always smiled when he looked at her and did his best to keep her spirits up. Karen became stiff from all the sleeping, so he would spend whatever time she wanted massaging her stiff musculature. He continually provided kind and encouraging words. On a daily basis he would start sentences with, "When you get better, we can…"

From horseback riding to hikes in the mountains, Drew constantly reminded her she had much to look forward to. He continually left books and magazines on her desk. In addition, he found brochures of the places they could visit when she was better. If nothing else, Drew would study at her desk while she slept. Occasionally Kim and Beverly would stop by to chat. Every evening, without fail, Oliver would greet her with a huge smile, ask how she was doing and if there was anything she needed.

Karen loved Saturday mornings. She didn't get up until nine- thirty or ten each day, but on Saturday mornings Drew would always be studying at the desk in her room when she woke up. When he saw she had awakened he would greet her by saying, "Good morning, snow angel."

"I'm being treated better than at any other time in my life," she told Ruth.

Without being asked she always helped around the house. She knew she shouldn't do a lot, but she managed to help Ruth with occasional meal prep, laundry, and sometimes a little ironing. Ruth kept a watchful eye on her and made sure she adhered to the doctor's orders.

"Karen, you know I teach languages at the university. Would you like to learn a language while you're healing?"

"What language do you think I should learn? I've already had two-years of Spanish in high school."

"Let's keep building on your former school work."

Gradually Ruth began incorporating Spanish into their daily routine. As Drew was fluent in Spanish and Italian, he also spoke to her in Spanish. Sometimes he would tease her by leaving her notes which included words in Italian.

An exasperated Karen kept an Italian-English dictionary next to her Spanish-English dictionary to help her decipher Drew's multilingual notes.

***

When Thanksgiving arrived, so did Holly and Jonah, as well as Oliver's and Ruth's parents. Holly commented how well Karen fit into the family.

As Jonah and Oliver listened to Karen conversing with Holly and Ruth, Jonah told him, "They sound like sisters."

Oliver watched them for a while. "You're right. They absolutely sound like sisters. Karen has even picked up some of Ruth's mannerisms."

"How's your Auburn running?" Drew asked Jonah.

"Like a watch." Jonah replied. "I wanted to talk to you about something on behalf of my Uncle Meyer." Jonah took out a series of photos of what could have been charitably referred to as pile of rusty metal.

The last photo was a beautifully restored Ford Gran Torino. "This is what it will look like when it's restored. Uncle Meyer asked if I wanted to rebuild it, but I start grad school next summer, so I won't have time. Drew, he was wondering if you would like to restore it. He'll pay for everything including your labor on the car. Also, he said to tell you you're only allowed to work on it during summers and vacations — it has the big block engine, by the way."

Oliver thought Drew's eyes were getting so big they would pop out of his head.

"Tell your uncle I'd love to."

"Looks like we need to finish installing a furnace in the garage," Oliver said, smiling at Drew.

Drew stared at the photos. "You started installing the furnace three-weeks-ago. Did you know about this?"

Oliver broke up laughing. "When I cleared out the last bay in our garage and started installing the furnace, I was sure you would start asking questions as to why I suddenly decided to open up the space and heat the place. I talked to Meyer a week before that. I was certain you would want to do the restore. The car was supposed to arrive early this morning but the driver ran into a snowstorm in Illinois. He's with his family in Pocatello today and tomorrow but will be delivering the car on Saturday."

***

Looking over the Thanksgiving feast, Karen marveled at all the food choices on the dining room table.

"I'm amazed the table can hold up all this weight," she quietly told Holly.

During Thanksgiving dinner, Oliver's mom offered a prayer of thanks and everyone was given a chance to say why they were thankful.

Jonah said he was glad the end of undergraduate school was in sight, as he couldn't wait to start graduate school. "I'm also thankful the Lord has given me another year with Holly."

Holly thanked Jonah for the happiness he brought to her life, and as she did every year, said, "I thank the Lord he put Ruth and Oliver in my life to raise me and help me become the person I am."

Drew declared quietly, "This year I'm thankful the Lord sent me a snow angel."

Ruth pointed out to those who didn't know that snow angel was Drew's nickname for Karen.

A smiling Karen stated in a reverent tone, "I'm thankful for family — this family."

"Thank you, Karen. We truly feel blessed you are with us," Ruth said.

***

On the Friday morning after Thanksgiving, the guys arose early and went out to the garage to complete the furnace installation while the girls went to the mall on a brief shopping trip. At lunchtime, Holly and Karen made Panini sandwiches and served them with minestrone soup. This was followed by leftover pumpkin pie from the previous day's feast.

By three o'clock, the furnace installation was complete, from gas and electric lines to duct work. The garage was feeling its first warmth.

On Friday evening, the Holts, Cases, Schulmans, Beckhams, plus Tina's family met at the Levins' house after dinner for desserts and a movie. David and Linda were in town visiting the Schulmans. "Hello, Aunt Holly," Linda shouted to Holly when she saw her.

"Hello, Aunt Linda," Holly replied as they hugged.

"Before the movie starts I need everyone to be quiet for a moment," Jonah announced. "This is the spot where I first met Holly."

Jonah opened a small box and showed Holly a beautiful engagement ring. "Holly, will you be my bride?"

"Jonah, I would love to be your bride!"

Jonah placed the ring on her finger and they engaged in a long kiss while the assembled families cheered.

Karen asked if Holly knew Jonah would propose to her.

She smiled. "We planned this last weekend. I also helped him pick out the ring. He might know amazing amounts of science and mathematics, but when it comes to jewelry, he doesn't have a clue."

Chapter Twenty-Two ~ *College Bound*

AS KAREN BEGAN TO heal, Ruth started teaching her skills which would allow her to return to school by the end of January. With Ruth's teaching and Karen's work ethic, by the time she returned to high school, she could keep up with her classmates in most of her classes.

When she had problems, Ruth or Oliver demonstrated endless patience working with her to ensure she stayed on top of her studies, and by mid-March she was scholastically indistinguishable from her classmates, though she had missed the entire fall semester.

When she brought home her first report card, it consisted of nearly all A's. She was amazed how proud Drew, Oliver, and Ruth were of her scholastic performance.

"With grades like these, you need to be thinking about a major when you attend university," Oliver said.

"I never considered going to college. I don't have a clue what I'd like to major in. I don't know what college would accept me. Besides, I have no way to pay for it. You're going to have to pay for Drew's college. I couldn't possibly ask you to pay for my college education."

"You just keep your grades up, young lady," Ruth told her. "I'm sure we'll work out something."

Two-weeks-later a letter arrived for Karen. It was from something called the J and M Family Foundation.

As she handed the letter to Karen, Ruth had a smile and huge tears in her eyes. Karen carefully opened the letter and read the following:

Karen Steele,

Based on your character and scholastic achievement, The J and M Family Foundation is proud to announce you have been awarded a four-year scholarship to the university of your choosing. The scholarship includes tuition, room and board, plus textbooks. Congratulations and good luck on your university education.

Joan and Meyer Minkowski.

"From the look on your face, you knew this was coming," Karen said. "I don't even know these people."

"They are Jonah's aunt and uncle. When I told Holly you would need money for college she told Jonah. They approached Meyer and Joan. They told them you deserved a chance at a college education. They took Holly and Jonah's word and there you are. Like I said, you're family now. We have to get busy, girl. We need to start planning which university you should attend, and which major would be right for you."

Karen was overwhelmed. "I have to call and thank them."

She reread the letter then joined Ruth in a long tear-filled embrace.

"I'd love to attend the university where you teach, Mrs. Holt, but I'm still not sure what I would major in."

"As I teach there, we can work something out. Tell me what you like to do and what your favorite classes were in high school."

"Actually, I enjoy working on anything mechanical. That's why it's been so easy for me to work with Drew and Oliver on rebuilding that old V-eight transmission for the pickup. I get a real sense of accomplishment when a machine runs right. As far as favorite classes, I find science endlessly fascinating."

"Drew is planning on majoring in mechanical engineering.

His goal is to design and build his own vehicles. You don't have to decide today, but spend some time online seeing what that major could lead to. Why don't you call Joan and Meyer to thank them? I have their number."

Chapter Twenty-Three ~ *Another Steele comes to Town*

IN MID-MAY, THREE-years after Karen and Drew started university, an eighteen-year-old girl knocked on the door to the Holts' residence. Ruth answered the door and saw a thin girl of average height, with a more-than-ample chest and a pretty smile. She wore torn blue jeans, worn-out flip flops, and an oversized, faded navy blue hoodie, which hung limply off her shoulders. Her thick, long, and bushy hair looked like it hadn't seen a comb or brush in weeks. She carried a large plastic trash bag.

"Is this the Holt residence?"

"Yes it is. Can I help you?"

"I received a letter from my sister a-while-ago and she said I should come see her when I graduated high school. So here I am."

"Karen's sister?"

"Yes, ma'am. I'm Lucinda Steele."

"Come in, Lucinda. I'm so pleased to meet you. Karen's in class at the university now, but since it's Friday she and Drew will be home later this afternoon. They usually come home weekends to study here, because it's quieter than in the dorms. It's lunchtime. Would you like something to eat?"

"I'd love something. I've only had a burger and a couple of bags of chips since I left Miami two-days-ago."

Ruth quickly put together a grilled Panini sandwich with sliced black olives, spinach, basil, roasted red peppers, mozzarella, and prosciutto. Lucinda wolfed down the sandwich like she hadn't eaten in a week.

"So, my sister is in university. I never imagined that for her."

"In this house, it's not a matter of whether or not those who live here go to university, but rather which university they will attend. Karen's an excellent student. She and my son Drew are studying mechanical engineering."

"Karen said you guys been treating her like she was your own kid. She said she got a boyfriend. Is that Drew?"

"Yes. They've been together for over three-years now. Would you like something else to eat?" Ruth offered.

"No, ma'am. I'm kinda tired. If I could just lay down some place for a while, I'll be okay."

"Why don't you sleep in Karen's room? I'll show you where it is."

"Thanks. She wrote me she got her own room and it was cool." Ruth led Lucinda up to Karen's room, and Lucinda smiled as she looked around. She slipped out of her flip flops and pulled off her hoodie, then walked around the room looking at all the photos and drawings of Karen doing things with the Holts.

There were lovely drawings of Karen playing a conga drum, dancing, being sung to, in the stands of a football game on a snowy day, cross country skiing, plus photos of her in a prom dress, her high school graduation, and many pictures with Drew and the Holts.

Ruth watched as Lucinda marveled at the framed *Snow Angel* drawing and a large acrylic painting of Karen and Drew wrapped in her Shared Spirits blanket during a snowstorm.

"She's smiling in all these pictures. I never saw her with such a happy smile."

"Yes, she is," Ruth agreed.

As Lucinda lay down on the bed, she looked up at the pink soft-sculpture letters. "Karen's Cabin. This is so cool."

Lucinda curled up on Karen's bed and Ruth placed Karen's

Shared Spirits blanket over her.

Three hours later, Drew and Karen arrived home from university.

"Karen," Ruth said, "quietly go and see who's sleeping in your room."

Karen looked at Ruth with curiosity, then went upstairs. She returned with a huge smile.

"I had no idea she was going to be here. Remember the letter I read to you when I asked if she could visit. I sent it two months ago."

Karen began helping Ruth prepare dinner while Drew set the table for five.

"I hear there is a snow angel living here," Lucinda said, as she walked into the kitchen.

"Lu, I'm so happy you're here." Karen embraced her younger sister.

"Me, too."

Oliver arrived then and was introduced to Lucinda. They all sat down to a tasty dinner of beef-based minestrone soup, a mixed- greens salad, sesame topped bread sticks, and apple slices with honey for desert. Drew and Karen talked about their week in university. Lucinda let them know she would like to stay with Karen until she got a job and rented her own place to live.

"I thought maybe we could get our own place together," she told Karen.

"I'm completely tied up with my studies. Besides I have a scholarship which pays for my food and dorm."

"Oh, I see." Lucinda looked very disappointed.

Oliver must have noticed her disappointment, too. "We have a spare bed frame in the garage which Drew and I can setup for you in Karen's room. Why don't you plan on staying with us for a while until you get things worked out?" he suggested.

"Thank you, Mr. Holt. That would be great. When I get a

job I could pay you some rent money."

Drew and Oliver maneuvered the spare bed into Karen's room. They arranged the beds on opposite walls. Karen and Lucinda took her plastic bag of clothing to the laundry room and started getting her clothes washed. While the clothes were in the dryer, they sat down in the family room with Ruth.

"That's all the clothes I own," Lucinda told them. "Our dad has been selling my clothes to buy booze. I ended up selling some stuff to buy the bus ticket to get up here, too."

"Did Mom know Dad was selling your clothing?"

"Karen, she and Uncle moved out about two-months after you left. I didn't want to tell you because I was pretty angry with you for leaving. But I didn't know why you left until I got your letter this spring. Uncle came into my bedroom just after you disappeared. He put a hand on me and I let him have it. I wasn't no little kid he could pick on. I clamped my teeth on the side of his face like an angry mother 'gater. He slugged me, but I told him I would be ripping parts off his sorry ass if he ever came near me again. A-week- later he and Mom moved out and I ain't seen or heard from either of them. Dad just kept getting more and more drunk. I saved up some money. The minute I graduated, I did what you said and bought myself a bus ticket—and here I am."

"We're pleased you decided to visit us," Ruth told her.

"Next weekend, a lot of my friends from the university will be here," Karen told Lucinda. "We're going to study here all weekend because we have finals the following week. I can't wait for you to meet them."

"Can I get to see the Gran Torino you and Drew are fixing up?" Lucinda turned toward Ruth. "Karen always loved cars, but for me, I always liked plants."

"Plants. You love plants," Ruth said making a mental note.

She walked across the room and pulled a book off the shelf. She handed it to Lucinda. "Oliver and I have been trying to plan a perennial garden, but can't ever seem to find the time.

Maybe you could look through this book of perennials which grow in this area. I'll show you where we want the garden and you can suggest what to plant."

Lucinda started paging through the book and her face was glowing with happiness. "Mrs. Holt, I can design and plant a beautiful garden from this book. You'll love what I can do with plants."

"Wow," Ruth said, "a future botanist."

Lucinda seemed confused by Ruth's statement, but Karen and Drew smiled at each other, knowing full well Ruth had just started building a case which would eventually convince Lucinda she needed to attend university.

***

When the two sisters curled up in bed later that night, Lucinda turned to Karen. "You really slimmed down. And your boobies really came in."

"I run every morning with Drew. Not that running has anything to do with the size of my chest, but I've been running since I moved in here. Oliver and Ruth run as well. I'll wake you up and we'll run together."

"The only shoes I have are flip-flops."

"I have an old pair of running shoes you can wear."

"You and the Holts talk real nice, using good words. I'm gonna try to use good words, too, 'cause I don't want them to think I'm some kinda hick."

"I'm sure they would appreciate that, Lu."

Lucinda was quiet for a moment. "Thanks for writing."

"You're welcome. I'm happier than I can tell you, having you here. The Holts have always treated me like family, but with you here it makes the feeling of family complete."

The next morning, Drew, Karen, and Lucinda headed out on a run. Lucinda was in terrible shape and was completely exhausted by the time they returned to the house. Karen hugged her and congratulated her on completing her first mile-run.

Then, much to her surprise, Drew gave Lucinda a hug and told her how great she did by managing to run a full mile with them. "You have your sister's determination, Lucinda. You'll be in great shape in short order."

Oliver and Ruth ran up to them, having completed their own run. "How far did you run, lady?" Oliver asked Lucinda.

"One mile," Lucinda replied, still out of breath. "Way to go," Oliver said.

"Lucinda, that's great," Ruth added.

After they showered, Lucinda asked Karen about all the praise. "Sister, get used to it and know it's absolutely sincere. We're all proud you worked hard to do something which is good for you."

"With you, and especially Drew, teasing me and joking so much, I just about laughed my way around the neighborhood."

Lucinda stared at her big sister. "You look great and you talk in such a kind manner to everybody. I'm going to try to do that. I'd appreciate it if you'll help me."

"I'd love to help you. Anything you want—because that's what big sisters are for." Karen hugged Lucinda.

***

After breakfast Lucinda asked for some tracing paper. Ruth found the paper and took her outside to show her the area where she wanted the perennial garden.

Lucinda made some measurements and began sketching some shapes. She began looking through the perennial plants book Ruth had given her and started laying out the garden in three-layers corresponding to plants which would bloom in spring, summer, and fall.

She shaped the garden on the bottom sheet of tracing paper

with a broad marker. Starting with what would become a forty- eight-inch circle in the center for a tree, she then drew straight lines from the top of the circle out to the sides. These lines were going away from the center to a length of ten-feet-each.

From the ends of the long lines she drew a curving radius line which started out moving away from the top lines but then gently increased its curvature as it came back to the center circle. Itlooked somewhat like looking down on a bird's wings.

***

Karen and Drew's university friends started arriving Saturday morning and were introduced to Lucinda. They were loaded down with textbooks and notebooks. They spread out in the living room, dining room, plus the family room, and were soon busy studying.

Drew's university roommate, Ryan Rifkin, entered the kitchen looking for a drink of water. He was wearing a black and gold university t-shirt with cutoff jeans and white and red running shoes. He had short, straight, blond hair and a thin body. He also had an incredibly warm smile. He looked at Lucinda's drawing. From his upside-down view, he said it looked like a bikini top.

Lucinda turned her design upside down and started laughing. "Let me know if you need help laying out this pretty design in the turf," he told her.

Lucinda thanked him. She thought he was funny and awfully cute.

She showed her design to Ruth. With the help of the perennial book, Lucinda then showed her what the plants would look like when they bloomed. The garden would contain a riot of colors, shapes, and textures which would change with the seasons.

"Lucinda, this is going to be gorgeous," Ruth told her. "As

soon as you have the ground prepared I know just the place to buy plants. Would you mind stopping for a moment and helping me prepare lunch?"

As it was turning out to be a warm day, Ruth brought out a cold Gazpacho soup which she had prepared the night before. She sliced three long baguettes lengthwise and buttered and toasted the baguette-halves on the flat-top. Once lightly toasted, she had Lucinda start layering provolone cheese, deli meats, sliced tomatoes, various roasted peppers, and shredded lettuce along the length of the baguettes. Lucinda sprinkled the layers with sharp raspberry vinaigrette and sliced them into six-inch-long lengths. They toasted the sandwiches in the Panini press and stacked them on a large serving platter.

"Let's put this in the dining room and set out some paper plates and drinks," Ruth said. Then, Ruth let the student-group know lunch was ready.

Lucinda was standing at the end of the table when she saw Drew pull out a chair for Karen. She thought pulling out a chair for her sister was a lovely gesture. She looked to her left and saw Ryan had done the same thing for her.

"Thank you, Ryan."

She and Karen raised their eyebrows at each other.

"What would you like to drink?" Ryan asked her.

"Diet soda would be fine."

Ryan retrieved a drink for each of them and sat down next to Lucinda.

The jolly group of students chattered about their studies. Every now and then, Ryan would find a reason to ask Lucinda about something so she was part of the conversations.

Lucinda wasn't sure what to make of the attention Ryan was giving her, but she was certain she enjoyed it. As soon as lunch was over, Ruth and Lucinda cleaned up the dining room and kitchen.

"About six this evening we're putting out a barbeque

spread. Would you mind helping me?" Ruth asked.

"I'd love to, Mrs. Holt. What kind of barbecue?"

"Oliver has had racks of pork ribs, two kinds of sausage, and a beef brisket in the smoker since eleven o'clock last night. I've had a big cast iron pot of baked beans on the stove since just before I ran this morning. We'll serve the meat and beans with two kinds of potato salad and coleslaw. I'm picking up cherry pies and apple strudel from the European bakery in town. It will be a feast."

"I'd love to learn how to cook barbeque."

"The lady who taught us will be here tonight, along with some of our other neighbors. Her name is Dell Beckham. She loves passing on her knowledge of slow cooking. I think most of the neighborhood learned from her. I'll be sure to introduce you."

An hour after lunch, Lucinda had laid out the circle and straight lines of the garden. She was perplexed about how to transpose the lovely curves in her drawings to the turf when Ryan came out of the house and asked her how it was going.

She shrugged her shoulders and explained the difficulty with the curved sections.

"I know what to do," Ryan said. "First we'll need some stakes and twine. Let's ask Drew's dad."

Oliver told them where the twine was and gave them some four-foot-lengths of one-by-one-eighth wood.

"Do you know how to safely use a radial-arm-saw?" Oliver asked Ryan.

Ryan assured Oliver that he did and proceeded to cut the wood into twelve-inch-lengths. He then restacked the wood and moved the saw to a forty-five-degree angle and made points on the ends of all the stakes.

Lucinda enjoyed watching Ryan carefully craft the stakes for her. "I really appreciate your help, Ryan, but shouldn't you be studying for your exams?"

"I'm lucky. School is easy for me. I don't forget what I've

learned, so I don't have to review for finals. I'm here to help other people, plus I like being with this crowd. They're good people."

Lucinda was delighted as Ryan took measurements off her drawing and scaled them up on the turf. He had one side laid out and then had Lucinda record measurements of the first side, which Ryan transposed to the other side. Both sides of the garden had identical curves. Lucinda was most pleased.

"Thank you, Ryan."

"You're welcome, Lucinda. Now for the hard part. Now we remove the turf down to a depth of one-foot."

Ryan secured two spade-shaped shovels from the garage and they began cutting out the turf. It was physically exhausting and sweaty work. Their pleasant conversation consisted of discussions of her life in Miami, and Ryan's life in Seattle growing up with a wheelchair-bound father.

"He's a well-known author of numerous children's and adolescent's books. I've learned quite a bit of how to get through life from watching my father deal with his disabilities."

As each section of turf was pulled up, they had to knock off as much soil as possible. They piled the turf into a wheelbarrow and Ryan took it out to a mulch pile at the back of the Holts' lot.

After sixty minutes of hard labor, Ryan said to Lucinda, "It's too warm for a t- shirt today," and he peeled off his sweat-soaked shirt to reveal a slim upper body with perspiration-covered skin glistening in the sunlight.

As she looked at his well-defined musculature, Lucinda felt a wave of warmth suddenly start spreading throughout her body. She couldn't believe what the sight of this guy was doing to her. She was from Miami. She'd seen plenty of guys without shirts. Lucinda was confused and beginning to get scared.

Ryan was steadily working the soil when Drew came out of the house. He had a legal pad in his hand and showed something to Ryan.

Ryan studied the paper. "Take the third derivative and use *l'Hôpital's* rule."

"Great!" Drew yelled and ran back into the house.

Lucinda did her best to work in a way where she could avoid looking at Ryan's body. Every time she looked at him, another wave of warmth ran through her—she could almost swear that he was trying to avoid looking at her as well.

"Let's see," he said, "I need to calculate the amount of soil we need to add. Can I see the numbers I gave you when we measured the sides?"

Lucinda watched as he started calculating the volume of soil they would need.

"Do you want to mix peat moss into the soil for moisture retention?"

"Yes," she said. "That would be good for the garden. A three- to-one ratio would be best."

"Okay then. We need nine bags of soil and three-cubic-foot-blocks of peat moss."

"Will that mix provide us a ratio of three-to-one?" Lucinda asked.

"We'll need one more bag of soil just to be sure," he told her. "Let's head over to the landscape supply store. We can take my Jeep."

They walked over to an old Jeep Wrangler, two-door-model, which had had its roof and doors removed. Ryan folded the windshield flat.

"So we can get as much air on us as possible."

Lucinda loved Ryan's open Jeep. It wasn't pretty, but seemed to express the feeling of that warm sunny day in an automotive style. As he started driving, she kept glancing at the well-defined muscles in his legs. She noticed that he seemed to be watching her from the corner of his eye as well—particularly when the Jeep went over a bump. She knew guys well enough to know he was probably watching her jiggle over the bumps in the road, too. In fact, she could tell that he was, from the bulge in his shorts.

"So, Drew is your roommate?" she asked.

"He has been for three-years."

"Any chance I can see your dorm room?"

Ryan grinned. "Sure. It's not too far from the landscape supply store."

He parked at the dorm and led Lucinda up to the room. Ryan unlocked the door and stepped aside to let her enter first.

Ryan turned to close the door, and when he turned back around, Lucinda was staring at him.

Silently, they stepped toward each other. Lucinda put one hand on the back of Ryan's head and pulled his lips down to hers. With her other hand she undid his belt and unzipped his shorts.

At the same time, Ryan was pulling her polo shirt up and unhooking her bra. He slid his hands down her back and inside the elastic band of her shorts, onto her buttocks, gently pushing her shorts down her legs.

Lucinda thought her heart was racing faster than when she went running. They tumbled onto one of the beds and he slowly put himself inside her. Lucinda firmly wrapped her arms and legs around Ryan's body as he gently caressed her breasts. Every time he stroked her, she moved her hips so he could get as far inside her as possible.

They moved faster and faster, until Lucinda felt like her hips would explode from the pressure building inside her. As they both achieved release, they started moaning and thanking each other. Lucinda relaxed and they lay still and satisfied.

Unlike the other times she'd had sex, Ryan remained inside her and held Lucinda after they finished. "You're incredible, Ryan Rifkin."

"You're not bad yourself, Lucinda Steele."

"I've had guys before," she admitted. "But not like this—

there's a little girl inside me who thinks I should feel guilty because we haven't even been on a date yet."

"I've always thought chemistry between two people was a myth," Ryan told her. "But now I know it's true. When I've done it before, I couldn't wait to get away from the girl after I finished, but I find I am incapable of doing that with you. What magic do you possess, woman?"

Lucinda laughed. "No magic here, just a plain girl from Miami."

"Not so plain," Ryan told her.

They engaged in a long kiss. "Remember when you said my garden drawing looked like a bikini?" Lucinda asked. "I just laughed. I usually get angry when someone criticizes my work."

"The moment I first saw you, I felt drawn to you," Ryan confessed.

"Ryan, I was in physical pain watching you garden. That's how badly I wanted you."

"I could hardly shift the poor Jeep due to the bulge in my pants."

She laughed. "We should get dressed and get out of here."

"I don't think I'm capable of pulling my shorts up right now."

Lucinda rotated her hips slightly and felt Ryan was again ready for her. Sliding her arms around his neck she pulled his lips to hers once more.

As Ryan began slowly moving inside her, she wrapped her legs tightly around his body for the second time that day, and if anything, the second time was better than the first. Again he didn't let go of her after they finished.

After a rest, they got dressed. Lucinda's body still tingled from the sensation of having made love with Ryan. She was worried he would have a low opinion of her because she had hopped into bed with him without as much as a date. She mentioned her concern.

He smiled at her. "So how about we head out to a movie tonight and spend the day tomorrow gardening, and then Wednesday, after my last exam, I'll pick you up and drive you to a special place called the IBG?"

Lucinda agreed but was still concerned.

Ryan put both of his hands on either side of her face. "While we talked to each other today, I felt like I've known you for a long time. That's never happened to me before. I promise I will not now, or ever, intentionally do anything to treat you in any way but a respectful and loving manner."

"Ryan, don't talk about love. We just met."

Ryan looked at her with his ever-present warm smile. "Tell me you don't feel the same way."

She put her arms around him and held him tight against her. "You know I feel the same way. I'm just frightened we've done this and I won't see you after today."

He held her in a firm embrace and kissed her cheek. "Then I'll have to prove to you there is nothing to be frightened about."

They drove to the garden center and purchased the materials they needed to complete the bedding for the garden. Then, as soon as they arrived back at the house, Drew once more came out with a math problem for Ryan.

Ryan studied the problem for a few moments, wrote something on the pad, and then told Drew, "Multiply the equation by this complex fraction and use Bernoulli's method."

"How can you do that?" Drew yelled. "We've been working on this for the last forty-five-minutes and you solved it in four-seconds!"

He then turned to Lucinda. "This guy is, by far, the smartest of my smart friends."

As Lucinda smiled at that, she turned to see Karen at the window, looking concerned. Most likely it was over her and Ryan. Lucinda knew Karen was aware that she had never had good relationships with guys.

Just then Ryan handed a large, heavy, bag of peat moss to Lucinda in an intentionally awkward manner, which caused her to lose her balance and fall into the soft plant bedding. She thought that if Karen was still watching she would expect her little sister to jump up and explode in anger. Instead, Lucinda was laughing so hard she couldn't stand up.

Ryan bent over to give her a hand. Lucinda grabbed his hand with both of hers and pulled him onto his back into the soil next to her. She quickly rolled over and sat on his stomach with her arms folded across her chest, looking at him with an expression of pretend anger.

"You're a bad gardening assistant, Ryan Rifkin. If you can't do better work than this, then you're fired."

"You can't fire me," he yelled. "I'm in a union—the peat moss spreader's union."

Lucinda threw her head back and began laughing hysterically before she stood up and helped Ryan to his feet. Lucinda looked back up to the window just in time to see Karen's expression of astonishment as Ryan bent over and kissed Lucinda, right on the lips. Clearly she was shocked that Lucinda didn't appear to be the man-hating little sister she remembered.

***

Ruth walked outside to see how the garden was progressing. "Ready for plants," Lucinda told her. She looked at Ryan and grinned. "I could have gotten it done sooner, but I had a terrible assistant today."

In a voice filled with mock rage, Ryan said, "You couldn't have gotten any of this done without me. Who did the math to lay out the shape you wanted and who calculated how much additional soil we would need?"

Lucinda looked at Ruth. "I apologize, Mrs. Holt. He's

talking math when all I needed today was a weak mind and a strong back."

Ruth laughed at them. She was pleased to hear all the teasing and laughter between Lucinda and Ryan. On the other hand, there was something else they shared that they had to get rid of before dinner.

"You two smell like you've been shoveling out a horse barn. Get in the house and shower. Ryan, I'll put out some of Oliver's clothes for you to change into. Dinner will be ready in an hour. It will take the two of you at least that long to get cleaned up."

"We'll put the tools away and get showered, Mrs. Holt," Lucinda told her.

Ruth smiled as they giggled their way into the garage to store the tools and then proceeded to giggle their way into the house.

"Someone's finally made an impression on Mr. Rifkin," Oliver mentioned to Ruth. "Besides that, I watched how he worked in the garden today. That kid has one solid work ethic. Once he had a rhythm established, he just kept digging and digging. He doesn't have big muscles like Andy or Drew, but I'll bet he's one hell of a lot stronger than he looks. Did you know he has a possible job for the summer working at some mathematics consulting firm?"

Ruth nodded. "Yes, Drew told me. Ryan started university in Seattle when he was sixteen. Apparently there's a huge math gene which runs through his family. Drew also said he's been taking nothing but graduate-level courses the last-two-years. He's only a year or so away from a PhD."

"He is one modest young man," Oliver agreed. "It's hard to imagine being incredibly smart and not being conceited."

"When I mentioned to him how smart he is, he told me, 'I'm lucky really. I was born with this gift, so it's not such a big deal. My father has MS and has spent all his life in a wheelchair, but has managed to write numerous books and be a wonderful father and husband. Now that's an accomplishment.' Holly mentioned to me he's the grandson of one of Meyer Minkowski's cousins."

"What a small world," Oliver said.

"Yes," Ruth agreed. "He also mentioned to me what an amazing woman his mother is. I hope we get to meet her."

***

As Lucinda put clean clothes on in Karen's room, she saw the *Karen's Cabin* sign had been moved from the side wall to directly above the headboard of Karen's bed.

Lucinda stopped moving, her jaw dropped, and eyes widened. Over the headboard of *her* bed were similar pink soft-sculpture letters which spelled out *Lucinda's Lair*.

"What are you staring at?" Ryan asked as he stopped by her room.

She pointed to the letters.

"Ruth must have done this while I worked outside today. She is so kind. You would think she's my mom. What did she call me? Right—I have to find out more about botanists."

Lucinda raced downstairs and gave Ruth a hug. "Thanks for the sign over my bed. That was quite thoughtful of you. I get a real family feeling being here with you guys."

She and Ryan helped Ruth get the tables setup outside. A number of neighbors came over to join in the barbeque feast. All the neighbors were excited to meet Karen's sister, and Lucinda was pleased to hear many positive compliments about her big sister.

Ryan and Lucinda continually laughed and teased each other. They also seemed to be finding reasons to touch or lean against each other.

After helping with cleanup, Ryan asked Oliver if it was okay for him and Lucinda to go see a movie.

"As long as you're going to get all A's on your finals, it is okay with me."

"Dad," Drew told him in a sarcastic tone, "Ryan probably wrote the finals."

Everyone laughed, and Ryan and Lucinda headed out the door. Lucinda was amazed at how the smallest remark from Ryan made her happy. As they stood in line to buy tickets, he held her hand and she leaned her head against his shoulder. She smiled up at him, and any time he touched or smiled at her, she loved it. He was certainly convincing her that they were a couple.

Please Lord, let there be a future to this relationship, she silently prayed.

When they returned around eleven o'clock, they heard Oliver talking to the students. "Okay troops, here are the sleeping orders. Girls who want privacy can sleep in Karen's or Holly's room. Guys who need some privacy may sleep in Drew's room. Committed couples may sleep together in the family or living room but *will* keep their clothes on. Everyone else can sleep in the family or living room as well."

Drew and Karen passed out pillows and blankets.

"Ryan wants to take me to something called IBG after his last final," Lucinda quietly told Karen in their bedroom. "Do you know what the IBG is?"

Karen thought for a minute and then a huge smile spread across her face. "Yes, I know what it is, but I won't tell you. I'll let him surprise you. Believe me Lu; it's incredibly thoughtful of him to take you there."

***

Ryan was curled up under a thin blanket. He lay on the floor in the living room with his head on a pillow from one of the couches. He was thinking about Lucinda and how she was fulfilling some need in him he didn't know he had.

He smiled and thought that if she were an equation, he

would understand this better.

Ryan believed it was going to be difficult to get to sleep with his mind absolutely spinning from thinking about Lucinda. In the darkened room, someone kneeled next to him. Lucinda lifted the blanket he was under and gently pushed him over onto his back. She lay on her side against him with her head and arm on his chest.

Ryan held her tightly against him. "Goodnight, partner," he whispered.

"Goodnight, gardening assistant," she replied. He giggled, and Lucinda kissed his cheek.

"Thank you for calling me your partner," she said and they both fell into a deep sleep.

Chapter Twenty-Four ~ *Things Botanical*

OTHER THAN OLIVER, Ryan and Lucinda were the first ones to wake up on Sunday morning. Oliver drove them to the perennial plants nursery, and they loaded his pickup truck with plants and cuttings for the garden.

"What's your favorite tree?" he asked Lucinda.

"I love fruit trees because they're so giving. I think my favorite is the orange tree, followed by the flowering crabapple tree for their exquisite, fragrant blooms and showy leaves. I can also cook delicious crabapple jelly with the fruit."

Before long, Ryan and Lucinda were on their hands and knees carefully bedding the plants. The students gradually woke up and began studying, waiting for brunch to be served around ten-thirty.

An hour before brunch, Karen and Drew came into the kitchen and sat down to talk to Ruth. "Ryan and Lucinda are acting like they've known each other for years," Karen commented.

Ruth glanced out the window at the two gardeners who were working side by side while they bedded the new plants. They had warm smiles for each other and could often be heard laughing.

"Sometimes two people come together and fill a need in each other they barely realized needed filling," Ruth told them. "When I met Oliver, I was this intellectual snob who thought she only wanted a man who had huge intellect. When I started spending time with him, I realized having someone who was kind, gentle, and caring made me supremely happy. From early on it was obvious he loved me without reservation—and still does. When we took Holly and Drew into our lives, he loved them the same way."

"Do you think it's the same for Lucinda and Ryan?" Karen asked.

"It's way too early to tell—it does look promising." Ruth thought for a moment. "They both work hard to take care of each other. Yesterday he was carrying one of those heavy bags of soil on his shoulder. He tripped and fell. Lucinda was at his side in an instant. Ryan kept telling her he was okay, but then she insisted they carry the rest of the heavy bags as a team. If they keep working together as partners, then I would say yes, they're a together- couple."

"Drew and I want to talk to you about something. We love each other. I would put my life on the line for him in an instant and I know he would do the same for me."

"But we've come to the conclusion," Drew chimed in, "we love each other more like good friends. Not like boyfriend and girlfriend. More like brother and sister."

Ruth smiled. "I think the two-of-you are wise to come to this conclusion before you try to force a relationship on each other which will end up failing."

"Drew and I have been close for over three-years. I previously thought I didn't want to have sex with him because of my having been abused. Now I realize it's because I've always, deep down inside, thought of him more as a friend, or maybe a brother." Karen looked at Drew and then back at Ruth. "Ruth, I need to talk to you about something privately. Is now a good time?"

Drew took his cue and immediately left the room. "Of course, Karen, we can talk any time."

"When I first met you, I was a frightened seventeen-year-old runaway girl who waitressed tables for a living. I didn't like who I was and hadn't given a thought to attending college.

Now, I believe in myself, and I'm about to start my senior year at university and complete an engineering degree. You and Oliver have given me a set of values to live by which made it all possible."

Ruth smiled and nodded, encouraging Karen to go on.

"You not only talked to me about those values, but you and Oliver demonstrated them on a daily basis. Holly told me recently, one of the things which made her the happiest in her relationship with Jonah, is they share most of the values you and Oliver live by. Whatever success and happiness I find in my life will be based on what you've taught me. I know I can never repay you, except to tell you when I raise my own children, they will be raised with the same values you gave me. You and Oliver have treated me like your own child since we first met. You're the one who guided me from adolescence to adulthood, so I have a request."

Karen hesitated a moment. "I would like to start calling you Mom."

Ruth welled up with pride. "It would be an honor greater than you can possibly imagine."

Karen walked around the table and embraced Ruth.

Ruth smiled. "That's enough talk for now, *daughter*. We have to get brunch on the table for all these hungry students."

Karen smiled back and her voice was filled with reverence when she replied, "Okay, Mom."

***

After lunch, Karen called Beverly to tell her she and Drew had decided they were brother and sister rather than boyfriend and girlfriend. Then a micro-second after Karen ended the call, Drew's phone started ringing.

"Hi, Beverly. Yes, studying is going well. Oh, okay. That would be great. See you at the coffee shop on campus around three o'clock Wednesday."

"That was Beverly. She wants to meet me for coffee after my last exam."

Karen had surprise in her voice, but wore a knowing smile. "She is certainly a thoughtful person."

***

Around mid-afternoon, Oliver arrived back home and pulled up in front of the perennial garden with a small tree on the back of his pickup truck. The tree looked like it was just coming out of hibernation. It was about five-feet-tall and had a root-ball about thirty-six-inches-in-diameter.

"We're going to need an opening deep enough so we can bury it up to the top of the root ball," Oliver said.

He smiled at Lucinda. "I bet you already knew that."

She smiled back as she nodded.

"I'll take one of the spades and help dig," Oliver said.

"What kind of tree is it?" Lucinda asked.

"I'm not real sure. It was on sale so I thought it was a bargain and snapped it up. I figured anything cheap is good enough for this garden. The tag on it says something about it being some kind of transcendental crabapple tree. It's self-pollinating, has flowers in the spring through June, and produces two-inch fruits from September through October but I don't know much about it."

Lucinda stared at Oliver. "You bought a crabapple tree for me."

"Don't you bother thinking like that, young lady! There's no way I'd spend my hard-earned money on a tree for some stranger who just recently showed up at my door, is bringing lots of joy to my family, keeping strange Mr. Rifkin laughing, and is putting a magnificent perennial garden in my front yard."

Lucinda walked over to Oliver and gave him a hug. "Thank you, Mr. Holt. This is amazingly thoughtful of you."

"Oh, that's real nice," Ryan complained, his voice dripping with sarcasm. "I've been shoveling for two-days and *he* gets a hug."

Lucinda shook her head, sighed, walked over to Ryan, and gave him a hug, too.

"The men around here are so demanding and so high maintenance," she declared, her hands on her hips. "It's a wonder I have time to get anything accomplished."

Oliver and Ryan both laughed at her as they started digging. "We're going to need more muscle to get this tree safely off the pickup and into the hole," Oliver said when the hole wascomplete.

Drew and two other boys were summoned to help. Oliver went to help on one side but Drew moved in front of him. "We have it, Dad."

When the tree started going into the ground Ruth walked out to look over the garden.

"Lucinda, this garden is going to be beautiful."

"Thank you, Mrs. Holt."

Ruth looked at Oliver and he smiled, letting her know how pleased he was with the work Lucinda and Ryan had performed.

"Did you see Drew wouldn't let me help with the tree?" Oliver quietly asked Ruth.

"That's fine with me," she said.

She was standing at Oliver's side and surreptitiously slid one hand behind his back and squeezed his behind. "You save all your strength for me, old man."

Oliver grinned at Ruth and briefly kissed her lips. Then they watched as Ryan and Lucinda filled the earth around the tree and Drew retrieved two steel fence-posts from the garage. He and Ryan took turns using a post-driver to force them into the earth.

Finally, Oliver took some wire and two-lengths of plastic-water-hose to secure the tree in a proper position, while

Lucinda and Ryan unrolled two garden-hoses so they could begin watering all the plants and the new tree.

Inside the house, everything seemed quiet, until Lucinda's screams shattered the silence. Everyone jumped up and looked outside. They saw Lucinda and Ryan engaged in a water fight. Ryan didn't have as good a nozzle on his hose so he had to deliver water in a more personal manner to get Lucinda good and wet. Naturally Lucinda was making the best use possible of the nozzle she had to completely soak Ryan.

Finally Lucinda yelled, "Truce!" and they spent the next ten- minutes giggling and actually getting some water on the plants.

***

After a good five-minutes of quiet, Ruth peeked outside just in time to see Lucinda checking to see whether or not Ryan was looking at her. When she saw that he wasn't, she briefly sprayed water high into the air which, of course, came down on Ryan.

As he was getting rained on, he looked up and then over at Lucinda, who gazed skyward and put her hand palm-up at shoulder height as if she was trying to detect rainfall. Ryan nearly fell over, he was laughing so hard.

"My word, those two seem so good for each other. They certainly know how to enjoy each other's company," Ruth told Oliver.

After putting away their tools and coiling up the hoses, the two drenched gardeners came into the house.

"I'm not going to let you children play in the garden again if you're going to make yourselves into a mess like this," Ruth teased them. "Go get cleaned up. Dinner will be ready in a few hours."

The gardener and her assistant giggled their way upstairs.

After they were alone again, Oliver turned to Ruth. "Did Karen and Drew talk to you?" he asked.

"Yes," Ruth replied. "Did they talk to you?"

"They talked to me first because they didn't want to say something which might hurt your feelings. I gave them a hard time by pretending to be angry because they weren't worried about my feelings"

Ruth laughed. "Oliver Holt, you're terrible!"

"Ruth, those kids of ours are special. The three of them have truly blessed our lives."

They heard Lucinda burst into peals of joyous laughter. The sound was coming from behind the closed door of Karen and Lucinda's room.

Oliver nodded in the direction of the sound. "Could be four kids…"

Ruth just smiled.

Karen came into the kitchen. "Mom, do you want me to explain the house rules to Lucinda and Ryan?"

"Thank you, Karen, but I think they need some time to be by themselves. I'll have a talk with them about the house rules."

Karen looked at Ruth with a puzzled expression for a moment, then asked, "How do you know that's what they need? I mean, I'm sure you're right, but how do you know?"

"It comes from being a mom. Sometimes I know things by sensing other people's feelings. Your wonderful sister puts on a great show of being a strong person, but underneath all her bravado is a frightened little girl. Ryan knows how to take care of her and she feels secure around him. You know, Ryan is the quietest and shyest of your classmates but look how outgoing he is with Lucinda. Before today, could you imagine him getting into a water fight?"

"I remember meeting him one morning during freshman year when Drew and I were stretching before a run," Karen said with a laugh. "We invited Ryan to join us. It was two-months before he could say hi or look directly at me. He's still the quietest member of our friends."

"But then your sister comes into his life and her warm smile and laughter made him feel comfortable around her, which resulted in his becoming more outgoing. I mean, if those two had done any more laughing they wouldn't have finished the garden. You're a feeling person, Karen. When you're a mom, you'll know."

***

Ruth was correct, of course, about Ryan and Lucinda.

"We're still having such a good time," Lucinda said, as they changed into dry clothes.

"But you're still worried, aren't you?"

Lucinda nodded. "As soon as I did it with someone, they disappeared from my life. That still worries me about us. You've been awfully kind to me, Ryan Rifkin, but I still worry."

"I knew I should have dumped you after we did it," he teased. She didn't have a hint of a smile.

"I'm sorry, Lucinda. That wasn't funny. I care about you."

Lucinda didn't say anything so he put his arms around her and kissed her forehead.

"I'm wiped out, so let's lay down for a while in Lucinda's Lair," he suggested. "Maybe if we hold each other you'll feel better."

"Let's open the door a bit so people won't think we're doing it up here. I don't want it to look like we're being disrespectful toward the Holts."

After leaving the door ajar, they lay on her bed.

"I'm going to call you after each of my exams this week so I can tell you how they went," Ryan told her.

"I'll look forward to your calls. I would love thinking I'm important enough to get a call after each of your exams."

"That's what partners do."

"Thank you, my partner." She briefly tightened her arms around him as they rested a bit before dinner.

***

After resting up and having a nice dinner, it was time for Ryan to head home.

"Call me so I know you arrived home safely," Lucinda told Ryan as he left.

Two minutes after he left, her phone rang. She started laughing. "I said to call me when you were home. Not from the end of the block."

"Hey, I didn't want you to worry."

After Lucinda hung up, Ruth had a private talk with her. She explained the house rules and how they had been the same for all her children.

"I know I just met Ryan, but he makes me feel like I'm important," Lucinda told her.

"Did you have boyfriends in high school?" Ruth asked.

"Not really. I mean, I was with a number of guys back then, but when Ryan holds me I feel like I could do anything if he was there with me. Does that sound immature?"

"No, it doesn't sound immature at all, Lucinda. From what I saw of the two-of-you, you were treating each other with utmost love and respect. That's how people who care about each other act." "I always felt like a kind of throw-away girlfriend. As soon as

something better came along, I was dumped. That still scares me." "Maybe you needed someone as intelligent as Ryan to see your true worth."

"I would love to think that's true."

Ruth got serious. "Lucinda, are you on the pill? Either you are, or you need to be. This is private between you and me only. If you need to see a doctor for a refill, we'll take care of that. Privately."

"Thank you for worrying about me, Mrs. Holt. I'm on the pill. Thanks for asking. I'll let you know when I need a refill. Karen's right about you. She said I could talk to you about anything. I feel better having talked to you this week. Thank you for your time."

She stood up and hugged Ruth.

Chapter Twenty-Five ~ *IBG*

ON MONDAY MORNING, RUTH took Lucinda out to the mall for some new clothing and a pair of running shoes.

"I'll pay you back for the clothing, Mrs. Holt." "Thank you, Lucinda. Karen and I have a favorite hairstylist at the mall. Why don't we stop by and see if we can get you an appointment with him."

"It's been a long time since I had my hair styled. I would love that."

Ruth bought her some underwear, shorts, a light jacket, sandals, and a few tops. With Lucinda's petite figure and large breasts it wasn't easy to find clothing which complimented her figure, but with Ruth's eye for style, shape, and color, she ended up with pieces which would combine into quite a few lovely outfits.

At a running store, a female clerk helped Lucinda chose running shoes and a proper bra for running.

"This thing could hold up a battleship," Lucinda said as she examined the bra.

"We want *the girls* to stay in place while we run, so the tissue doesn't stretch," the clerk told her. "Also, bouncing tends to attract unnecessary attention from guys when we're trying to concentrate on our running."

"As big as Lucinda's are, she could be charged with assault if they bounce into someone," Ruth added.

Lucinda and the clerk both laughed.

"That's enough humor at the expense of my big *girls*, please," Lucinda said after a moment, which only served to cause more laughter.

At the hair salon, Ruth's stylist recommended a radical change in the length of Lucinda's shaggy locks.

"It's time for a grown-up look, if you don't mind me saying."

Lucinda said she was scared to death at the thought of losing as much hair as the stylist was recommending.

Ruth thought she would look lovely in the new style, but had to rely on the biggest gun in her arsenal of persuasive techniques.

"I know Ryan will love this look on you," she said.

Lucinda reluctantly agreed to the new hairstyle, although Ruth saw she seemed to be in pain watching so much of her hair hit the floor.

***

On Wednesday, at one o'clock after his last exam, Ryan knocked on the Holts' front door. Lucinda opened the door for him with an ear- to-ear smile. Ruth was standing behind and slightly to the side of her.

"How was your last exam?" Lucinda asked.

"Not too difficult," Ryan said. He proceeded to give them more specific detail concerning its content.

Ruth started pointing at her head and nodding to Lucinda. Ryan looked confused until Ruth started making a scissors motion with her fingers.

Then he caught on. "Lucinda, your new hairstyle looks fantastic!" Ryan said in an enthusiastic manner. "I like your outfit as well."

"Thank you, Ryan. I have to get my purse. I'll be right back."

Lucinda turned her back on him and faced Ruth. She mouthed, "He likes it."

"She's been a wreck for two-days worrying herself silly

hoping you would like her new hairstyle," Ruth said to Ryan, after Lucinda was out of earshot. "Even if she had Cauchy or Schwarz inequality equations pasted on her forehead, you probably wouldn't have noticed!"

"Possibly not, but if it was a Hardy inequality…" Ryan said seriously.

Ruth laughed and then grew serious. "You will, please, be good to her."

"Mrs. Holt, Lucinda is the best, therefore she gets my best," Ryan solemnly replied.

***

As he started driving them to IBG, Ryan mentioned he would be working in Boise over the summer. "I may have a job I want to talk to you about. I need your thoughts on this."

Lucinda was quite pleased he valued her thoughts.

"I'm supposed to start working on my PhD this September, but I've been thinking of working for a year to pay for my graduate degree by myself. My family is willing to pay for it, but I think it would be better if I did."

"Where are you going to go for graduate school?" "Most likely I'll be in Seattle, Washington."

"If you stayed here to work for the next year, where would you live?"

"I have an apartment I'm using for the summer. It's about fifteen-minutes from here. I can extend the lease if I decide to stay." After carefully considering Ryan's question, Lucinda said, "I think you should start graduate school. That way you can start your career one year sooner. You can pay back your parents when you start working."

"Thanks, Lucinda. That is absolutely logical. What are you going to do next year?"

"I don't have a clue. Work probably. Ruth mentioned something about my becoming a botanist. I looked up the definition and I'd become an expert with plants."

"Would you like to do that?"

"I've never been a good student and I never thought about college. Ruth said she would help me get going in school like she did for Karen."

"Lucinda, would you like to become an expert in plant life?" Lucinda thought.

"I think I would love that," she said.

They were both quiet for a while. They crossed downtown Boise and were heading south. Ryan turned left onto a small two- lane street. Much to her surprise, Lucinda saw an abandoned old prison up ahead.

"We're going to the IBG prison?"

"It's the IBG at the old prison," he replied.

As they turned into a driveway, Lucinda saw a sign that read, Idaho Botanical Garden. She threw her arms around Ryan's neck.

"Hey," he yelled. "I'm still driving!"

The instant the Jeep came to a stop Lucinda gave him a long kiss.

Ryan bought their tickets and they walked back to the incredible gardens. To say Lucinda was fascinated would be an understatement. One of the garden's volunteers saw Lucinda's excitement while they were touring the historic iris collection. For the next three-hours, Lucinda was in heaven talking with her and examining plants.

Ryan used his cell phone to take numerous pictures of Lucinda with the beautiful gardens in the background.

"Are you bored out of your mind?" Lucinda asked him after the three-hours had gone by.

"I'm with you, so I'm fine," Ryan replied looking deep into her eyes.

"I've seen enough for today. Thank you for bringing me here. I love your taking me to a place where I could spend the afternoon surrounded by what I love."

"You were so excited, it was delightful to watch."

"But there was nothing for you to enjoy." Lucinda was starting to feel guilty that the afternoon's activity was exclusively centered on her interests.

"The purpose was to show you a good time. Obviously you enjoyed being here."

"But you didn't."

"Yes, I did. It was a delight watching your face. That made the whole day worthwhile—and you haven't seen the gift shop yet."

Lucinda slipped her arms around Ryan and held him tightly against her, placing her head on his chest.

He put his arms around her, using one of his hands to hold her head against him. "Lucinda, you are more special than you realize."

"That's just it. I'm not special. I'm not smart like you. I can't talk using good vocabulary like you do. I'm just a plain-looking girl from Miami."

"Lucinda, look at me," Ryan said, his voice tinged with anger. "Don't you ever think you are not a special lady. In fact, you are without a doubt, the most special lady who has ever been a part of my life. The way your face sparkles when you smile or laugh is a long way from plain."

"How can you think I'm special? You have smart college girls around you all the time. I'm sure some of them would be more interesting than I am."

"But who did I decide to spend the day with?"

Lucinda rested her forehead against his chest for a moment then looked up at him. "Thank you, Ryan. Every time we're together you make me feel special and I love when you do."

Following a tour of the gift shop where Ryan bought her a shirt with the emblem of the IBG, they drove over to Ryan's two-bedroom-apartment. There were a number of pieces of furniture with boxes and bags of stuff scattered everywhere.

"I haven't unpacked yet," Ryan told her.

"I'll help, if you like."

They arranged his furniture and started putting his clothes in dressers and closets. Lucinda was pleased Ryan let her decide the placement of the furniture so it would be to her liking.

"That's enough for now," he told her after a couple-of-hours. "You haven't held me enough today."

"Ryan Rifkin, you are so high maintenance."

He sat on one end of his big overstuffed couch. Lucinda lay across his lap with her head on the arm of the sofa. As soon as she felt his body against hers, she felt him relaxing.

"The warmth of your body against mine feels so wonderful… and secure," she told him. "I could stay like this for hours."

They kissed a few times then Lucinda asked, "Why are you going to school in Seattle? Isn't there a good math department in town here?"

"There's a great math department here, but the one in Seattle is one of the top in the nation. I could have gone there for undergraduate school, but I was fighting with my parents and especially with my grandfather. They wanted me to attend school with a certain major and I wasn't going to be pushed into doing it their way. That's why I came out to Boise. I have a cousin, Holly's husband Jonah, who went to school in Seattle, as well as my grandfather's cousin Meyer so it would have been easy for me to get in there. With my scholastic background I could have pretty much gone anywhere."

"What did they want you to major in?"

"Hold on to your horses when I tell you."

"So tell me."

"They wanted me to major in Jewish studies and become a rabbi."

"A rabbi?" Lucinda said slowly, trying to decide if that's what he said.

"It's been a tradition in my family going back at least five generations. My father, being the oldest son, was supposed to be a rabbi but with his MS there wasn't much chance of that. His younger brother, my Uncle Nathan, was supposed to pick up the mantle and become the next generation's rabbi. Nathan only wanted to study physics and he moved to Europe to avoid the problem. My grandfather tries to talk to me about it every time I see him. When I decided to go to school in Boise my mother understood why. When my dad and grandfather complained to her about letting me go to school out here, she told them that at least I wasn't running away to Europe like Nathan. She warned them that if they kept pushing me, I might. They were heartbroken to hear that, but they knew she was right."

"Ryan, do you want to become a rabbi?" "Does that scare you?"

"I would think a rabbi's wife needs to know something about Judaism and I know nothing."

"I'm familiar with your background. Karen told me last year, when you were both young your mom lit candles on *Shabbat* and you celebrated Hanukkah and Passover, but over the years it all stopped and you've had no Jewish education."

"You didn't answer my question." Lucinda was getting nervous. If Ryan wanted to become a rabbi, she feared there would be no place in his life for her.

"The answer is yes, but not like you may be thinking. I'm going to be a fulltime mathematician and a part-time rabbi. I intend to work fulltime as a mathematician for a few years before becoming a rabbi."

Lucinda was quiet, staring at Ryan.

"Lucinda Steele, we are embarking on a life together. I repeat, together. It is our joint responsibility to be open with each other concerning our feelings. That means you have to talk to me if I'm doing something which in any way upsets you. As our partnership grows, we will make more and more of our decisions based on what's best for us as a couple."

"Ryan, you are so different from me. What if we were married and had a kid who was as smart as you are? How would I answer his questions?"

"My parents know nothing about mathematics. I mean zero, zip, *nada*! When I had a math question I called my dad's cousin, Meyer Minkowski. Their lack of mathematical sophistication didn't stop me from loving my parents. It was my parents who taught me a set of values to live by. I know I don't always act like it, but the most important thing in the world is not mathematics. Love is. That's where you come in."

Lucinda looked up at him, her smile growing as he continued. "What am I supposed to do if one of our children asks me about monocotyledonous plants? I'll send that child to talk to you and I'll be proud to do that."

"Ryan, I can't so much as cook for us, and we're talking about having children and building a life together."

"Great. I can't cook either. This is surely a problem we can solve as a couple. Let's head out to the bookstore and find a cookbook—and some pans, silverware, plates, glasses. What do you think?"

"Well, Ryan Rifkin, I think we need to go shopping or the partners are going to starve to death."

As they were about to leave, she grabbed him once more and gave him a long kiss. "I hear what you're saying, but you are the special one because you make me feel so loved," she told him.

He wrapped his arms firmly around her. "I can't wait to see what the Lord has in store for us. I know there will be good times and difficult times, but with you at my side, the good times will be better and the bad time will be easier."

They arrived at a bookstore and they were looking at a myriad of cookbooks without any idea where to start.

"My mom has this cookbook." Ryan looked through a three- inch-thick tome.

"Ryan, some of these cookbooks are simple and some are

involved. We won't know if the dishes we prepare came out right!" "Pardon me for nosing in, kids," a short, casually-dressed elderly woman told them. "I'm Ellie Weiss. How many people are you cooking for?"

"Just the two of us," Ryan replied.

"How much do you know about cooking?"

Lucinda smiled. "He doesn't know anything, and I know less." "May I make a suggestion?" the little lady asked with a twinkle in her eye.

She handed them *Campbell's Weeknight Cooking*. "Follow exactly what's in the book. No changes, no substitutions. All the ingredients are easy and there are generally less than four-ingredients-per-recipe."

Ryan and Lucinda leafed through the book. "Kids, do you have pans?"

"We don't have anything."

"*Oy!* Go over to the restaurant supply store. The pans aren't pretty but they're rugged, cheap and they cook well. Get a small pasta cooker and a small two-quart sauce-pan with a lid. Get one plastic spoon for stirring and a wide spatula. That will get you started. Here's my card. When you are tired of the recipes in this book, which believe me will take a while, call me and I'll tell you what to get next."

"Thank you, ma'am," Lucinda said.

They bought the book and headed over to the restaurant supply store. Then, after a quick stop at the department store for utensils and the grocery store to get the ingredients for their first recipe, they headed back to the apartment where Lucinda called Ruth to tell her she was having dinner with Ryan.

They made chicken and broccoli Alfredo. "Our first meal we've cooked together," he pointed out as they sat down to eat. They each tried a forkful and Ryan looked up at Lucinda in surprise.

"This is wonderful."

"I can't believe it. Mrs. Weiss was right. This is delicious."

For the next-ten-minutes the only sounds were of forks and knives on plates.

"Great meal, partner," Lucinda said as they moved to the kitchen to clean up. They embraced and enjoyed a long kiss.

"That's enough of that," Lucinda said, "I can't afford to get too excited today."

"What's wrong?"

"I'm busy down there. My period started." Lucinda thought for a moment. "That's funny. I've never mentioned my period to a guy before without getting embarrassed."

"That's because we're partners," he told her as he kissed her forehead.

"You think I'm special?" Lucinda asked, looking for reassurance.

Ryan gave it to her. "Lucinda Steele, from the bottom of my heart, I know you are."

Chapter Twenty-Six ~ *Lucinda's Gardens*

THE FOLLOWING WEEK, A letter arrived at the Holts' addressed to Lucinda. It was from the IBG and it included a lovely membership card and a welcome letter.

She showed the letter to Ruth. "Ryan must have done this. Mrs. Holt, he is so good to me."

"Don't forget, Lucinda. You're awfully good for him as well."

"I don't think I do anything for him."

"Lucinda Steele, why do you think he looks at you the way he does? Why does he call you and talk to you about every little thing in his life? You can see the happiness in his face anytime you talk to him. That is what you do for him. You appreciate Ryan for being Ryan. That's all guys want—they want to be appreciated for the person they are. You let him know that you appreciate him."

"I know what you're saying, Mrs. Holt, but I still feel like this is just a dream and it will end at any moment. I know I'm not pretty, and I'm sure not as smart as he is. I'm amazed he wants to spend any time with me."

"Tell me, Lucinda, when you're together, do you feel like you are taking care of each other?"

Lucinda smiled. "Yes… I mean he absolutely does that—and I love when he does." Lucinda held up the letter. "I mean, look at this."

"You've been disappointed so many times in your young life when it comes to relationships, I can understand how frightened you are. Give it time. You will be surprised. I can honestly say every year with Oliver has been better than the last. Not many people can make that statement."

Lucinda was carefully considering what she had heard.

"You may not think you're pretty, but the way Ryan looks at you, I know he does," Ruth continued. "As far as how smart you are—you're obviously smart enough to make him happy. Besides, if Ryan wants to talk math, he can call Jonah and they can math together. You and Holly can do something else together during those times."

Ruth's cell phone began ringing. After a brief conversation, she excitedly turned to Lucinda. "Jonah and Holly are coming down to visit. They'll be here for the weekend, plus a few days next week. Apparently, Jonah has some research to do in town. I can't wait for you to meet them."

***

Ryan and Lucinda were admiring their garden handiwork on a Saturday morning. A car was driving by as they were looking over Lucinda's plan for the garden, comparing it to how it was turning out.

The car parked in front of the house and the couple called to Lucinda and Ryan. "Do you mind if we take a look at your new garden?" the woman asked.

"Not at all," Lucinda said. "My name is Lucinda. This is Ryan."

"I'm Natasha Omondie and this is my husband, William. We're trained botanists and we teach at the university during the school year, but we run a landscaping business during the warm months."

They examined the multi-layered plan, and then Natasha looked at Lucinda. "You've got a great start. It's going to be magnificent. I see you've included some plants that will maintain some color during the transition between seasons. I love how the heights of the plants will be increasing toward the middle. Who designed this?"

"I'm the guilty party," Lucinda said.

"It's great, Lucinda. We get requests from our customers for garden designs almost every week during the summer. Being botanists, we know how to take care of plants but we're not as artistic as you seem to be. Would you consider designing gardens for us?"

Lucinda was taken aback. She couldn't believe someone wanted to hire her to design gardens.

"We'd drive you out to the client so they could tell you what they want, and you could see the location," William said. "If they like what you've drawn up, we'd be willing to pay you five-hundred- dollars-per-design that we install."

Lucinda was too shocked to speak.

"That would be great," Ryan answered for her. "What do you think, Lucinda?"

Lucinda nodded. "I'll give you a phone number you can reach me at."

"Let me call the Esterbrook family. They asked about a garden design last week." Natasha pulled out her cell phone. "Hi, Mr. Esterbrook. This is Natasha Omondie. I wanted to tell you we have a garden designer on our staff now, and we'd like to come over and discuss a design for you."

After a pause, she looked at Lucinda. "Next Saturday morning at ten?"

Lucinda nodded.

"We'll see you then."

They all shook hands and worked out the details.

"Will you come with me next Saturday?" Lucinda asked Ryan. "I'd rather not go alone."

"Of course, but I expect assistant's pay."

"You'll get paid according to how much aggravation I have to put up with!"

"If that's the arrangement, I'll end up having to pay you."

Chapter Twenty-Seven ~ *Intrigue*

WHEN JONAH AND HOLLY arrived on Friday, Ruth thought it was curious they didn't want to be picked up at the airport. They arrived in a full-sized black SUV which, according to Oliver, was being driven by some military-looking types.

Ruth was walking on air as she watched Lucinda, Karen, and Holly move around the kitchen helping her prepare dinner. Every time a new technique was on display, from chopping and dicing to sautéing and brazing, Lucinda practiced every move.

"They talk like sisters," Ruth whispered to Oliver. "That makes me so happy."

"You should hear Ryan, Drew, and Jonah talking automotive engineering," he added. "Drew is in heaven now that he can teach Jonah and Ryan about something technical. He was showing them some harmonic equations which are useful in intake manifold design. They haven't looked at the Gran Torino yet. Drew is under strict orders from Karen not to uncover the car until she is out there. She is so proud of what she's done—and she has every right to be." Oliver looked outside.

"Hmm," he said. "There's an older full- sized van with dark windows sitting across the street. And come to think of it, I have also seen the local police coming by the house quite a bit this evening."

"I wonder what that's about," Ruth said.

During dinner Holly had an announcement to make. "Jonah and I have a wedding date set. We will be getting married on Sunday, the last weekend of August. We have some other good news as well. We are buying Ari and Leah's home on Lake Washington."

Everyone was congratulating them, but Ruth sensed something was bothering Holly. Having the opportunity to start married life with a home on beautiful Lake Washington should be every girl's dream. Holly appeared to be forcing a smile when she talked about their new home. Ruth decided to wait before she asked her about it. After dinner, Ryan and Jonah remained sitting in the dining room with Drew. Jonah asked for a legal pad and wrote something down. "I've been having a hard time solving this equation. Can you take a look at it, Ryan?"

After forty-five-minutes and six-pages of written work, Ryan handed the solution to Jonah. Jonah thanked him and then spent a lot of time looking at Ryan's work leading up to the solution.

***

The following morning everyone headed out for a run. Jonah said a couple of his friends would be running with them.

"They're from the company I'll be working at next week," he explained.

Oliver noted an extremely fit young man and woman arrive. After introductions, they all set off. It was a warm morning, but the two friends ran in short-sleeve sweatshirts. Oliver saw that they were continually glancing around during the run—it didn't seem like they were just enjoying the scenery.

When the three-mile run ended, Oliver was standing to the

side of the group and nodded to Jonah's friend.

"You need a bigger sweatshirt," Oliver told the friend when he walked over. "Your forty-five semi-auto pistol shows when you shorten your stride."

The man displayed no reaction. "Are you ex-military, sir?"

"Yes, I am," Oliver replied. "May I ask what this is all about?"

"It would be better if you didn't, sir."

Oliver stared at him a moment. "You make damn sure you take good care of them."

"I don't know what you're talking about, sir, but if I did, I would tell you that taking care of them is my one-and-only-job."

After breakfast, Jonah and Ryan began talking mathematics again when Oliver suggested that he and Drew head over to the aviation museum to see some new acquisitions.

The girls headed off to the farmers' market and the outlet mall. Holly was working hard to get to know Lucinda and before they left, Ruth told Oliver she was pleased, but that it almost seemed like Holly was trying too hard. Lucinda didn't seem to mind, simply enjoying having Holly's attention. Karen didn't seem to mind either as she enjoyed more time with Ruth.

The rest of the weekend was spent doing things as a family. When they drove out to see some recently discovered artifacts along the Oregon Trail, Oliver saw that Jonah was carrying a concealed pistol. To his absolute shock and amazement, Holly had one as well. When he had a chance to talk to Jonah away from the others, he asked him about it.

"Is that a Springfield or an HK?"

"I'm carrying an HK compact in forty-five, and Holly's carrying an HK compact in nine," Jonah told him without batting an eye.

"Can you shoot straight with it?"

"I practice on three-inch-sized-targets at seven-yards. I

have an eighty-five-percent hit-rate. Holly has an eighty-seven-percent hit- rate."

Oliver smiled. "That'll do." While he knew whatever was going on didn't concern him, Oliver did begin looking around more often and watching the people around them.

***

Ryan was nervous about his Monday morning job interview. Someone from the company called him and told him a car would pick him up, and to his surprise, Jonah said he would be going to the same location.

When the car picked them up, they were driven to a National Guard facility at the local airport. Quite a few people seemed to know Jonah.

Ryan was ushered into an interior office which had no windows. "Is this where I'll be interviewed?" he asked Jonah.

"The interview was Saturday, and you passed."

"What's going on?"

"I'm doing classified research. I want you on our team, but I can't tell you more until you put your signature on some papers." He slid some documents in front of Ryan.

Ryan was confused, but he trusted Jonah so he read through the non-disclosure agreement and signed.

Then Jonah and two other people began a long presentation on the genetics research they were pursuing.

"While this could lead to cures for numerous genetic-based defects and diseases, obviously this also has terrible implications for using genetics in warfare," one of his briefers told him. "We need to get, and stay, ahead of everyone else."

"Will my family be in danger?" Ryan wanted to know.

"The long and short of this is, yes, they will," Jonah told him. "I'm sure you've heard the family story about how Holly and I stopped two people who were trying to kill everyone in my parents' home. It turns out they were going to kill all of us to try and stop my father's research and send a warning to other people in the field. There is some evidence he didn't die of a heart attack, but rather was killed by a chemical that mimics a heart attack. A fellow researcher named Elizabeth Lipinski also died of a similar heart attack a few- years-later. Back then no one suspected that the deaths were related."

After a pause, Jonah added, "You'll be listed as an employee of my Uncle Meyer's company, just like I am. We get paid a lot of money, but have to live a different lifestyle. You'll be given an initial assignment that will allow you to complete your PhD while you work. Every Monday morning, you and I will fly to Austin, Texas for the week. We'll be flown back to our homes on Friday afternoon. We hope to have a secure facility here in Boise by the end of the summer. This is not a just a summer job, Ryan, but for the next year you'll be listed as a student at the university. Eventually our work will be moving to Seattle. We're not sure exactly where, but most likely at one of the military bases up there."

"Does Holly know?"

"She knows I can't ever tell her what I do for a living. Holly was only concerned we would have a life that would allow us to raise our children. I've assured her we would. If you decide to give Lucinda a ring, Holly and I will meet with both of you to help you talk to her. You and I can't talk about what we're doing unless we're in a secure area, like this office."

"All I wanted to do in my life was work on math. This sounds like what I've dreamed about, but it doesn't sound like I'll have time to become a rabbi."

"Think about it, Ryan. You don't have to decide today but I need to know this week. There is a sign-on bonus worth half your annual salary if you decide to work with us."

Ryan sat quietly for a while, then he stood up and walked over to a whiteboard and began writing a series of equations. "This is a better solution to the equation you gave me on Saturday. Seeing as we're going to be working together, I thought I should give it to you."

Jonah reached out and shook Ryan's hand. "Come on, I'll show you our office. We'll be flying to Austin tomorrow."

After an intense day of briefings, Ryan was happy to be on his way back to the Holts' to have dinner with them.

Lucinda greeted him expectantly. "Well, how did it go?"

"I have the job." He grinned.

Lucinda hugged him. "Ryan, that's great."

"It's a project that will require me to spend my weeks in Austin, Texas for the summer, but I'll be home on weekends."

"Ryan, is it the kind of job you wanted?" Karen asked.

He felt someone's eyes burning a hole in his back. He turned around and Oliver was looking directly at him.

He returned Oliver's gaze, then answered Karen's question. "It's not *exactly* what I wanted, but it's an important job which I'll be quite proud to perform."

He noticed Oliver smiling and nodding. "Plus, I'll be working with Jonah."

"Holly, did you hear that?" Lucinda exclaimed in an excited voice. "Ryan's going to be working with Jonah."

"That's wonderful," Holly said.

That evening Ryan and Lucinda drove over to a hardware store.

He had two keys made, which he gave to her.

"This one is for my apartment and this one is for my Jeep. You can use them anytime. If anything seems strange with the Jeep, have Oliver or Drew check it out. I'll call you every night when I get off work. I'll be coming home from Austin on Friday at five o'clock. Do you want to meet at my apartment?

"Yes. Definitely yes. I'll have dinner ready for us."

"By the way, how about coming up to Seattle with me over the July fourth weekend? You can meet my folks. Holly and Jonah said we can stay with them."

"That would be great. I like Holly and Jonah. They are so easy to be around. Holly treats me like a sister, and Jonah teases me like you do—not in a mean way, but funny."

Chapter Twenty-Eight ~ *A Busy Shabbat*

ON FRIDAY NIGHT, RYAN returned from Austin to his apartment. Flowers in hand, he arrived to the smell of freshly-baked bread wafting under the door.

He opened the door and saw Lucinda dressed in a white peasant blouse, white slacks, and white tennis shoes. She looked excited to see him and ran to the door to greet him with a kiss and a long embrace.

"These are for you." He handed her the flowers. "It smells wonderful in here."

She smiled. "Thank you for the flowers."

After another quick kiss, Ryan headed toward the bathroom. "I'm going to shower and change."

After his shower, he came out dressed in light slacks and a white shirt.

Lucinda turned to him as he walked into the room. "Would you please join me while I light *Shabbat* candles?"

Ryan placed a *kippah* on his head and was positively ecstatic as he saw their dining table adorned with a *Shabbat* candleholder, a *Kiddush* cup, and a lovely *Challah* covered by a beautiful *Challah* cover. "Lucinda, this is wonderful. I mean the table and place settings are beautiful and the lovely plants you've added here— you've really turned this place into a home."

"Thank you, Ryan, it's been fun."

He listened to Lucinda chant the blessing over the candles, then they embraced and wished each other a good *Shabbos*.

Ryan chanted the blessing over the wine with tears in his eyes, and by the time they joined hands and said the blessing over the *Challah*, he could hardly see the table for his tears.

"I thought, I mean—you've obviously remembered a lot from your childhood. Lucinda Steele, this is so thoughtful and so lovely that you've done this for us."

She beamed proudly and offered Ryan a warm smile. "I am so glad you appreciate it. I knew you would. I spent the week with Anna Levin, and she taught me how to set the table, chant the blessings, and bake the *Challah*. She bought us the lovely *Challah* cover, too. We made gefilte fish from scratch yesterday. And look at the lovely white-porcelain soup-tureen, fish-serving-plate, and two- complete-sets of Lenox Autumn-pattern dishes, silverware, and glasses. Anna gave them to us as a house-warming present. The dishes are so lovely and formal. I think we should only use them on *Shabbat*. She invited us over for dessert tonight. I can't wait for you to meet Michael and her. You won't believe her wonderful children. Her daughter Carrie helped me learn the blessings."

Ryan embraced Lucinda. "Lucinda, bliss is coming home to you."

"Bliss is certainly creating a *Shabbat* meal for you to come home to."

"You've truly made this place a home for us." He glanced around his modest apartment. "You bring more peace and love to my life than I deserve."

"Anna and Carrie taught me a song she said we should sing tonight."

"*Shehechianu*?"

"Yes, that's it."

As the sound of their voices filled the room, they sang that ancient melody which celebrates significant beginnings. Ryan thought he couldn't possibly be happier.

Lucinda pulled out a piece of paper. "Would you like to discuss this week's *Parsha*?"

Ryan dissolved into sobs. "What's wrong?" she asked.

"I don't deserve all this, and I certainly don't deserve you. I love you so much, Lucinda Steele."

"I know." She put her arms around his neck. "When I felt lonely this week, I only had to think of how you treat me and the memory brought a smile to my face every time." Lucinda kissed his cheek. "Let's eat."

After a lovely dinner that included Anna's all-night-cooked brisket, followed by cleanup of their new dishes, they sat together on the couch in the living room.

Ryan talked about his week in Austin. "I have so much to learn. My head was spinning by the end of the week."

"We need to watch the time," she said. "I still live with the Holts, you know. Seeing as its *Shabbat,* I was hoping to have enough time for the traditional *Shabbat mitzvah.*"

"Are you sure?"

"My body is sure. I've been in pain down there the last two days whenever I thought about what we did at the dorm."

"Well, it is a *mitzvah.*"

***

They walked into the bedroom and undressed. There was no hurrying this time. Lucinda placed soft kisses all over Ryan's face and neck while he caressed her. She gasped at the sensation his attention produced.

She grasped him and found him ready for her and guided him inside her. He stroked her slowly, almost teasing her.

It had a different feeling this time. Instead of satisfying themselves, they were satisfying each other. For the first time inher life, Lucinda experienced the difference between having sex and making love.

They held each other tightly as they reveled in the joy their relationship brought to each of them. As they luxuriated in the afterglow, Lucinda's cell phone started ringing. Ruth was calling her. "Oliver and I just saw a news report that there is going to be a terrible snowstorm tonight in Nome, Alaska, so we thought you should consider spending the weekend at Ryan's place."

Lucinda felt confused but before she could ask Ruth what she meant, she continued. "Joking aside, Lucinda, we understand how close you two are, and you're certainly a woman, so it's your decision. We just wanted you to know it is okay with us."

"Thank you. I'll talk it over with Ryan," she grinned at him, "but I'm sure he'll want to avoid the snowstorm."

"If you can make it, we're having brunch Sunday morning on our patio around ten-thirty."

"We'll be there, and I love you guys."

"We love you as well."

Lucinda hung up and turned to Ryan. "That was Mom. She said there's a snowstorm in Nome, Alaska, so we should think about spending the weekend together."

"Do you want to?"

"Do I want to have a chance to hold you all night? Do I want to wake up in the morning and find you next to me? I can't think of many things I'd rather do."

Ryan beamed.

"Let's head over to the Levins' home for dessert!"

***

They had a lovely apple crisp for dessert, which was accompanied by a slice of sharp cheddar cheese and a tiny wedge of blue cheese.

"Can I show you my room?" Carrie asked Lucinda. "Sure you can."

She took her on a brief tour of her room. "Let's sit down on my bed. I have something personal I wanted to ask you. If you don't want to talk to me about this it's okay. Sometimes it's hard to talk to your parents about some stuff. Anyway, I'm almost a teenager and my mom told me that I'm going have a body like my birth mom which means I'm going to be more like you, and I have some questions about that."

"How will you be like me?"

Carrie looked nervous and kept her head down as she continued. "My boobs are coming in and Mom thinks I'm going to be big like you."

"Oh. What would you like to ask?"

"Will it be hard to find clothes that fit?'

"Not really. It *will* take patience plus a sense of style and shape. You have to be careful and dress modestly. With a big chest, you don't need plunging necklines or tight tops to show off. If you do end up being my size, you won't have to work at showing any cleavage either. I mean, I have cleavage even if I'm wearing a turtleneck! The minute you enter a room, Carrie, your feminine form will be apparent."

"Does it hurt when they bounce?"

"Yes. The discomfort you feel is the tissue stretching so you will always need properly fitted bras. If you go jogging or exercising where the girls are going to bounce you need a properly fitted sports bra."

Carrie nodded.

"And guys will stare and they'll want to touch them."

"I don't think I want guys to do those things to me," Carrie said.

"You will when the right guy comes along."

"He's going to have to be awfully special."

"That's how it's supposed to be."

"Is that how it is for you and Ryan?"

"He absolutely takes me to a place I've never been before."

"So you did it with guys before Ryan?"

"I did, and it was a huge mistake because I thought I *had* to do it with them to have a boyfriend. If someone loves you, he'll wait until you're ready without putting pressure on you.

Believe me, when it's the right guy, you'll want him at least as much as he wants you."

"How will I know when it's the right guy?"

"You'll know when you see how you and he are taking good care of each other, and you find that it doesn't matter what you are doing, you want him next to you."

Carrie thanked Lucinda for being honest with her and they returned downstairs.

Then, after a lovely evening with the Levins, Lucinda and Ryan returned to their apartment and curled up on the couch to read.

"I was thinking," Lucinda said. "Staying here tonight will give us another opportunity to perform the *Shabbat mitzvah.*"

Ryan laughed, leaned over, and kissed her lips. "You are such a loving partner."

"Thank you, Ryan. I think Carrie and I are going to be close. We had an interesting talk tonight."

"Did you have a sex talk with her?"

"How did you know?"

"I didn't. I was trying to be funny."

"You can't tell anyone."

"Who would I tell?"

Chapter Twenty-Nine ~ *A Life Changing Decision*

WHEN THE JULY FOURTH weekend rolled around, Ryan pulled up in front of the Holts' home to pick up Lucinda for their trip to Seattle. He was in a large navy-blue SUV with two people in the front seat. Lucinda noted they were the same people who brought Ryan home the previous weekend.

"They work for the same company so they drive me around when I'm in Boise, until I can get a company car."

Lucinda thought this was strange, but she was with Ryan and that's all she cared about.

The car was driven to the back of the airport and stopped in front of a small jet.

"Here's our plane," he said. "It's a company plane," Ryan added when he saw Lucinda's surprise.

Lucinda *was* pleasantly surprised. She didn't think a new employee would get all this special treatment. As they entered the plane, she heard the pilots greet Ryan as *sir*.

When they took their seats Ryan let out a long sigh. He leaned over and kissed her.

"Has it been a tense week?" she inquired.

"It has certainly been a tense week. I've had so much to learn. I'm going to have to find a way to deal with the stress." Ryan looked at her and continued. "I can't believe how at peace I feel when I'm with you."

She put her head on his shoulder and wrapped both her arms around his arm. "I've decided to tell you I love you."

"It's about time," he said with a smile. She laughed.

"You're terrible!"

"Please clear your weapon, sir," one of the other passengers said to Ryan just before takeoff.

Ryan withdrew his pistol from its holster, removed the magazine, and cleared it. At the same time, the two other passengers on the plane took off their sports coats. They were both wearing side arms which they also cleared.

"You all have guns," Lucinda said, feeling panic.

"Lucinda, you're going to have to trust me. I can't tell you what's going on until we're at Jonah and Holly's home."

"I don't like this. I don't like this at all," she said crossing her arms against her chest and looking out the window.

***

When they arrived at Jonah and Holly's new home on Lake Washington, which they had purchased from Ari and Leah, Lucinda was still concerned by the display of all the guns on the plane.

Holly took her on a tour of the house. Quite a bit of remodeling was taking place. Many new cables were being run and it looked like some walls were being modified.

"Holly, this is beautiful," Lucinda told her. "You have a wonderful home, which practically begs to have family events."

"Thank you, Lucinda. We're going to have our wedding here next month. How's your relationship with Ryan?"

"It's better than I ever imagined a relationship could be. I surprised him with a *Shabbat* dinner with gefilte fish and homemade *Challah*. While I learned how to prepare those from Anna Levin, she and her daughter Carrie taught me how to chant blessings. Ryan was so happy I did all those things that he cried. He appreciates every little thing I do."

"Ryan comes from a religious family. I suspect he

appreciated your learning those things for him more than you know. I didn't tell Jonah I was converting to Judaism until I had completed all the requirements. I was secretly studying with Ryan's grandfather. Jonah thought I was just improving my Hebrew. We went to dinner at Ryan's grandparents' home and his grandfather asked me to light the candles. We did the other blessings and as we sat down to eat I analyzed the week's *Parsha*. Ryan's grandmother then presented me with a beautiful necklace with a Star of David which came from Israel. That's when I told Jonah. He tried to talk but just cried. I'll never forget his expression. I don't think I've ever seen his face filled with more joy than at that moment."

When they arrived at the wine room, Ryan and Jonah were waiting for them. The décor of the wine room was setup to look like a garden in the middle of a vineyard. A table and chairs were arranged for dinner. Jonah filled their glasses with a Chateau Ste. Michelle, *Chenin Blanc*.

They all sat down at the table. Holly had prepared a spicy, cold Gazpacho soup, a spring-green salad with blue cheese dressing, plus herb-onion bread sticks.

"All right. No one starts eating," Lucinda said loudly. "No one takes a bite until you tell me what's going on."

Ryan reached out and grasped her hand. "Jonah and I have jobs working on a classified project. We can't tell you what we do for a living. Not now. Not ever. You and Holly are the only ones who get to know we do something classified. We suspect Jonah's Uncle Meyer may know, as well as Oliver, but they're both ex-military and know not to say or ask anything. We get paid through Meyer's company. They bill the agency we work for."

"This isn't just a summer job," Jonah told her. "For the next year, the work will be based in Boise and Austin. Ryan will be coming home to Boise every weekend. The work will be moved to Seattle within the next couple-of-years. You will have the opportunity to finish whatever schooling you desire here in Seattle."

"Lucinda," Holly said, "you and I would be close in the sense we would understand what we are going through with partners who do this kind of work. We could provide support for each other."

"Do all the guns mean people may try to kill us?"

"There will be security people around at appropriate times," Jonah said. "Our families would have lots of protection."

"But the answer is yes," Holly added. "We may be at risk."

"I can't even shoot a gun."

"You can begin learning while I continue my training. Tomorrow Uncle Meyer's friend Gene will be over in the afternoon to give us a private, ladies-only lesson. He's an NRA instructor and taught Ari, Leah, Jonah, and Joan to shoot. He's been a fantastic instructor for me. Our lives, and the lives of our families, may depend on our skill."

"Our children would attend the best private schools in the country," Ryan told her. "The house next door is being torn down. A new house is being built, and it's a similar size to this one, but a different style. I can show you the plans. That will be our house. There will be a secret security tunnel between the two houses. All the wiring you saw upstairs is for security. Our house will be similar."

Lucinda was starting to shiver with fright. "You guys—this is too much."

"Lucinda, I beg of you, please take the time to consider you and I know each other," Holly pleaded. "You wouldn't be in this alone. We would have, and I suspect need, each other. I know it's hard for Ryan to admit it, but he needs you too."

Lucinda sat quietly for a long time while they began eating.

"You come first in my life," Ryan finally said. "If this is unacceptable to you then I'll quit and do something else."

"Ryan Rifkin, I love you more than life itself," Lucinda told him. "What you are doing must be important, or you wouldn't be willing to risk our lives. If this is the path you've chosen then I'm taking that path with you."

Ryan kissed her. "Thank you."

"What will this do to your plans for school in Seattle this fall?" Lucinda asked.

"To answer, let me tell you a story about the Primrose flower. It grows wild on the central plains of our country. A perennial, it's one of the first plants to emerge in the spring. Winter in the plains is a time of freezing cold temperatures, where everything turns gray. During the previous fall, the Primrose used the last of its strength to store energy in its roots so it could grow in the spring. The Primrose must push through the previous year's growth and often struggle through ice and snow to reach out to the sun. Even when it gets through, there is sometimes a late-season blizzard, but the Primrose is ready for all it may have to endure. The struggle a Primrose endures is what we human beings endure growing up. Both the good times and bad help us push through our childhood, so in our adulthood we can reach for the sun."

By now everyone had stopped eating. They were carefully listening to his story.

Ryan once again took Lucinda's hand. "Last May I found a Primrose. She had shaggy hair and ill-fitting clothing, but she was unmistakably a Primrose. Just the thought of her brightened my days and warmed my nights. My Primrose was frightened at first— afraid I would be attracted to the other flowers. I did my best to reassure her through reason, laughter, and love that she was the only Primrose of my life. This fall, I'll be going to graduate school where I work and that will allow me to be home weekends so that I can be near my Primrose."

Lucinda eye's widened and as she looked at her dining companions—Holly had tears in her eyes.

Ryan pushed his chair back, dropped down on one knee, and showed Lucinda a beautiful engagement ring.

"Lucinda Steele, you are the Primrose of my life. Would

you do me the honor of becoming my wife?"

Full of shock and joy, Lucinda replied, "Ryan Rifkin, becoming your wife would make me the happiest Primrose in the world."

Jonah and Holly were all smiles as Ryan put the engagement ring on Lucinda's finger. Hugs and congratulations were exchanged around the table. Then Jonah broke out a bottle of champagne and filled glasses.

Jonah raised his in toast. "To Ryan and Lucinda—a long, happy, and healthy life."

Ryan and Lucinda thanked him.

"I need to call the Holts," Lucinda said. "I have to give a huge thank you to Ruth and Oliver who took Karen into their home and hearts. If they hadn't, we might still be alone and waitressing tables some place. It was in the garden of their love that this Primrose was able to bloom."

Lucinda excitedly called the Holts. "Ryan asked me to marry him," she blurted out when Ruth answered.

"Well?" Ruth asked. "Well what?"

"Lucinda Steele, for heaven's sake, what was your answer?" Lucinda started laughing. "Of course, I said yes!"

After congratulating her, Ruth called Karen to the phone. "Lu, I'm so happy for you. Oliver just told me to tell you he's angry he's going to lose his gardener. Wait, here's Drew." "Congratulations to both of you," he told her.

They decided to wait until the following day to tell Ryan's parents in person.

Later-that-evening, Ryan and Lucinda were sitting on the patio looking out at the lake. It was a cool evening so Holly brought out a blanket for them to wrap themselves in.

"Before you came into my life, I felt like I was on a ship being tossed around by uneven seas and stormy weather," Lucinda told Ryan. "After we met, I felt like the seas had calmed and we had sailed into smooth waters. I have to admit, all this need for security makes me nervous. Will we have people driving us around all the time?"

"Not much longer. We're getting armored cars. They look like normal cars but have bullet resistant windows and doors, plus special tires. Sometimes the threat level might change. There are people who do nothing else but worry about the security of our project and the people involved in it. We'll be the first to know if the threat level changes."

They both looked into the darkening night sky. They wrapped themselves around each other as tightly as they could, wondering what impact their decisions that summer would have on the rest of their lives.

Chapter Thirty ~ *The Inknr Ayfri Foundation*

IT WAS WITH GREAT expectations Lucinda looked forward to her education as a botanist. She decided she would commute to the university the first year, since she didn't have enough money for room and board. While the Holts had offered her financial assistance, she decided that she would pay the cost for her studies out of the money she received for doing garden designs and take out loans for the rest.

On Friday, the first week of August, two envelopes from the university arrived. The first envelope was large and contained Lucinda's acceptance letter and the information she needed to register for classes. She and Ruth poured over it. It was hard to tell who was more excited. Even though Ruth had been through this three-times-prior, she said she was still just as excited as the first- time.

The second envelope was from the admissions department and was only one-simple-typed-page that read:

Lucinda Steele,

The Inknr Ayfri Foundation has notified this university that you have been awarded a full scholarship to our university. Your room and board, plus tuition and books have been paid for under this multi-year scholarship.

Congratulations and welcome to the U.

Lucinda and Ruth both screamed at the same time.

"Do you know who Inknr Ayfri is?" Ruth asked her.

Lucinda shook her head no.

The screaming caused Oliver, Karen, and Drew to rush into the room.

"Lucinda received a great scholarship, but it's from someone we've never heard of," Ruth told them.

Lucinda was staring at the letter when she suddenly sucked in her breath and starting crying.

"What's wrong, Lu?" Karen asked.

Lucinda was wracked with sobs. She couldn't talk, but kept pointing to the name of the foundation on the letter.

Drew looked at it, smiled, and showed it to Oliver who also began smiling.

"We engineers get it," Drew said.

Karen looked at the letter and a broad smile crossed her face. "It's from Ryan. He spelled his name inside out and backwards."

Lucinda could only nod as she was desperately trying to get control of her emotions and when she finally did, she said, "He must be spending the sign-on bonus he received for joining the Texas project. He knew I needed the money and mentioned he didn't want you guys to go into debt to give me an education."

Lucinda immediately called Ryan. "I believe I'm speaking to the head of the Inknr Ayfri Foundation," she said when he answered. "You better come directly over here after your plane arrives today, Ryan Rifkin."

"Dinner's at six tonight," Ruth yelled.

***

The minute Ryan's new Jeep pulled up in front of the house, Lucinda ran out to meet him. She threw her arms around him and started crying again.

"Don't cry," he said as he embraced her. "This is supposed to make you happy."

231

"I'm so happy—you can't imagine how happy I am. I love you so much, Ryan Rifkin."

He held her tightly against him. "I know you do and that is one of the greatest pleasures in my life."

They walked up to the house with Lucinda tightly holding his hand in both of hers.

Ruth walked over to Ryan and hugged him. "Thank you. You should have seen her expression when she realized who setup the scholarship for her."

"This is your fault," Ryan said quietly to Ruth. "You're the one who said to be kind to her."

Ruth stood on her toes and kissed his cheek. "You are most kind, Mr. Rifkin."

Oliver came over and shook his hand. "Your folks would say you're a real *mensch*. I'd say they were right."

"Thanks, Mr. Holt. I'm earning a comfortable amount of money. It will easily cover her school costs. Also, the company I work for is going to pay for my PhD."

Chapter Thirty-One ~ *The Girl with Six Toes*

ON A FRIDAY IN mid-August, twenty-three-year-old Andy Schulman, his best friend Drew, and Drew's fiancée, Beverly, attended a bluegrass festival near Pocatello, Idaho. They had a small group of friends from school which assembled occasionally to play bluegrass music, and they were meeting them there. They were going to play a couple-of-times at the festival which was for professionals and amateurs alike.

At their first performance on Friday evening, Andy noticed a girl who kept staring at him. She had raven-dark hair and a petite, slim body, wearing a lovely western-style dress. Andy thought she was awfully good looking. He was somewhat surprised that such a pretty girl was watching him. He even glanced around to see if she was looking at someone behind him.

There was something about her, though. He thought she looked familiar, but couldn't imagine where he'd seen her before. He was wracking his brain trying to remember where he had seen those sparkling blue eyes and that lovely smile. Was she from another band or summer camp? Andy pointed out the girl to Drew, who swore he had never seen her before.

After their performance, Andy joined the audience to hear the other groups, and he found himself standing right next to the lovely mystery girl.

"Don't you wish you were on stage now?" she asked.

"I'd love to get good enough to play with them, but these

are the fast pickers now. I'm not that skilled. We mostly play for fun. We don't record or anything as I'm sure these guys do."

A band started playing the lively tune "Roll in my Sweet Baby's Arms." Andy saw she was moving in time to the music so he asked her to dance.

At one point they were both facing in the same direction with their arms around each other's waist. As they executed coordinated forward kick movements, Andy suddenly realized that he had experienced having his arm around her previously.

"Hi, Shelly," Andy yelled over the sound of the music. "Hi, Andy," she yelled back.

"It's great to see you again," he said when the music ended.

"I feel the same way," she replied. "I'm glad you remember me."

The song "Rocky Top" started playing and they began dancing again. Andy couldn't believe how her eyes sparkled just like they did when he first met her.

"I'm amazed you remember me," he told her when the music ended. "You were just a little kid."

"You weren't so old yourself as I remember. While you drove me down that mountain, you kept talking to me and making jokes so I wouldn't be scared. You made me laugh the entire ride. I owe you."

Shelly stood on her toes and kissed a rather astonished Andy. "Shelly," he said. "Hmmm...are you the famous six-toed Shelly?"

"Do you remember how silly you were?" she asked, laughing and smiling at Andy. "You owe me another dance because that was a bumpy ride," she said as the next song started.

Andy laughed and they started dancing again.

When the music ended, Ruth Holt and Holly walked over to Andy and Shelly.

"Mrs. Holt, Holly, I want you to reintroduce you to someone you met about twelve-years-ago," Andy told them. "This is Shelly."

"Shelly!" Holly shouted. "I'm the one who held your hand while Jonah put bandages and splints on your leg and arm."

Shelly smiled at Holly and then looked at Mrs. Holt.

"And you're Ruth. Thank you so much for what you did for me back then. As you can see, everything's healed."

Shelley's bright expression sparkled like her eyes. Andy searched his mind to think of things to say to her so that he could have a reason to stay close, which was a good thing as she had not only kissed him, but also seemed to have a death grip on his hand since the last dance.

Holly suggested they talk outside where it was quieter. Ruth and Holly led, and Shelly turned to follow them. As Andy was still firmly attached to her hand, he followed after.

They engaged in pleasant conversation for a few minutes. Shelly reminded them that the first aid they provided at the scene probably saved her and many other lives that night.

"At a minimum I would have lost my leg if it hadn't been bandaged to close the wounds and stop the bleeding."

"Will you be here through the weekend?" Ruth asked.

"We're going back to Ogden Sunday morning."

"Good," Ruth told her. "I have something for you. I'll give it to you tomorrow."

"My mom is here and I'd love to have her meet you again," Shelly said.

They walked back inside as the last band started playing.

Shelly looked at Andy as they walked. "By the way, my full name is Shelly Birnbaum." She pronounced her last name slowly while she gave two quick squeezes to Andy's hand.

He realized she was letting him know she was Jewish.

"I was a scared-to-death little girl when you drove me down that hill. I'll never forget the silly things you said to me to make me laugh. Every time we went over a bump you asked me to count my toes to make sure they were still attached. When I told you I counted six toes, I remember that you yelled, 'Oh no. You're supposed to have seven toes on that foot.' I was laughing so hard I nearly forgot my pain. You were so kind to me. I remember how gently and carefully you lifted me off the litter. You carried me into a big camper and gently placed me on a bed."

Andy smiled at the memory, too.

"I attended NFTY camp as a counselor earlier this summer," Shelly continued. "I met someone from your high school who told me about you. She said you're an accomplished violin player, you work out with weights every day, and you're starting your PhD in chemistry. I didn't expect to meet you here, but I hope we can get to know each other."

"I may have to do that if only to be near my fingers." He lifted their hands, noting the still-firm grip she had.

Shelly giggled. "You can certainly still make me laugh, sir."

They arrived where her mother was standing wearing a curious expression.

"Mom," Shelly said, "I'd like you to meet Andy Schulman."

"How do you do, Mr. Schulman. Please tell me about yourself and how you know Shelly."

"Well, I live in Meridian, Idaho. I've just graduated from the University of Idaho with a degree in physical chemistry, and I start working toward my PhD in chemical engineering in two-weeks. I speak Hebrew and Spanish, and I've been making Shelly laugh since she was a little girl."

Mrs. Birnbaum looked at her daughter with a questioning expression.

"It's true, Mom. When I was in the plane accident, Andy drove the ATV that brought me safely off the mountain. He's the one who made me laugh the whole ride."

Shelly looked up at Andy and continued, "He's also the one who gently lifted me off the litter and carried me inside a camper." Recognition dawned across her mother's face.

"Shelly's mentioned you at various times through the years, but I never imagined you'd meet again."

Ruth, Drew, Beverly, and Holly walked over then and were introduced to Mrs. Birnbaum, too.

"Andy lives in our neighborhood," Ruth said, "and I've known him since he was seven-years-old."

"I'm Holly. I'm the person that found Shelly at the wreck."

"You also held my hand while I was being bandaged," Shelly added.

"What happened to the boy that bandaged and splinted Shelley's injuries?" Mrs. Birnbaum asked.

"That boy is about to become my husband," Holly proudly said. "He's just completed a PhD in mathematics."

"I'm surprised he didn't become a doctor. How old were you when the accident occurred?"

"Jonah and I were sixteen."

Mrs. Birnbaum smiled at Holly. "How wonderful the person you did all those wonderful things with will become your husband."

"It was a struggle at times," Holly admitted. "But we continued to grow closer over the years, and we made it."

***

The following day Andy met Shelly around mid-morning. "Let's go for a walk." he suggested.

They talked about their years apart and caught up on what their lives had been like since they met. Andy related that he had a few girlfriends over the years, but the relationships never amounted to much. He had decided to concentrate on his school work for the time being and pretty much gave up on dating.

Then they stopped walking and sat on a small park bench. "When I was at NFTY camp in Utah three-years-ago, I met a girl then too, who said she knew you," Shelly told him. "She said you were one of the kindest boys she had ever met."

"I paid her to say that," Andy quickly told her.

"You don't know who it was." She laughed.

"That's only because my reputation is so poor, I have to pay a lot of people to say kind things about me."

Shelly laughed again and they resumed walking.

"Are you this silly with everyone you meet?"

"Only with Jewish girls from Ogden, Utah," Andy replied in a serious tone.

Their conversation started changing to attitudes about family, friends, and religion. It was obvious to Shelly that Andy had strong family values. She shared many of the same values, but his attachment to religion was much stronger than hers was and she wondered if that would be a problem for them.

Andy, Drew, and their band played again that afternoon, but Shelly and Andy were inseparable the rest of the day.

They decided to take a break from dancing to enjoy the cool evening air. They walked away from the music area to a more secluded location.

Shelly experienced a bit of sadness. "You're going back home tomorrow and I don't know if we'll ever see each other again, what with you living in Idaho and me living in Utah. Would you please hold me for a minute?"

Andy held her and she put her arms around his neck, laying her cheek on his. "I've held guys before, but I can't believe how wonderful this feels. I want to spend more time with you."

"I'm starting school again in Boise in a couple-of-weeks, but if you're free next Friday through Sunday, I'd be willing to fly down to Ogden in my dad's plane. It would only take an-hour-and-a-half to fly there. That way we could have a chance to get to know each other."

That made Shelly happy. "I still live at home so I have to ask my parents."

"Great. Let's find your mom."

***

Holly, Ruth and Mrs. Birnbaum met for dinner. She asked them about Andy. "He seems to have quite an interest in Shelly. In fact, they seem to have quite an interest in each other."

"If I was picking a husband for your daughter, I would love to think she would have a partner like Andy," Ruth suggested. "He has been a faithful friend to my son Drew since their childhood and he is one of the kindest boys I know. If the day comes when you meet his parents and sister, you will find they are wonderful, family- oriented people."

Mrs. Birnbaum appeared quite relieved to hear positive comments about Andy.

Ruth gave a bag to Shelly's mom. "This bag contains the blanket that I used to cover Shelly the night she was injured. As she is completely healed, I think that blanket must have brought her good luck. I want her to have it. It's thirty-years-old but still looks like new. I've carried it in our camper for a long time, but I think this is a good time to pass it on."

Mrs. Birnbaum pulled an intricately patterned, all-wool blanket from the bag. She looked at the label. "This is a Pendleton Chief Joseph pattern. No wonder it still looks like new. This is a precious and thoughtful gift. Thank you. Shelly will be pleased, as am I."

Just then Shelly and Andy arrived. "Mom," Shelly said, "Andy wants to fly down to Ogden to see me next Friday through Sunday. He can stay with a friend of mine. Would that be okay?"

Andy took out a personal card and handed it to Mrs. Birnbaum. "You are welcome to call my parents and ask them about me."

"Thank you for the card, but you took good care of my

Shelly before," Mrs. Birnbaum said. "I'm sure you'll do the same when you come to visit us in Utah."

***

Early the following Friday morning, Andy and his dad were reviewing Andy's flight plan down to Ogden. His father kept asking to make sure Andy had checked and double checked everything he needed for the flight.

His parting words to Andy were, "Be safe and don't think about Shelly until you shut the engines down in Ogden."

Andy smiled and thanked his dad for coming out to the airport to help preflight the four-passenger, composite, twin-diesel- engined-aircraft. Then his dad stood off to the side and Andy started each engine, verifying that each engine's oil pressure and temperatures were in the green.

He gently advanced the throttles and headed onto the asphalt taxiway and over to the active runway. He didn't see any other aircraft, so he announced on the radio that he was beginning his takeoff roll. As he advanced the throttles, he felt a reassuring push in his back and heard a roar in his ears as the plane accelerated down the runway. After a brief run he began slowly lifting the nose of the aircraft, and within a couple more seconds he felt the plane lifting off the runway. The hydraulic pump hummed as he retracted the gear, and the electronic flight instruments helped establish his climb to altitude and set his heading for Ogden, Utah.

The sky was mostly clear and only a few puffy clouds appeared. He listened to air traffic control and watched his instruments as he carefully navigated to the Ogden airport, landing safely.

As Andy left the active runway he saw Shelly waving to him.

She was standing off to the side of the taxiway he was entering. He taxied the airplane near her and pulled off the taxiway, driving it onto the grass. He shut off both engines, slid the canopy back, felt the warm Utah sunshine on his face, stepped onto the wing, and jumped to the ground.

Shelly walked over to him. Without saying a word she put her arms around him and held him tightly.

"That's the best welcome to a new town I've ever received," he said as he embraced her.

"I am so glad you're here." Shelly kissed his cheek.

"I have to do some more airplane stuff and then we're on our own." He showed Shelly how to climb into the plane and seated her in the copilot's seat. Then Andy climbed in and fired up the engines. "First we'll fill up the fuel tanks and then find a place to park.

Are you afraid to fly? I mean after your accident and all?"

"I'm okay," Shelly told him. "Besides, you wouldn't do anything to put me in danger."

As they taxied over to the fuel pumps, Shelly looked around at the plane's interior. The extremely comfortable leather seats were set low, and her legs almost went straight forward. A control stick came up from the floor between her knees and the canopy window provided a great view out the front. Andy explained what some of the instruments and gauges were for.

"This would be a great way to travel," she said.

After fueling the plane and moving it to a parking spot, Andy mentioned that they could fly over the mountains the next day and he could take her up in a glider. He closed up the plane and they started walking to Shelly's car.

"Sounds like you've planned things for us to do, sir."

He grinned. "I checked into a couple of things." Andy thought she looked nervous and mentioned it.

"I've been planning all week and now you're here and I'm hoping we'll have as good a time as I've planned," Shelly said, looking down as they walked.

Andy didn't have much experience with girls, but he knew

exactly what his father did when his mother was nervous like this. Andy wrapped his arms around her and in a happy voice said, "Shelly, it's already a great time because we're together again. We had fun at the Bluegrass Festival and we had fun getting you off a mountain. All we need to know is that you have the right amount of toes on your feet and we'll be fine."

"After all these years, you still can make me laugh with silly jokes," she told him through her laughter.

As they walked over to her car, Shelly called her parents to let them know Andy had arrived safely. Before she popped open the trunk to put away Andy's things, she pointed out the two mountain- bikes mounted on the back. "We have some gorgeous trails around town, if you'd like to try them."

"Find me a place to put on some shorts and off we go!"

Andy changed into shorts and they drove about twenty-minutes to the outskirts of Ogden. They parked near the base of a line of beautiful mountains to the east of town.

Andy noticed that Shelly had helmets, riding gloves, hydration packs, homemade energy bars, and sunscreen. "You're ready for me. That's very considerate of you," Andy told her.

"Thank you, Andy. I love to mountain bike and I was hoping you would as well."

As she led Andy up the first trail he was amazed that Shelly was so easy to engage in conversation. She was obviously well-read and could understand when he explained some of the chemistry he had studied in college. Shelly was also physically fit—they headed up some steep runs and she stayed seated on her saddle the entire time. She didn't seem to be breathing hard, either.

After an hour on the trail, they stopped for their first break. Andy looked out to see a magnificent panorama of mountains, lakes, and cities. He and Shelly sat on the side of the trail taking in the scenery.

"Shelly, this is beautiful!"

"I'm glad you like it. I've looked at these mountains all my life and I still love seeing them."

"Have you seen the Tetons?"

"I've only seen them in pictures. You need to take me there some day."

"How about visiting them tomorrow?"

Shelly looked at him with surprise. "You're serious, aren't you?"

"Sure. If we fly out of here at eight o'clock tomorrow morning, we can be landing in Jackson Hole about ten o'clock. There is a great ATV rental place near the northern end of Jackson. We could be out on the trails by ten-thirty or so. I can call and make reservations for us today, if you like."

Shelly smiled at him without saying anything, then leaned over and kissed him on the cheek.

He turned toward her, put his hand behind her head, and kissed her warm lips.

"Wow, thank you, sir."

"Does that mean you trust me to take you on an ATV ride again?" Andy asked.

She laughed. "Only if you promise not to make any toe jokes."

"Oh no! That kills the trip. No toe jokes, no go."

Shelly giggled and pretended to concede. "Okay, toe jokes allowed."

She slipped her arm around his arm and held his hand with both of hers. "Have you thought of me since the accident?"

"I have to admit I did wonder what happened to you."

"You mentioned the relationships you had previously didn't amount to much."

Andy shrugged. "Each of us expected something different from our partner such that the relationships never grew. I always dreamed about having a girlfriend who I enjoyed being with no matter what we were doing. When you and I were sitting together on the bench at the music festival last week, a sense of serenity came over me. I don't know how else to describe it. It left me as soon as we separated that weekend. When I thought back on that feeling last week, I started to believe it was just my imagination…but when you sat down next to me in the airplane earlier today, I felt it coming back. I feel it now. We barely know each other and I'm starting to worry. Well, maybe I'm trying too hard. Maybe we're both trying too hard to make this a great relationship."

Shelly seemed to think for a moment, and then rested her head against his shoulder. "Remember when we hugged each other at the Bluegrass Festival?" she asked. "Not only was that the best a guy has ever made me feel, but I felt elated this past week just reliving the moment. Andy, that's not only special for me but unique as well. Besides, I don't think I need a perfect relationship. I think I just need happy."

Andy stood up and helped Shelly to her feet. He was about to reach for his bike, but instead he put his arms around her. "Do you know what *Bashert* means?"

"I'm sorry but I don't know any Hebrew."

"It's *Yiddish*. I'll tell you what it means later. Let's get more riding in and then find a place for lunch."

"My mom is expecting us at one o'clock."

Andy glanced around. "Do we have time to keep riding?" he asked. "I love this trail and the scenery, though the company is a little non-descript."

Shelly smiled at his teasing.

"Be sure to keep drinking water," she advised. "The air is pretty dry around here this time of year."

Andy took a long drink of water and realized he should have had some water sooner.

"Hey, mister, we have to get some sunscreen on you or you're going to burn."

Andy glanced where Shelly was looking. The back of his calves were turning red. He hadn't noticed.

Shelly quickly applied sunscreen to his calves and

forearms.

"Water and sunscreen—do you always take such good care of the guys you ride with?"

"Only if they're Jewish boys from Boise, Idaho."

They mountain biked for another hour and took turns leading on the various trials. Andy couldn't help but see that there wasn't any fat on Shelly's body. She obviously kept herself in wonderful condition. His eyes kept glancing at her cute little behind.

Shelly must have noticed where his gaze kept wandering because she teased him. "What are you looking at?"

"I was trying to count your toes."

She tried to reply but was too broken up with laughter to get any words out.

On the trail back to her car, she told him she ran or rode her bike every day, and Andy described his running and weight routine.

"No wonder you have such a muscular body."

"Thank you. You look pretty good yourself."

Shelly thanked him, then she looked down at her modest chest and wrinkled up her nose. "Not too much up front, though, I'm afraid."

Andy turned his grin serious. "I have a wise friend who has informed me, more than a handful is wasted."

Shelly burst out laughing. "Stop making me laugh or I'm going to fall off this bicycle!"

Andy smiled at her. Being with Shelly was one of the best things to happen to him in a long time. "Let's plan on getting up early enough to go running tomorrow," Andy suggested.

Shelly agreed. They cycled back to the car and loaded the bikes onto their rack. "You're not just another girl, Shelly Birnbaum."

"Thank you, kind sir." She smiled and then asked him to drive them over to her home.

After greeting Shelly's mom and meeting her older brother, Andy sat in their family room talking to him while Shelly and her mom went into the kitchen to put lunch on the table.

"How's it going with him?" Shelley's mom asked her.

"He's kinder than I imagined him to be. He makes me laugh and he makes me feel good about myself. It's like he appreciates who I am. Momma, I think I like this guy."

"Well, Shelly, I wanted to warn you about the dangers of falling in love too quickly, but I've seen a special glow on your face every time you've talked about Andy the past week. It's already too late to warn you, I think."

Shelly smiled at her mom and then called Andy and her brother, Gary, to lunch.

"The smell coming from the kitchen is wonderful," Andy said.

"Shelly is making *sambusas*," Gary told him. "She learned how from a Nigerian friend. They consist of a spring roll wrapper with ground beef inside. The ground beef is seasoned with cumin, cardamom, white pepper and a dash of smoked Tabasco. You add chopped onions and scallions to the meat mixture, and since we had peas for dinner last night, Shelly probably added some of them to the filling for a little color as well. You form them into triangles and then deep fry them."

"Wow, Gary, you know the recipe pretty well."

"It's one of the first things I learned to cook. Sometimes I go over to the Mexican deli and buy shredded beef to put in them instead of the ground beef. I like the texture better."

They sat at the table. Each person had a plate in front of them which had a small bowl of cold beet borscht with a dollop of sour cream floating on top, two spicy *sambusas*, and a little bowl with fresh fruit.

After the rigors of the morning trail ride, the lovely meal disappeared quickly. Andy thanked Shelly and her mom for putting out such a delicious lunch.

Shelly suggested they drive across town to see the annual art show.

Andy asked Mrs. Birnbaum if she would like to go with them.

"Thank you, Andy," she said with a smile, "but I want you two spending as much time together as possible so you can get to know each other."

They arrived at the art show to find there were many rows of small white booths. They both loved the sculptures. Shelly loved anything made of glass, but Andy said he preferred the metal and wood sculptures. Also Andy preferred photography to paintings.

"I can hear it now," Andy told her. "We're going to have knock-down, drag-out fights over how we decorate the places we're going to live in."

Shelly giggled. "I don't know if I should be worried we're going to have arguments or be happy you are talking about our future home."

Andy turned and briefly kissed her lips. "Not to worry, pretty lady. My folks do their best to resolve any arguments before they go to bed and always share a kiss before sleeping. We should try and see if that works for us."

She nodded and planted another kiss on Andy's lips before they resumed walking.

As they walked past a music stand they saw the drummer of a blues band being helped off the stage.

The leader of the band made an announcement. "We were going to play BB King's song 'Bad Case of Love'—it won't sound like much without a drummer, though."

"I know that song," Andy yelled without any hesitation. "I can cover for your drummer."

The band leader looked down at Andy and waved him up to the stage.

Shelly grinned and spoke to no one in particular. "He

drums...besides playing the violin. I don't believe it. No wonder I like him so much. I've always been a sucker for drummers. If he's a good drummer this could seal the deal for us, whether Andy knows it or not!"

The band started the song with a gentle electronic keyboard solo. This was followed by Andy coming in with an energetic up- tempo rhythm accompanied by a driving bass guitar line.

He was a superb drummer and he was playing a wonderful blues song. Most of the time Andy was swinging out, he was smiling and looking directly at Shelly. Her knees were getting weak and her smile was so broad it nearly hurt.

Halfway through the song, Shelly's brother came by the bandstand with some of his college friends. He looked surprised to see Andy drumming. He walked over to Shelly. "Did you know he could drum like that?"

Shelly shook her head.

He saw that she had tears in her eyes. "Are you okay, Shelly?"

"I'm happier than you can imagine. I'm going to marry that guy!"

Gary seemed shocked at his sister's words. "I thought you two hardly knew each other."

When she didn't reply, he shrugged his shoulders.

After the song ended, the band leader spoke into his microphone, asking if Andy could play a couple more songs. Andy replied that it was up to his girlfriend.

The band leader looked at Shelly. "Would you mind?"

"It's fine with me," Shelly yelled up to him. It was actually more than fine with her and she enjoyed every beat.

Andy and the band played Stevie Ray Vaughan's song "Voodoo Chili" and followed it with a song which had a drum solo in the middle—Shelly felt even happier as they played Brian Setzer's "Rock This Town."

As they ended their set, the band members came over to thank Andy. He waved Shelly up to the stage and started to help pack up the drums.

"Hey you," she called out to him.

He turned and she jumped into his arms, putting her mouth on his. He held her off the ground as they engaged in a long passionate kiss.

"The hell with it," one of the band members declared. "I'm switching to drums."

Andy agreed to return to play in the band's evening set with one condition. "My girl gets to sit next to me on the stage."

As they rejoined the audience, Gary introduced Andy to his friends. Shelly was proud of Andy as everyone complimented him on his drum solo. She was so excited she felt like she was walking six-feet off the ground.

As they climbed back in Shelly's car, she slid across the seat and kissed Andy again. It was slower this time and Andy put his hand on the back of her neck to hold her lips against his. It was clear that they each felt their love, not to mention their excitement, for one another growing.

Shelly put her right hand on his upper arm inside his shirt sleeve. She squeezed his bicep and he flexed for her. "Your bicep is huge!"

Andy just smiled and starting driving them back to her parents' home.

As Shelly and her mother prepared dinner, Shelly's dad said he was pleased to meet Andy, especially after hearing so many stories about him from Shelly and his wife.

In the kitchen, Shelly enthusiastically told her mom that Andy was also a superb drummer.

Mrs. Birnbaum looked up at the ceiling and spoke quietly, as if pretending she didn't want Shelly to hear. "Oh no! Please Lord, not a drummer. That's it for her. He has her forever now."

Shelly smiled at her mom.

During dinner, she proudly talked about how Andy had

jumped onto the stage and played with the band.

***

Andy loved hearing the pride in Shelly's voice but was disappointed they didn't light *Sabbath* candles. He had a commentary on that week's *Parsha*, but just left it in his shirt pocket. When Shelly asked about the paper, he said it was notes for his flight plan for the next day.

They returned to the music venue and there was a chair waiting for Shelly near Andy's drum throne. Andy had time to warm up properly, so his performance was even more inspired than during the day.

Gary had called around and invited quite a few of his and Shelly's friends to hear Andy and the band. Andy watched as Shelly sat smiling and clapping on stage, and her brother and their friends clapped and danced to the music.

After a fun evening that included dancing to other bands when Andy wasn't on stage, they returned to the apartment where Andy would be staying.

"This apartment belongs to my friend, Janine," Shelly said. "She's gone for the weekend. I'll call my parents and tell them I'm staying at Janine's tonight."

Andy smiled and went to take a shower. When he came out, he was standing naked in the middle of the bedroom when Shelly entered.

She was wearing a long robe which was loosely held closed with a belt. She also carried a blanket which she threw onto the bed. Closing and locking the door behind her, she walked up to Andy, put both hands on either side of his face and kissed him. As she did, she shrugged off the robe to reveal it was the only thing she was wearing.

Andy held her body tightly against him. He loved how her warm body felt against his bare chest, and he could feel Shelly's heartbeats coming faster and faster.

They began to slowly make love. The two of them were just as in sync as they had been with everything else so far.

When they were done, they rested in each other's arms. Andy finally looked at the blanket Shelly had brought into the room to cover them.

Shelly must have noticed his curiosity. "This is the blanket Ruth Holt covered me with after you put me on the bed in her camper," she told him. "She gave it to my mother, who gave it to me. She thought it gave me luck then and I should have it as it might continue to give me good luck."

"I can guarantee you at least one of us feels he got lucky!" Shelly laughed and kissed Andy again.

***

They following morning, they pulled on clothes for a run. Once outside they talked while they stretched.

Andy learned Shelly volunteered with organizations which helped the elderly.

"It's not like I can relate to them, it's just I feel good when I know I can alleviate some of their loneliness." Shelly explained how the town had named an office for her.

"That's mighty fine, Shelly," Andy told her.

"At Christmas I help them decorate their homes and make sure they have an appropriate meal on Christmas day. At the Jewish center, I always volunteer at holiday time to do similar things."

"Shelly have you thought of getting an MD and specializing in geriatrics?"

"I love you for thinking I'm smart enough to attend medical school, Andy, but I haven't sufficient brain power. I work hard in school to get a mix of A's and B's. I can barely understand my math and science courses."

They began their run, and Shelly covered the ground with smooth gentle footsteps. It almost looked like she was floating above the pavement.

Then after showering and changing, they headed out to the airport and were soon winging their way up to Jackson Hole.

Shelly seemed mesmerized by the scenery which passed beneath them.

"Oh, my God. Oh, my God. Andy, this is so beautiful," Shelly repeatedly declared as the white-capped Grand Tetons came into view.

Andy chuckled. "Shelly, please make sure your mic is turned off. If your words get out over the radio someone's going to think we're having sex up here."

Shelly's intense laughter filled the little plane and was only minimized by the amazing sights spread out before them.

Before long, Andy was busy getting the plane ready to land. They were approaching the airport from the north, which meant they were flying with the Tetons close by on the right.

"They're so beautiful and we're so close, I want to reach out and touch them," Shelly said.

Andy smoothly touched down, and Shelly seemed to be so entranced by the view, Andy wasn't sure she realized they were even on the ground.

Once he had parked the plane, he slid the canopy back. The air in the valley was substantially cooler than the temperature was when they left Ogden. They pulled on light sweaters and jackets, and Andy came around to help her get off the wing and onto the ground.

Shelly stood on her toes and kissed Andy's lips. "You get a kiss for flying me to such a beautiful location," she told him.

A brief taxi ride took them into Jackson where Andy rented a small side-by-side ATV just like the one he had used to rescue Shelly many years before.

With maps in hand, and helmets on heads, they headed out with three others on ATVs. They climbed a small rise and paused to take pictures. They were on a low range of hills that were on the eastern side of the Jackson Hole Valley. As they gazed to the west they were confronted by the majesty of the Teton mountain range. "Look at all this beauty, Andy," Shelly said as she wrapped her arms around him. "Thank you so much for bringing me here. I don't think you could have found a more magnificent and romantic location."

Andy was proud to hear that. As he looked at Shelly's bliss-filled face while she took in the gorgeous surroundings, he thought that he'd really have to remember to thank his dad for teaching him to fly. In the distance they saw the crooked Snake River carrying people on a float trip. Andy handed his binoculars to her and indicated where she should look to see them.

"I've done that with my family," he said. "The views are great and the float trips vary from mild to wild. We should plan to do that next time we come up here."

"Thinking about our future again, Mr. Schulman?"

"I can quit doing that if you like."

"You better never stop doing that," she said with a stern expression.

"We keep doing things to make each other laugh," Andy said. "This is almost too good to be true."

"I hope you don't find this childish, but ever since you rescued me, I've fantasized about meeting you again," Shelley told Andy as they motored up a long slope. "I made up stories for myself where I was on an adventure and you would always be there to rescue me when I was in trouble. As I became older the stories changed so we rescued each other. Does that sound childish?"

"I like how that sounds."

They drove around some tight turns which exposed more of the Tetons' majesty.

"When I was at an eighth-grade graduation party, this guy was saying awful things about my best friend and me. I told him, if Andy was here you wouldn't dare talk to us like this.

Everyone stared at me because they didn't know who I was talking about."

She got quiet. "I have to admit something else," she said. "I thought of you last year after I finally did it with someone. It was an awful experience. I immediately imagined it would have been better with you. After last night, I know I was right."

Shelly started to giggle. "I found out that jerk was only good for what my best friend refers to as two-pumps-and-a-squirt."

Andy began laughing hysterically. "A lousy ten-seconds, eh?" he finally said when he regained a semblance of composure.

Shelly laughed. "It wasn't half that long."

They both busted up laughing now. After their laughter died down, Shelly asked, "May I call you Andrew?"

"Sure you can. Why?"

"Well, I started calling you Andrew in my mind a-year-ago when I realized you wouldn't be a boy any longer."

Andy brought their ATV to a halt. He leaned over and kissed her.

"Thank you, sweet lady. That's a lovely thought."

They followed more trails, took more pictures, and soaked in the beauty of the incredible landscape before they returned the ATV to the rental location.

"I know a great barbeque restaurant at the other end of town," Andy told her.

As they walked to the restaurant, they stopped in many of the interesting shops in Jackson, then after returning from a wonderful lunch they continued exploring the small shops.

Andy took her into his favorite one — By Nature. It displayed ancient fossils that were in beautiful condition and priced according to their uniqueness. They were both fascinated and excited to see such a novel collection.

"This is a clutch of Oviraptor dinosaur eggs found in China," Andy pointed out. "I would love to own something like this one day."

They both gazed at a huge Ichthyosaur which was still in its Holzmaden shale.

"I can't believe how well all the detail is preserved. Wouldn't this be a treasure to have in our home?"

"Another reason to study hard," Shelly reminded him. "That's for sure." Andy admired the magnificently preserved fossil.

As they flew back to Ogden, Shelly again expressed her joy in the spectacular sights along the way.

"This is so beautiful, Andrew. Thank you so much. I know we still have Sunday morning to be together, but I am concerned about when we will see each other again."

"I'm renting a small apartment near school," Andy told her. "Once I'm settled you can come and visit. But I have to warn you, I'm a serious student, and I don't know how much time I'll have for you."

"I'm sure I'll be fine," Shelly replied, smiling.

***

In a handful-of-weeks, Shelley will visit Andy at his apartment… and never leave. They find joy in each other's hearts as only two individuals who are meant to be together would find.

Chapter Thirty-Two ~ *The Wedding Weekend*

KAREN WAS INTRODUCED TO Ryan's brothers at the Friday night dinner before Holly and Jonah's Sunday wedding.

Benjamin was two-years-younger and Avram was the youngest.

The family was gathered on the outdoor patio which overlooked the swimming pool and lake. A translucent acrylic sheet covered the pool turning it into a dance floor for the wedding party to come.

"I'm not a math and science geek like my brother," Benjamin told Karen. "I'm double majoring in psychology and Jewish studies."

He was slim like Ryan with a playful look in his eyes. He also had Ryan's warm smile.

"I'm a senior majoring in automotive engineering," Karen told him.

Benjamin slapped his forehead.

"Nothing but techies in this family! I feel like an escapee from the law of averages by majoring in a social science." Karen laughed.

"I guess you and Holly are the only exceptions," she said. "What will you do with your major?"

"I'm going to become a rabbi."

"Oh."

He laughed. "Don't sound so disappointed!"

"I'm sorry, I didn't mean—"

Their conversation was interrupted by Marsha and Esther running into the room, screaming, "Hi, Aunt Holly."

"Who are the precious twins?" Karen asked.

"They're Esther and Marsha Minkowski. They are Ari and Leah's children. They've become quite close to Holly and Jonah. Let's walk over, I'll introduce you."

Anna and Michael Levin arrived with their two children, who were both twelve-years-old. Carrie and David Linn stayed near their parents while they walked around and were introduced to people. That is until they saw Jonah and Holly. They ran over to them and greeted them in excited voices. Then they were introduced to Esther and Marsha. A friendship began between the four of them, which everyone thought would last a lifetime.

Jonah spent some time talking to Michael Levin. "I know this is your wedding weekend," Michael told him, "but I'd appreciate it if you could find time to talk to Carrie. She has a math problem she's dying to ask you about, but she's nervous you won't have time for her. You know that huge math gene which runs through Ryan's family? Anna and I are starting to see Carrie may have a huge math gene as well. I don't know if it's a coincidence or not, but Carrie's name sake, her great-great-grandmother, supposedly was quite skilled at math. Please talk to her if you have time. I think you'll be shocked at her level of mathematical sophistication. Her school doesn't know what to do with her."

"Thanks for telling me, Michael," Jonah said. "I can always find time to math."

Before dinner, Marsha and Esther, who were studying for their *Bat Mitzvah*, led everyone in the blessing over the candles. During the meal they discussed the week's *Parsha*.

At dinnertime, Carrie managed to sit next to Jonah.

Ruth and Oliver smiled at each other as Benjamin pulled out a chair for Karen.

"They're talking to each other like the rest of us aren't

here," Ruth said.

Then Drew and his fiancée, Beverly, sat with Benjamin and Karen.

"We may be empty-nesters before long," Oliver told Ruth.

As the dinner began Jonah asked Carrie about the math problem. She took a folded page from her pocket and opened it up revealing a polynomial based complex fraction.

"I picked up a book last winter and have been doing all the problems in it. It's one of those *For Dummies* books about high school algebra. I got stuck on this problem."

Jonah quit eating and began quizzing Carrie on the properties of basic algebra. She had an excellent understanding of most of the properties. A smile grew on Jonah's face. When he finally asked about an algebraic property she didn't quite understand, he patiently explained it to her. As he talked, he saw a knowing grin slowly spread across her face.

"Oh, Oh, Oh!" she suddenly exclaimed. "Wait! I can solve this now."

She began writing on the page she had brought from home then showed her work to Jonah.

"Correct," he said.

"I was looking ahead," Carrie said, "and they have a section on imaginary numbers. What's that about?"

"It's easy, i is simply another direction off the number line. It is used for complex numbers of the form a plus bi where a and b are real numbers. Real numbers are a subset of the complex numbers when b equals zero."

Michael and Anna watched with pride as their daughter looked off into space and took in what Jonah had just explained to her.

"That's cool."

"If you think complex numbers are cool, we need to teach you about quaternion numbers."

At the mention of the word quaternion, Ryan's head

swiveled in Jonah's direction. He excused himself from the group he was sitting with and grabbed a chair to sit with Carrie and Jonah.

Jonah drew a graph and put a real number and an imaginary number on the graph.

"Now if $a + bi$ is a complex number in the plane of the page like this, then a number of the form $ai + bj + ck$ is a number in three- dimensions like this, while a quaternion number is of the form $a + bi + cj + dk$, where a in this case is some scalar value."

As Jonah graphed a quaternion number, Carrie's eyes widened. "I get it," she exclaimed. "I absolutely get it. How can I add and multiply them together? And what about dividing and subtracting them? When would I want to use them? Oh! I know! A satellite in orbit could have its position be described by the last- three-terms of a quaternion relative to its own spatial reference frame and the first-term could describe the magnitude of the distance from the center of the satellite's reference frame to the center of its orbit. Wow. This is so cool."

Carrie looked as excited as an explorer discovering a new world. "She absolutely gets it," Ryan said.

Jonah looked over at Michael and Anna, saying to them in a slow manner, "She…absolutely…gets…it. We need to talk."

David Linn was busy talking to Holly in Italian, Hebrew, and occasionally, English. The twins looked excited to meet David Linn. Even though he was two-years-younger than they were, they seemed quite aware that he had inherited his father's good looks. They said they were amazed he spoke to them in English, but spoke to Holly in Italian and Hebrew.

"I think Italian is a pretty sounding language," Marsha declared.

"I have to help get some things ready for dessert," Holly told them. "Would you two mind walking around with David Linn and introducing him to your side of the family?"

They agreed and David Linn looked in heaven with a twin on each side of him. As Leah watched the trio, she said she wasn't sure who was having more fun—the girls or David Linn.

Moshe and Samantha arrived with their sons, Sam and Dov, and then when David and Linda Kaplan arrived, they received an especially warm greeting from Moshe and Samantha.

Jonah and Holly had a long talk with Michael and Anna concerning Carrie's understanding of mathematics.

"You guys are right," Jonah told them. "She absolutely has one huge math gene. The problem is she may get burned out if we push her. As long as she enjoys the mathematics, then she will push herself. I believe she will, but you can't always tell. I know of a program for gifted students here in Seattle which takes place for eight-weeks over-the-summer. I can loan Carrie the books she will need to prepare for the class. How do you think David Linn will feel about that?"

Michael smiled. "He has a huge language gene, plus he has already built his own website. We'll manage to do special things with him next summer and he'll be fine."

Ruth overheard them and came over. "I have a couple of students from Italy who will be studying at the university in Boise next summer," she said. "I can setup an advanced Italian language program for David Linn if you like."

"He would love that!" Anna exclaimed. Then Carrie was called over.

"Jonah wants to give you some math books to work through,"

Anna told her. "Your father and I will help you. Your regular school work must come first, but if you complete the books by the end of the school year, we are willing to send you to live with Holly and Jonah for eight-weeks next summer while you attend a special math course for gifted students at the university. You would be studying mathematics the entire-eight-weeks. Would you like to do that? You would also do summer things as well. When they go camping and sailing, you would be invited as well. What do you think? Would you like to do that?"

"Could I continue to study math while we go camping and sailing?"

The four of them laughed and told her she could.

"Now if this doesn't work, you can quit anytime and there will be no hard feelings concerning your decision," Michael told her.

Carrie looked surprised. "Why would I want to quit? Dad, I was made for this stuff."

"When you live with Holly and Jonah, you will have to follow their rules," Anna advised. "And do what they say, just like when we talk to you at our home."

"For heaven's sake, Mom," Carrie said, sounding exasperated. "I've been doing what they tell me since I was a baby!"

She looked up at Jonah. "Thank you for this."

"Don't thank me yet. This is going to take a lot of hard work." "Like you've told me so many times, if all it takes is hard work, then I can do this." Carrie smiled.

Beverly came over and stole Holly away for a while to chat. "Holly, how did you come to the decision to convert to Judaism?"

"I agonized over my decision for much longer than I should have. I finally realized Jonah and I shared nearly all the same values. Jewish values helped shape who he is, and I love who he is."

Beverly pointed out she had been introduced to Jonah's mother, Michelle. "If her smile gets any bigger, I think her face is going to break. She is so happy for you two," Beverly told her.

"Believe me when I tell you," Holly said, "Michelle has a heart bigger than her smile. Knowing she's going to be my mother-in-law delights me no end. Look at her with Linda. You would think she's Linda's mom the way they laugh and joke together. Not to mention how lucky I am to have Linda for a sister-in-law. And now you. You're going to fit right in with us."

"Thank you, Holly. That's so kind of you to say that. Personally, I can't believe how lucky I am to have your parents for in-laws."

All the Holts were staying at Jonah and Holly's home, as well as Ryan and Lucinda, while the Levins were staying in the Minkowskis' in-law apartment.

Late in the evening Karen and Benjamin walked out the front door and up the drive way. As Benjamin was about to head down the street to begin his walk home, he turned to Karen. "It's been a lovely time today. I enjoyed talking to you. I'll be at the brunch tomorrow. Will I see you then?"

"If you want to see me tomorrow," Karen said mischievously, "then you better be over here at seven o'clock in the morning with the rest of my family to go for a run"

"I think I can manage," he replied.

At that, Karen put her hands on either side of Benjamin's face and slowly kissed his lips. That was just a test to see if you're a good kisser," she told him.

"Did I pass?"

"The jury's still out. We may have to try again tomorrow."

"Goodnight, Karen. Our time today was quite special for me."

"Goodnight, Benjamin, and thank you for spending so much time with me."

When she walked in the house, Lucinda asked her sister about Benjamin.

"We just met, but I don't think I've ever felt this way before. At the end of the night he said our time together was quite special, and he said it in such a sincere way. I can't believe how wonderful that sounded. He's somewhat like Ryan, but also kind of like Oliver."

"Karen, that's a combination worth fighting for. Get going with this guy and we can have a double wedding," Lucinda said. "Two brothers and two sisters. I think that would be great."

"I just met him today. Besides, your wedding is your day."

Chapter Thirty-Three ~ *A New Relationship*

ON SATURDAY MORNING, KAREN walked outside at ten minutes before seven. Benjamin was already waiting for her.

"Good morning," he told her with a sincere smile.

"Good morning, Benjamin," Karen replied warmly.

As they began stretching, the Holts, Levins, plus Ryan and Lucinda came out for their run. From up the street, Moshe and Sam, Ari, Leah and their twins, as well as Meyer and Joan came out to run as well. They stretched and began discussing various routes that would take them different distances.

Holly and Jonah, including his security people, as well as Benjamin, Karen, Drew, Beverly, Ryan, Lucinda, and Oliver decided on a five-mile run. The others decided on running either two- or three-miles.

The group running with Oliver knew he would set a fast pace. Most of them were accustomed to this, but it seemed to surprise Benjamin.

"He's in great shape," Benjamin told Karen.

"When he became a dad, he decided that setting a fitness example would be good for his children. He and Mom head out every day there isn't snow on the ground, and when there is snow on the ground, they cross country ski."

They completed the long run and began walking to cool down. "My mom always told us setting an example for our children is more important than what we tell them," Benjamin mentioned.

"That's why my goal is to have a relationship like Oliver

and Ruth have," Karen said.

Benjamin paused, seeming to think. "I've heard about your parents from Ryan," he said. "From what he's told me, that is a worthy goal. Perhaps I will be fortunate enough to be the person who will work with you on achieving that goal."

Karen's heart skipped a beat on hearing his words. "Thank you Benjamin. That's kind of you to say that."

Meyer and Joan were walking along a path to the lake front. "Look at them. They're in their sixties and still hold hands," Benjamin said.

Karen eyed him and he offered his hand to her.

"Thank you, kind sir," she told him, taking his hand in hers.

Oliver looked over the group and, in a voice, dripping with sarcasm said, "Oh, this is nice. I'm the only one who doesn't have some pretty girl to hold my hand."

Karen and Benjamin were the closest to him and Karen reached out and grabbed Oliver's hand.

Lucinda grabbed his other hand, then looked at Benjamin. "The men in this family are *so* high maintenance."

The whole group began laughing.

***

"Isn't it wonderful to hear all that laughter?" Joan asked Meyer.

"Nothing could be better than having all this family around us for the weekend."

"We've come a long way from a small town in Iowa." Joan kissed his cheek.

"It's been one wonderful, loving, family adventure."

"Larry and Danielle are coming in today with their children and grandchildren as well," Meyer reminded her. "I can't wait to see them."

Michael approached Meyer. "We're not broadcasting this yet, but we're going to be moving back to this area in the next year, probably over the summer. When we moved to Boise, only twenty- five-percent of our business was in Seattle. Now it's up to sixty- percent, and if we add in work from the Portland area, it's over eighty-percent. We have an office in downtown Bellevue. I'm coming up here a few times a week already, so it makes sense to move the whole operation up here. We're aiming to move the family sometime next summer, after the kids are done with school. I could use the name of a good realtor."

"I have the name of a good man. But if you're thinking about moving, please consider our house. We've decided to sell and get something smaller. As you know, it's about three blocks from here, so you'd be near all the family."

"That could be a great idea. I'll talk it over with Anna. Thanks, Meyer."

Meyer paused for a moment. "It's a crazy life. It's so difficult to plan."

Michael chuckled. "You have no idea. We're keeping this quiet, too, because this is the kids' big weekend, but Anna's doctor advised her to go on a special supplement a short-while-ago. It made a big difference for both of us—a multiple-birth-seven-months- from-now kind of difference."

"You're kidding!"

"No. The end of March next year should see a two-person addition to our family. Anna was shocked at first, but is in heaven now, as am I."

***

Ruth was waiting at the entrance to Holly and Jonah's home. As the group approached her, a loud hammering started up on the home under construction next door. "I hope that hammering doesn't keep going all day long," she said.

"Mom, that racket is music to my ears," Lucinda told her with a smile.

Ruth thought for a moment. "Is it going to be your house?"

Ryan smiled. "Next time you visit us in Seattle, you will be staying in that house."

Ruth hugged Lucinda and Ryan. "That's wonderful, kids. And right next to Jonah and Holly. What could be better?"

Ryan looked at Karen and Drew. "Well, it would be better if we could get Karen, Bev, and Drew moved up here."

"Oh, no," Drew said. "I'm an Idaho kind of guy."

Much to everyone's delight and laugher, Karen looked at Benjamin and said, "I thought I was an Idaho kind of girl, but I may be getting confused on that account."

Before the brunch began, Ryan took out drawings of their new home to show Ruth and Oliver. Lucinda cheerfully explained what all the rooms would be.

"I am so happy for you guys," Oliver told them.

From the kitchen, they heard Holly calling Lucinda and Karen. "Excuse me," Lucinda said in a happy voice. "My sister needs me."

"I think I need to go as well," Ryan told them as he put thedrawings in a locked cabinet. "I see Carrie looking at me and she has her I-have-a-math-question expression."

"They're so happy," Ruth said as Lucinda and Ryan went to the kitchen.

"They have a tough road ahead of them," Oliver commented. "Holly and Jonah, too, but I think their relationships are strong enough to see them through the rough times."

"Does this have anything to do with the security people who always seem to be around?"

Oliver nodded. "How serious is it?"

"When we walked through the front door we were walking through a metal detector."

"Do I want to know what's going on?" Ruth asked.

"No."

"Is that why you, Beverly, and Drew have been going to the

shooting range so often and you convinced them to get concealed carry licenses?"

"I heard Karen tell Benjamin one of her goals in life is to have a relationship like ours."

"Oliver, please don't change the subject."

"Ruth, this is the path they've chosen. They know what dangers they may face. I trust Ryan and Jonah. If I had to trust my daughters' lives with someone it would certainly be those two. Jonah has already put his life on the line for Holly. They must be doing something important to warrant all this security. If you looked carefully at the drawings of the new house, there were some rooms indicated which didn't have doorways."

"I don't think I want to know any more about this." "Good idea."

***

When Ryan's parents and grandparents arrived they were introduced to the families from Idaho. Ryan's grandfather, Rabbi Rifkin, spoke to the Levins.

"I understand your family is becoming fluent in Hebrew," he told them. "Next spring my family is traveling to Israel. We will be celebrating Passover in Jerusalem. Ryan and Lucinda said they would like to join us. It would be an honor if you would join us as well."

"Thank you, Rabbi Rifkin," Michael said. "We will definitely consider your offer."

Rabbi Rifkin looked across the room at Benjamin and Karen. "I have a feeling from the way Benjamin is looking at Karen we may have another of the Holt sisters with us as well."

Michael and Anna smiled.

"Ruth Holt helped us learning Hebrew," Anna told him. "She is an amazing teacher."

"I've heard about her, and I've heard the west side of Meridian, Idaho is the place to visit for amazing meals, because a woman named Anna Levin is brilliant at teaching cooking skills, too."

"We have a number of great cooks in our neighborhood, and they've been teaching each other," Michael said. "We've been taking part in neighborhood events since the day we arrived. We love the area we live in."

The Rabbi seemed to think for a moment. "Wouldn't we all be better off if we loved the neighborhood we lived in?" he said. "Is Meridian the town where those teenaged children shaved their heads for a classmate who had lost her hair due to an illness?"

"If you've met Linda Kaplan then you've met the girl whose idea it was."

"David's Linda?" Rabbi Rifkin asked. "I had no idea."

"Not only was it was her idea," Anna told him, "but she's the one who convinced a large group of her band friends to do the same."

"I'll have to make a point of talking to her."

***

Jonah's Uncle Meyer had docked his sixty-four-foot trawler-type yacht at their dock. As people began eating, Meyer made an announcement. "For you nautical types, we will be having lake cruises at one o'clock and three o'clock this afternoon."

Jonah turned to Holly. "My uncle asked me to pilot the one o'clock cruise. Do you mind?"

"You never told me you could drive a big boat, Jonah."

"Is that a yes?"

Holly smiled, pointed out the window, and yelled to Drew. "Get over here. Jonah's going to teach you how to drive that big ship."

Drew looked out at the gleaming white yacht sitting majestically at its dock. He immediately walked over to Jonah, holding out his hand. "I knew you were going to be a great brother, but I had no idea how great," he said as they shook hands.

"Meet me down there at fifteen-before-one and we'll get the old girl ready," Jonah told him.

"Don't boats that big have engine rooms?" Beverly asked Jonah.

"Yes, they do."

"Well, if I lose track of Drew this weekend, I bet I know where I'll find him."

Holly laughed. "I know exactly what you have to put up with, Beverly."

Carrie, David Linn, and the twins came over to Jonah. "Will you take us on your cruise, Captain?" The foursome snapped to attention and saluted Jonah.

"You can go with me, but *only* if you can talk like a sailor." He returned their salute.

"We don't know how to do that," Esther complained. "Go ask your dad. I'll bet he can teach you."

They ran over to Ari who immediately started laughing and took them to another room to teach them how to speak sailor.

Drew and Jonah performed an engine room inspection on the yacht and fired up one of the generators. Then they went out on deck and started helping people get onboard.

Beverly, Holly, Linda, and Michelle brought out trays of munchies for the cruise.

Jonah saw the twins, Carrie, and David Linn marching in step down to the pier. He quickly told the others already on the boat they needed to get on the deck to see something.

The foursome came to a halt on the pier next to the boat. "Right face," David Linn called out.

They turned and were facing Jonah.

"Salute," David Linn yelled.

With serious faces they each snapped their right hand up to their forehead. Over his shoulder Jonah could see Leah had a video camera directed toward the foursome.

"Request permission to come aboard, Captain."

"Can you speak sailor?" Jonah returned their salute.

"Affirmative, Captain," David Linn said as they dropped their salute.

Carrie took one step forward. In as deep a voice as her twelve- year-old throat could likely manage, she shouted, "A-vast there you barnacle encrusted keel-hauler."

Next Esther stepped forward. "Hoist the main sail up the boson's mate and mate the boson!"

Marsha joined them. "Stuff the ensign in the binnacle and wrap him in a spinnaker."

David Linn took a step forward. "Flim-flam the boson's bottom, Captain," he called out.

As the onlookers started applauding and laughing, Jonah did his best to maintain a straight face. "Permission to come aboard granted, you caterwauling porthole polishers!"

The foursome immediately changed into giggling and high- fiving young teens as they scrambled onboard.

"Can we sit on the bow?" Esther asked Jonah. "Yes, you can, but what are the rules?"

"Stay together," Marsha said. "Keep your life preserver on. When you're on the bow and we're under way, stay away from the rail."

"Sounds good to me," Jonah told them.

"Come on, you guys. I can show you where the life preservers are," Marsha said.

As they watched the foursome help each other into their life preservers and get them adjusted properly, Anna said, "Look how well they get along. I was worried Carrie and David Linn would feel like outsiders. Everyone is treating us like we're family."

"Leah told me she's helping the foursome put together a play for tonight," Michael said.

It was a sunny day so Jonah piloted the trawler from the fly bridge. He explained his careful maneuvering to Drew, while he moved the ship away from the dock. Then Drew took over at the helm, which had two side-by-side captain's chairs.

Jonah called to Beverly and she came up to the fly bridge. "When Drew is at the helm, this is your seat," he told her.

"Thank you, Jonah." She took the seat next to Drew. "This is an amazing view from up here," she said.

She gestured at all the instruments arrayed in front of them. "Do you know what all these do, Drew?"

"No, but I'm working like mad to learn them."

Beverly twisted in her seat to take in more of the view. "Leah told me she and Ari have been to Alaska in this ship. Wouldn't this be an amazing way to travel there?" She wrapped her arms around Drew's arm.

"I would love it." Drew leaned over and kissed her.

Jonah and Holly sat on the fly bridge as well. "Do you think your brother is having a good time?" Jonah whispered to Holly.

"If Uncle Meyer needs a pilot for the second cruise, I know who he can ask."

***

On the boat deck, Karen approached Dr. Rabinowitz. "I'd like to talk to you sometime, Dr. Rabinowitz."

"Anytime is okay with me. Would you like to talk now?"

"That would be great."

They sat somewhere private and Karen began. "I'd like your advice on something," she said.

"Go ahead, Karen."

"Well, I was repeatedly molested by an uncle when I was a child. I have a huge concern. When I find Mr. Right...I am worried I won't want to do anything with him because of my past."

"Do you have nightmares which cause you to relive those experiences or times when you feel like you're reliving those experiences? Flashbacks, in other words."

"I did have nightmares, but they ended shortly after I moved to Idaho. I haven't had any since then, and I haven't had any flashbacks."

"Please be aware, flashbacks can happen. If you have found Mr. Right, he won't mind being patient with you while you work things out."

"I'm scared I'll disappoint him. I would hate to do that."

"The way you and Benjamin look at each other, I don't think it will be a problem for the two of you to work out. How long have you known each other?"

"I met him yesterday."

Dr. Rabinowitz raised his eyebrows in surprise and then looked contemplative.

"Benjamin has demonstrated huge patience in dealing with his father's speech and physical disabilities. I'm certain he'll have whatever patience you need until the two of you work things out. If you need help, you can call me. If you'd rather discuss this with a woman, I can arrange that as well."

"Thank you, Dr. Rabinowitz. I'll let you know."

"You're welcome, Karen."

Karen got up and asked where the washrooms were. She was told to use one in the cabins on the lower deck, so she walked down the winding stairway and into the guest cabin, admiring the lovely wood work. She ran right into Benjamin.

"I guess that's a sign," she said.

He looked at her with a confused expression.

"I need to talk to you about something, Benjamin." She took his hand and pulled him into the guest cabin and locked the door. "First, I want you to hold me," she said.

Benjamin put both his arms around her and Karen put her

cheek against his, wrapping her arms around his neck. She felt an amazing sense of serenity come over her. Her mind started telling her she belonged with Benjamin. To her absolute amazement, she felt her body telling her the same thing.

"Benjamin, when it comes to a physical relationship, we have to go slow…because of some problems I've had."

Benjamin tightened his embrace. "This kind of slow I can enjoy."

She loved his embrace and wanted him to continue holding her. Karen was ecstatic at the mental and physical sensations his embrace produced.

"When you have a relationship that is *Bashert*, and you are meant to be together, you can work out anything," Benjamin told her, as if he knew everything about her concerns. "From the first moment we started talking, I knew we belonged together. Karen, I knew it in my heart. When I see how Lucinda and Ryan look at each other and hold each other, I know they belong together. I feel the same way about us."

"We live so far apart. Who knows when we'll see each other?"

"The Lord knows, and little by little, he's going to let us in on his plan for us."

"Us…I love that. Two-days-ago I was alone, and today I feel like I have a partner in my life. Thank you for letting me into your life, Benjamin."

"Thank you, Karen, for becoming part of my life."

They engaged in a long kiss while trying to stay as wrapped around each other as two-standing-adults possibly could.

"I'm going to help Leah prepare the children," Karen said, "for a play they are going to be performing this evening. Would you like to help me?"

"I'd love to."

Chapter Thirty-Four ~ *To Family*

THAT EVENING ESTHER, MARSHA, Carrie, David Linn, and Sam put on a play for the assembled families. Carrie walked out to the front of the media room with a sign.

Three Couples in Love—Act 1.

Marsha walked to the center of the media room and sat cross legged on the floor. Esther then walked out with her hair tied up to look as short as possible. She sat on the floor next to Marsha.

In as low a voice as Esther could manage, she said, "Did you see the main power amplifiers have Type B push-pull design with eight- BM-eight-SG pentode tubes?"

In a high-pitched voice, Marsha replied, "It's certainly interesting to hear you speak in audiophile."

"How about the pre-amplifiers? They have one-percent resistors and I see the speakers are planar panels with quasi- ribbon- tweeters."

"I speak Italian, by the way."

"We're a perfect couple. If I ever buy some Italian stereo equipment, you can translate the manuals for me. I love you, Holly."

"*Te amo*, Jonah."

The two stood up, and in the midst of much laughter and applause, bowed to the audience.

Then Carrie came by with her sign again.

Three Couples in Love—Act 2.

Fifteen-year-old Sam walked out to the middle front of the media room and pretended he was on a phone call.

"That's right. I want to go to medical school to become an obstetrician, but it's hard to get into medical school without something special on your resume."

He listened on the phone for a while and then acted all excited. "What a great idea, Linda. As soon as the weather gets cold, I'll fly out to Boise. When we think your neighbor is about to deliver her baby, we'll drive her to the mall as soon as we know a big snowstorm is coming."

Sam listened. "Right. When we leave the mall, we can pretend to get stuck in the snow so she'll have to have the baby in her truck and we can deliver it. This is so great! Medical school here we come!"

Sam pretended to listen for another moment and then yelled, "I've got it! I've got it! This is so diabolical. After we deliver the kid, I'll pretend to get a phone call from my little brother and suddenly know how to get the truck unstuck. Not only that, we'll have them so fooled, they'll probably name the kid after us."

Sam paused, listening again. Then got a big smile on his face. "I also love you because of the way you think."

He then took a huge bow in front of the appreciative and laughter-filled audience.

Anna Levin was laughing so hard, they had to wait until she calmed down to start the third act.

This time Esther ran out with the sign.

Three Couples in Love—Act 3.

Carrie and David Linn walked out to the center of the media room. She carried a shovel.

David Linn said, "I see you've used twine and stakes to inscribe an enclosed polygonal figure just above the earth which contains four-right-angles."

Carrie stared at him for a moment and said in a droll voice, "Yes. It's called a square."

She held up the shovel. "Do you know what this is?"

He smiled at her. "I certainly know that device. It is a steel-bladed and wood-handled manual implement which is used to move solid material from one location to another."

"Please then, get busy using this manual implement to remove dirt from inside the square."

David Linn started to use the shovel but then stopped.

"Excuse me, but precisely how much dirt would you like me to remove each time I insert this device into the ground."

Carrie slowly turned and looked out at the audience in disbelief. She shrugged her shoulders and turned back to David Linn, shaking her head dramatically. "Precisely one shovelful, please."

David Linn smiled and pretended to shovel. "What do you intend to plant here?" he asked.

"*Akebia Quinata, Arctostaphylos Uvaursi, Echinacea Purpurea,* and *Rhododendron Impitum*—among others."

David Linn looked out at the audience. "Wow. Did you hear that? I think I'm falling in love."

He returned to shoveling for a while, and then said, "I'm getting tired over here. I think I need a hug."

Carrie turned to the audience and put her hands on her hips. "The men in this family are *so* high maintenance...but I think I love him."

David Linn sighed. "Now that you've spoken to me using the plant's Latin names, I can logically deduce we belong together!"

They hugged and then bowed to the loudly applauding family. Marsha walked out with a huge grin and a sign that said *Fin.* "That means it's the end," she said, to more laughter and applause.

***

Holly and Jonah's wedding was a jubilant and tasteful celebration. It was the culmination of many years—two loving people whose lives had begun to intertwine during their childhood.

With all their family surrounding them, it was everything

they dreamed it would be.

As the family members and friends sat down to eat, many lovely toasts were offered to the newlyweds.

Jonah stood up. "Holly and I wrote this together, but she wants me to read it to you." He cleared his throat and smiled.

"Thank you, family and friends, for being here today. We are grateful beyond words for the myriad ways you have helped us become the happy and loving couple we are. You've been there to get us through the worst of times and helped us celebrate the best of times. We've laughed together, cried together, and saved lives together. As tiny tributaries contribute to create the great rivers of the world, so have the strong values of individual family members contributed to making our great family what it is today. Having been brought up in the midst of those great lessons, taught to us by word and deed, we look forward to living a life governed by those values," Jonah raised his glass, "and we look forward to teaching them to the next generation. To the family!"

"The family!" Everyone toasted and cheered.

~ ~ ~ The End ~ ~ ~

If you enjoyed this contemporary romance, please leave a review on the website from which you purchased the book. Thank you!

Also by Richard Alan

Meant to Be Together series

Book 1 Finding a Soul Mate
Book 2 The Couples
Book 3 Finding Each Other
Book 4 Growing Together

American Journeys series

Book 1 American Journeys: From Ireland to the United States
Book 2 American Journeys: From Boston to the Pacific Northwest
Book 3 American Journeys: A Female Doctor in the Civil War